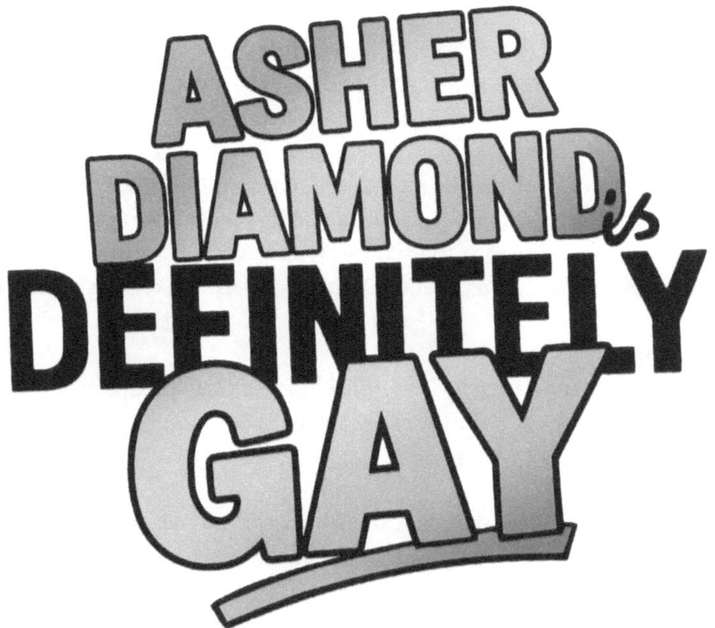

ASHER DIAMOND is DEFINITELY GAY
ANDREW EXTEIN

Cover art and design by Terrorifico Napalm (0800drnapalm.com)
ISBN 979-8-218-65318-7

Printed in the United States of America
First Edition

*To Florida, for raising me*

## *Prologue*

THE thing about my body? Total stranger—until nights like this. Long and locked in, wild and confusing, buzzing with...something. No fucking clue.

1:53 a.m., Thursday, March 6, 2003. Pantheon Nightclub, Fort Lauderdale.

A goddamn school night.

Finally, a chance to catch a breath. So. Much. Dancing.

My mouth's like sandpaper and my face is Jolly Rancher red, but I keep going. The strobes give me a seizure even when my eyes are closed, and all the fake fog's choking me out. *Get it together, Asher. You're not done. Swallow that air.*

The spazzy beat finally drops and it's all flying limbs, like the ground turned to lava.

*Thump, thump, thump.* Juvenile tells me to "Back That Azz Up," so I do.

Every beat pumps vodka Red Bull through my blood like CPR. My body's spinning out and possessed, straight-up *Poltergeist*. I'm trying like hell to keep up my bounce, and my tongue's wagging like a thirsty dog.

The Abercrombie polo I hate to iron is totally drenched. At least my arms look decent for once. This sweaty hair-gel humidity glob tickles my face, so I smack it. My eardrum's losing its mind.

I spot this hot girl across the dance floor, all confident in this magic kinda way I'll never be. The tube top's nice and full, and her tight denim shorts make me wanna touch her butt, even though I never will. That flat stomach's, like, grinding in circles, rubbing up on some lucky bitch. Long braids whip around like rat tails, and she looks cool times a million in fresh Jordans.

Suddenly there's this knee wedging its way between my legs, locking me in like Stone Cold. The guy's got his arm tight around me with a fist so I can't get away. *Don't run. Remember, Asher, act like you're into it.* So I just punch my body back, and we keep grinding so close and jumpy I get Tilt-A-Whirl dizzy.

That girl's right next to me. Her grinding buddy's everything I'm not—shit ton of swagger and a buzz cut, baggy jeans and a wife beater. But that person's actually *another* girl. They make out like crazy and now I'm snapped back to reality—ish.

I don't know what's real anymore, and it's like I'm cracking apart. It's like this ghost pops out of me and floats up, watching.

But all this insanity's totally normal now. Everything's electric and hazy and confusing and fun all at once. My new life—a psychotic, twisted Frankenstein shitstorm.

While the cool girls make out and I push my butt up against a gay guy's crotch, the hip-hop beat's ticking like a digital countdown to the messed-up truth, total TNT nuclear fallout. And all night I've had this sick question rushing through me like toxic waste in my pipes.

*When's it all gonna blow the fuck up?*

*Opossum*

LAND, tap, attack. Crushed it.

Draw, buff, attack again. Blocked.

No moves left. Fuck me.

I slam my cards onto the crusty cafeteria table, and a puddle of pizza sauce sprays on my jeans like I'm stuck in Shamu's splash zone. Lost again. Whatever.

"Damn, Asher, you kinda suck at this game." Robbie and me have been best friends since forever, so we know how to piss each other off. This is him being nice, which he basically always is.

*Breathe, loser.*

It's so dumb that I'm thrown off by this shit. This stupid game. The saddest part? Me and Robbie still play *Magic*—alone—at lunch. That little dork inside me's facepalming hard.

It's Monday, September 9th, 2002. The first day of the last year I'll *ever* see *any* of these people.

I tear a bite off my little circle pizza, but my pissed-off teeth stab my tongue mid-chew. I chuck the food like it's out to get me. A useless mana card's glued to the table, so I yank it and flick it across the caf like a paper football.

Oh, no. The card hits Sam Coolman's fake-blonde hair and drops dead. God, I hope she didn't feel it. Sam's scary-hot and crazy-vicious —but her boyfriend's worse.

I turn back to Robbie and death-stare his orange Kipling backpack with the dumb monkey. He never takes it off at school. Like, *actually* never. A goddamn life jacket on a sinking ship.

I can't stop looking at this car crash. Robbie's dorky blond bowl cut screams fifth grade. He's got these big ears, and his chubby body's just kinda...there.

"Rematch? Can't deal with your downer Asher vibe the rest of the day, so I'll go easy on you."

"I'm not a downer, I'm just...realistic."

Robbie's playing with this ugly thick leather cuff he got at Hot Topic. "That's what downers say to make themselves feel better."

"Okay, Buffy." I toss a card at his nerdy *Buffy the Vampire Slayer* T-shirt.

"Buffy Summers is a goddess." Robbie stuffs my *Magic* card into his ratty seventh-grade cargos. Suddenly his eyes open huge and dart down to the table.

"Buffy's for faggots." Luke Baker's annoying voice creeps up behind me.

"Faggot" has gotta be Luke's favorite word. My name's basically Faggot Diamond at this point. Let's get this bullshit over with.

Luke isn't fat anymore, which sucks for me. He's got this god-complex personality of a kid who grew up a lardass. I don't know how, but he got the whole school to eat up his cool-guy shtick and worship him, even as the biggest dickhead in South Florida.

"Go away, Luke." I don't even try to sound tough anymore. I've said it a million times and he never listens.

Over the years he's come up with lots of new ways to screw with me. The stupidest thing Luke ever did—it was sixth grade—was spread a rumor that I fucked my Nintendo 64. Like, *literally* fucked it. As if that's even physically possible. The school went apeshit anyway. Even now some kid'll yell, "It's a-me, Mario!" when I walk down the hall. So what nonsense do I have to put up with today?

Luke plunks down next to me and pulls my shoulders into him close. Like some mindfuck hug. His hand feels like a tarantula. "I *mith you guythhh.*" He's got his arm hanging around my neck. Doing one of those voices with the gay lisp thing.

Robbie's totally checked out, so *I've* gotta deal with this shit. He's just staring at the floor, rubbing that lame fire-juggling scar on his eyebrow. He does it when he can't deal.

It's weird to think about, but me, Luke, and Robbie used to do sleepovers and Dorito binges in second grade. Then one day Luke just, like...changed his mind about us, I guess? Spread some lie about catching me and Robbie kissing by the swings. Been total hell ever since.

I throw my shoulder forward to push him off. "You *don't* miss us. And you smell like shit."

Luke's Tommy cologne is really gnarly. Sugary and desperate. It follows him around like cigar smoke. Cancer-causing garbage—kills you eventually, like Luke'll do to me. "You love that *muthky man thent.* Here, take a sniff." He throws his arm in the air and yanks his polo sleeve down. He shoves his sweaty armpit right in my face, and these damp hairs swipe me like some nightmare car wash.

Vomit. I scramble to push his arm away.

Luke and his gang of copycat jocks crack up like my face just strummed an Adam Sandler song. Total wastes of space.

Then—oh no. There's this tickle in my nose and I spew out a big sneeze.

Now they *really* can't stop laughing their asses off. Luke stands up and gives me these wolf eyes. He rubs his hands all over the table and pushes my cards around. He flips my pizza over and rubs a bunch of cheese and sauce and gnarly shit all over the cards. Jesus.

"Fucking nerd." Luke grips my face like a basketball, smearing the pizza all over, in my eyes and my nose and my mouth even. Like instinct, I spray out this gnarly mix of tomato sauce and saliva. I must look like a real spaz.

Luke walks away, and Silas Ryker, his dumbass best friend, hangs back for a sec. Silas's dad runs some testosterone cable channel, so grades don't matter. And his porcupine hair's straight-up wannabe Green Day. He's just standing here with this mouth hanging open like an idiot, staring at me. He's tapping a beat-up lacrosse stick against his shoulder, like a threat or something, then backs away.

Super bizarre. The hell was that?

Back at the preppy kill-me table, I spot Luke grab at Sam's waist.

Sam is *way* too hot for him. Like, his hair's all greasy and he's got these small, mean eyes and gross lips and dry pale skin and just...no. I don't know how Sam can kiss him without blowing chunks. Or maybe I've got no clue what I'm talking about and Luke's a hot sex god or something.

Sam swats the prick's hand away before he can ruin her supermodel hair with pizza slime. She stands up and Luke puts his arm around her with this shit-eating grin. Like he's the goddamn Riddler.

They're walking over. No.

Normally I'd just roll over and take it like a bitch, but today, I don't know, something feels different. Senior year, my last chance to stop being such a pussy. Or maybe I just really wanted to eat that pizza. It's confusing, but something inside me's, like, *growing*.

Mario's getting a power-up.

I punch my hands against the table and shoot up. "Go *fuck* yourself, Luke." My front teeth dig into my lip when I spit out that loud *f.* Damn, I don't think anyone's seen me like this. Actually standing up for myself—kinda.

I rub my hand over my face to get it all messy, then I slam it out, not even thinking. My hand smacks against Luke's cheek. There's a big clap and now he's got pizza mush all over.

His face scrunches up and he pushes my girl Sam away, maybe by accident. She stumbles back and grips her short denim skirt for balance, awkward for maybe the first time in her life.

"What the hell, faggot!" Luke throws his body at me, like that'll stop me.

Silas jumps in and blocks Luke before he can do damage. "Dude, chill. That kid isn't worth it."

Luke paces around and wipes his arm over his gross face in one big swoop. "Bad move, Diamond." He clenches his jaw and marches away like a goddamn coward.

Did I...*win?*

Sam looks like she's about to go after Luke—but then stops. In front of me. Her eyes are, like, staring at me. Honey-brown and blank and perfect and—uh, what?

Sam's the hottest girl in school by a long shot. Ask anyone. She got these nice tits freshman year and that was it. One day she's, like, this *Maxim* hot chick, then the next it's girl-next-door Alex Mack stuff. But she's also a total evil bitch—not that anyone minds.

There's no point in having an *actual* crush on her, but of course I'd hook up with her. Maybe if I was, like, a Josh Hartnett clone.

Sam reaches up to me, out of nowhere, and touches my face. Our eyes lock and her soft skin gets me all shivery and tense. Then she pulls her long sleeve over her hand and wipes it all light across my forehead. Slow, getting some cheese and sauce off. My brain's pumped with helium, floating so high it disappears.

My eyes move down to that silver chain necklace all the popular girls have. It's sitting right on her famous cleavage, blinding me under the harsh caf lights. I can't look away.

She leans in and I space out. "Stare at my tits again, Diamond, and I'll cut your tiny little dick off." She's got this low, serious voice.

Yeah—definitely didn't win. Robbie's just sitting there quiet, big blinking eyes. No help.

Right before Sam runs off, she flips her hair at me and—I swear to god—her eyes, like, *smile*. This girl's toying with my head so bad. Zapping me with electroshock, even though she's being a total psycho and making me feel like some creepy perv.

I shake out of my Sam trance and pull Robbie's arm up so we can bolt outta here. His scuffed-up white Skechers squeak the linoleum floor.

Then I realize. The caf's *dead* quiet. Just lots and lots of eyes.

This angry voice breaks the quiet. "Hey! Are you boys just going to leave this mess for me to clean up?" One of the lunch ladies is next to our disgusting table, apron and hairnet and everything. She's got her hands on her hips like we're real pieces of shit. Hell, maybe we are.

After scurrying out with our heads down, I lean back against a wall and drop. I yell into my shirt. "I'm so fucking over that guy!" I don't tell Robbie what Sam said—too embarrassing. Something feels different this time. Like maybe I can finally destroy Luke. End all this crap, once and for all.

Or maybe I'll stay a little bitch.

"I have to say, dude, that was a badass move. Asher strikes back.

Bam! Bam!" Robbie punches the air like Sylvester Stallone. "But, uh...you kinda look like shit."

I grumble something out and wipe my hand on my face. It comes back, just, orange. Before I even think, I rub my grubby hand on my baggy jeans. I get up quick and dart down the hall to the boys' room. I scrub my hands, hard. Gotta get this dipshit off me.

As I'm washing, I look in the mirror. My face stares back, all scribbles and pink. Streaks of pizza melting off my skull like *Hellraiser*.

I gotta look. Who's this Asher kid?

Too tall. Too skinny. Dandruffed hair, thick and blah. Dark circles under my eyes, like I'm a drug addict. Muddy, shit-green irises. Nose that's too long and sticks out. Patchy stubble like a middle schooler's. My wrinkled blue polo looks like it's been lying dead for weeks like a lonely murder victim. I gotta get it together.

When I'm done cleaning, Robbie's gone. Fending for himself, I guess. Still four periods until the bell. No way I'm hanging around here looking like a freak. Screw it. I'm done for the day.

I breathe deep on my way to the senior parking lot, trying to chill out. If I focus on the plants and stuff maybe I'll get outta my head— tropical flowers, twisty vines, everything green and messy and making me feel less insane.

Forever ago, Palm Reef Prep got plopped down on a big-ass swamp outside Fort Lauderdale, and sometimes it still feels wild. One weird thing about growing up here is that Florida's like this jungle. Kinda surreal, like those post-apocalyptic movies where dead cities have grass growing on buildings and stuff. Slimy creatures hiding who knows where. Spooky as hell.

One time in second grade I was walking by myself, and I saw this opossum hanging upside down from a tree by its curly tail. I was super freaked out by its sharp teeth and ratty fur. I just froze cause I knew they attack. That thing looked terrifying.

But now I think about that little guy a bit different. He's basically an outcast in the animal world. Ugly, weird, just trying to survive without getting his ass kicked. No one really *gets* him. Maybe that's why I still can't get him outta my head.

I only saw him that one time. He's probably dead.

Finally, I get to my green Nissan. It's kinda chipped and full of crushed Coke cans, not exactly Luke's BMW or Silas's Hummer or Sam's Lexus, but whatever. Total freedom on wheels.

I hop in. Sometimes I get this fantasy of putting a brick on the gas and standing through the sunroof, speeding down I-95. My hair getting crazy in the wind, like a music video. Maybe blond or something girls go crazy for, like a Kurt Cobain moody thing.

I turn on Y-100, the Top 40 station, to feel like a normal teenager for a sec—but it doesn't work. That Britney "I'm Not a Girl" song where she's on the cliff comes on and I sing before catching myself. I picture Luke in the passenger seat right next to me, looking all disgusted. *What's that, faggot?*

I shake my head and change the station quick, my finger stabbing the button like it burned me, landing on Papa Roach. The screaming music blasts through the speakers and pounds in my skull. Better. I cruise down the highway back home to Boca. All my car's glass and metal can't really protect me. One bad crash, and—that's it.

No more Asher Diamond. Whoever the fuck that is.

If this year doesn't change—with Luke, with all of it—I'm not making it out alive. Something's gotta give. Soon.

I crank the volume and headbang to the heavy drum. I open up and shout the words, cracking my voice like a glow stick.

*This is my last resort.*

*Leeches*

*POSER.*

That's what Luke called me in eighth grade, right after I ate shit ollieing off that curb behind the library. I almost thought he was gonna help me up—crouching down and giving me this sick Joker smile. But of course he didn't. He just grabbed my board and took off like a total dick.

A few days later he tossed it back, and it was covered in these *Get well soon!* messages. Silver Sharpie and Wite-Out scribbled all over. Signed by kids, teachers—everyone. He told them I had *terminal cancer.* Like, full-on dying. When he forked it over, he goes, "Now you're a *real* poser."

I've been rotting in my cave, living in *Tony Hawk's Pro Skater* land since I ditched. When I'm doing my PS2 thing I can actually not suck, landing 900s and everything. I can be someone else—like, this totally different version of me. Cool and confident. Pulling off these insane tricks that would make Luke shut up for once.

I've hoovered so many Twizzlers and Tostitos I'm waiting for orange sludge to barf outta me. My only company's Michelangelo, this orange gecko my mom got me when I was six. Named him after the Ninja Turtle, duh. Can't believe the little freak's still alive. I hope my dad'll take care of him when I leave for college. Only a psycho would show up to the dorms with an ancient reptile.

I flop out of bed and scoop Michelangelo from his tank. We hop under the covers and he sits on my lap while this non-Asher Asher crushes a half-pipe.

Dammit. I wipe out on screen and I'm so mad that my body just, like, flinches out. Michelangelo goes flying. I'm army-crawling around all ADD looking for him, Tostito shards stabbing my knees, praying I don't squish my friend into gecko juice. I'm half under the bed when I hear my door swing open.

"Asher!"

The sudden *boo* makes me smack my head into the bed frame. Of course it's my dad. There's no fucking privacy in this house. "Can't you knock?" I squirm out but still can't find my lizard friend. I spit out a bunch of crumbs and filth and wipe my face. "Watch out! Michelangelo's...somewhere."

My dad plops on my bed, all hyped up like he's gonna drop the biggest news ever.

I spin into my desk chair and grab my controller to space out. "And this is about...?" I definitely don't tell him about Luke or ditching.

He's too checked out to even ask. "Guess who's coming to the Miami Beach store this weekend?" My dad's this total ham who owns Diamond Video—you know, the corny guy yelling about new releases in those cheap commercials.

"Ummm..." I keep skating, trying to zone out.

My dad snatches the controller and throws it onto Dirty Clothes Mountain. "Come on, Asheroony, guess."

I *hate* when my dad calls me that. Like I'm some wacky cartoon character. "Tony Hawk?"

"It's Mike Myers! Can you believe it? He's coming in dressed as Austin Powers, with the velvet suit and everything. It's gonna bring in a huge crowd. *Lots* of business."

"Wow. Thrilling." But the truth is me and Robbie are gonna totally spaz quoting every line like the nerds we are. I try to scare my dad off, glaring at him all serious like a bratty teen.

"Ah, yes. My teenage son—moody. There's Chinese in the kitchen...oh yeah, and Piper's not coming. Patient emergency."

My dad's girlfriend is a therapist and talks to me like I'm some broken thing she needs to fix. She doesn't live here but might as well, considering she never fucking leaves.

"Oh, yeah, and we want to talk to you about...college. Soon. I know, I know, it's only day one, but...we have to talk about it sometime."

*We?* He better have dug my mom up out of her grave, cause Piper isn't talking to me about jack.

I always just assumed I'd end up at Florida State cause that's where my dad went. I think I could get in? But motherfucking Piper's got this hard-on for NYU, like I'm gonna morph into some New York cappuccino-breath genius just cause that's her fantasy. My report card's basically toilet paper. Can't she just leave me alone? Let me be un-special on *my* terms? "Not talking about it, Dad." I grab the PS2 controller and skate.

My dad finally gets up, but turns around at the last sec. He gives me this laser-beam stare. "What's on your...?" He makes this circle around his neck.

Oh no—the pizza. I dart to the bathroom and zoom in on this red mark on my neck. Looks like a hickey, but never even had my first kiss.

"Everything okay, Asher?" My dad barges in while I'm attacking my neck with soap. This must look fishy, but I'm not telling him zip. My dad's watched Luke torture me forever, like when the prick "accidentally" spilled fetal pig guts on me in bio. But since I stopped talking about it? My dad's living in this magical world where his son isn't getting his ass destroyed daily.

"I'm fine."

My dad just comes at me and kisses the top of my head, like my mom did—even after I shot up taller than her.

I'm dying inside, like Luke's peeping through my window, seeing some weak little kid who needs his daddy.

The video king starts heading out but turns. "It won't be like this forever, you know."

My eyes don't roll cause I'm actually kinda spooked. I collapse back in bed as he leaves, wiggling my fingers at the game controller. Can't reach so I flip on the TV instead. *Fear Factor* is on. Holy mother, perfect timing.

*Fear Factor* is fucking amazing—totally deranged. Airhead hot girls and braindead buff guys getting launched across the ocean or stuffing their faces with nasty worms or shitting themselves hanging off high-rises.

This hot girl in a blue bikini's dangling off a helicopter, freaking out. But all I can see is Sam up there, being all perfect and badass about it, probably making that same face she made at me in the cafeteria. God, I hate how hot she is.

Why the hell does Luke get to have her? What does she even see in him?

I can't get that look she gave me outta my head. Pissed, full of herself, fucking hot. Torturing me. It's all so confusing, like, static in my head. That TV fuzz ya gotta smack off your set in a storm.

My hand's somehow ended up in my pants, didn't even notice. I could jerk off, I guess?

Just as I'm about to dip into a pathetic wank sesh, I realize—fuck. Michelangelo's still gone.

After trashing my room for half an hour, I find Michelangelo curled in my Airwalk looking more chilled out than I've ever felt. I pick up the shoe all careful and bring him into bed. I know he doesn't want it, but I hold out a red Twizzler anyway. A peace offering for losing him.

It hits me that I probably look totally insane. Snuggling with a sneaker, watching hot crazy people barf from eating too many cow testicles. Alone and horny for some terrified girl on TV who'd never even *look* at me in real life.

So this is gonna be senior year? Evil Luke. Helpless Robbie. Crazy Sam. My clueless dad and that wannabe stepmom.

I could just keep my head down for nine months until graduation saves me. Survive a summer in Europe with my dad and his tagalong. Show up at Florida State and start over.

Or I could focus on destroying Luke Baker.

Throw him in a tub of blood-sucking leeches, watch his d-bag bros pull them off his screaming face. Squeeze rotten pig intestines into Luke's mouth, laugh as he gags. Tie him to a crane and let him drop just enough to survive my torture.

Maybe that's just, like, the only way to stop all this shit.

Maybe only *one* of us can make it through senior year alive.

## *Balls*

SECOND day of school, and of course I'm already dripping wet, freezing my balls off in the locker room.

Coach Henley threw us in the pool for PE this week cause it's still summer-hot. Made me jump off the super-high high dive. Ate total shit cause the sun was blazing my eyes. Couldn't hear the guys laugh underwater, but yeah—they were losing it.

Worst part about swim? Walking around half-naked. Like idiots. Me? All ribs and bones and puny muscles, and the dickwads in class don't help.

Having Robbie here makes it a little better. We're hiding in our corner of the locker room like cowards. If I look away, it's almost like the asses getting rat-tailed aren't here. "What are you gonna do next year?" I ask Robbie while I wipe myself down with a grungy towel.

"Uh, what do you mean?" Robbie looks at me like I'm dumb. "Going to Carnegie Mellon, duh."

Silas grunts in the background, Luke's shadow doing his gross thing. These guys sound like animals. Loud and foul. Like pigs rolling in shit.

"You know, when we don't have to deal with all..." I spin my finger in a circle. "This."

Locker room culture's fucking mayhem. First off, it smells like moldy socks and old meatloaf. Then there's these wild guys everywhere, too much energy, all handsy and loud. Can't tell if they wanna fight or fuck each other. It's weird.

"Well, I'm definitely not gonna *choose* to hang out with a bunch of naked, low-IQ bros. Pretty sure it's not mandatory in college."

"Yeah, poor Luke's gonna be devastated."

"I'm sure he'll find another way to touch the male butt." Robbie raises his eyebrows. "He's very, uh, resourceful."

I wrap my towel around me so I can change quick. No way I'm letting anyone see me. I'm trying to tug my bathing suit off under the towel when I spot Luke across the room. The big stinky cheese just chatting it up with the guys, hanging out in his towel. Fucking with fat kids and ruining lives. Like last year when he told everyone my nipples were too small. That's not even a thing. There's those nasty leeches draining his blood again.

Then Luke swivels toward me, slow, and his face explodes into this sick smile. Something clicks in his brain and he's heading for me. Shit.

I'm trying to shimmy my suit down but it's tough since I'm so wet. Luke walks right up to me, yanks his towel open, and—bam. There's his gross dick, just like...flopping. Then he covers up real fast, and I'm like...what? Did that actually just happen?

"What the fuck, bro?" Luke's booming, all pissed, face twisted up like he didn't just flash me. Like I'm the disgusting one here.

"Uh..." What the hell's even happening right now?

"The fuck, Diamond. You just look at me?" He's getting scary loud. "Yo, Asher just looked at me! He looked at my fucking dick! You guys, this homo just tried to grab my dick!"

"W...what?" My eyes dart around the room like a schizo. "No...no. What are you talking about? You flashed *me*, you...you psycho."

"Dude, what's wrong with you?" Now Silas jams in, defending his butt boy Luke.

"Asher's a fuckin' *fag*, bro." Luke's all hyped now, like he cracked some huge secret. "Knew it! I knew that kid was a fag."

Laughing everywhere. I can't breathe—is this...real?

"Dude, stop looking at me! Stop looking at me!" Luke's voice is rattling my skull.

"Aw, man." Silas butts in. "That's fucked up, Asher."

Luke steps back, then lunges at me—hands out, grabbing at my towel.

I smash against the lockers like that's gonna stop him.

And then—shit—he lunges again.

This time he gets it. My towel's gone. Oh my fucking god. My skinny-ass body's ice-cold from the AC, shaking like a wet dog. Pretty sure I've had this nightmare before.

Now Luke's naked and spinning his towel in the air. He gets the towel all wound up nice and tight while showing off his douchebag muscles. He snaps the towel back and it whips forward into my hip.

Aaaah, fuck. Ow!

And here I am just taking it like a pussy. Probably how he wants me to feel.

My instincts finally kick in and I try to get the fuck outta here, but my suit's still loose around my ankles. I stumble across the wet locker room like a dumbass while these evil jerks laugh and stare. Where's Robbie? He's gotta be back there, probably scared shitless.

The floor's flooded from everyone's wet bathing suits and I slip. Like, full-on cartoon banana peel. I try to catch myself but it's too late. I fall forward and this old wood bench smacks me right in the face on my way down.

Ow, fucking hell. It doesn't get any worse than this.

"Step back! Back up now!" Coach Henley holds his arms out to keep them off me, shouting. "Get away from him!" He squats down in front of my naked body and pulls my head up to get a better look. Maybe to see if my face is busted open.

Coach pulls me up slow and sits me on the bench. His face looks crazy—it must be bad.

I spot Robbie behind him, all blurry. So humiliating for him to see me like this, even after everything. I wouldn't blame him if he finally cut me loose.

Coach grabs an ice pack from his office and holds it against my face.

I can't feel shit. Probably shock or whatever.

"Luke, my office. *Now.*"

Robbie's hand is warm on my shoulder when he sits next to me. "It's gonna be okay." He's whispering. "I've got you, okay?"

*Don't cry, Asher. Keep it the fuck together.*

Why is it always *me*? Am I a random target, or am I, like, rotten inside and everyone can smell it but me?

Robbie throws a towel on me to cover up my dick and stuff. It's dead quiet in here.

I barely manage to kick my bathing suit off. Robbie wraps another towel around my shoulders, like one of those emergency blankets they give people freaking out.

Eyes shut tight. Lots of feet shuffle out to get away from this mess. Silent now, except for my breathing—shaky, too loud.

"I'm gonna give you some space. I'll be right outside if you need me." I hear Robbie walk away and the door swing shut.

I'm alone now, pulling my clothes on slow because I can't stop shaking. Pain everywhere. I should leave, but I'm just...stuck. Sitting here like a loser, trying not to cry. My head's fuzzy, and Coach Henley's yelling at Luke like that's supposed to help. It's gonna take a lot more than one trip to the office to stop Luke.

I feel stuck, so I just stay here. No way I can go looking like I just got clocked. Gotta chill before I pass out.

Luke can't get away with this. He just...*can't*.

I finally let it the fuck out and cry. The tears are cold in the AC. No clue how long I'm here for. Can't think straight enough to check the time.

Suddenly, a rush of adrenaline. Need to get the *fuck* outta here.

I can sneak out the back all quiet so no one sees me, then flee to the parking lot. Coach isn't screaming at Luke anymore, so I creep past his office to the back door.

"Hey! Asher!"

Shit. Don't wanna deal with Coach, so I freak and bolt. My legs go faster than my brain, like I can outrun everything. But Luke's voice is in my brain, digging itself in. Fucking endless.

I round the final corner before I'm home free, just one more hall then—

*WHAM*. I smash into some random person.

They slam back and the impact almost feels good. "What the fuck?"

That voice—oh god. I blink the blur outta my eyes, and it sinks in who I barreled into.

Sam Coolman. Rubbing her shoulder, glaring at me like she wants me dead. Or worse.

The space between my eyes tingles, and I think a couple tears bump out. "Oh shit, I...uh, I'm sorry, I didn't see...fuck me."

"No thanks, freak." Sam fires back, making me feel like the

slimiest worm that ever was. She crouches for her Hello Kitty backpack, and—shit—her underwear flashes.

My stomach flips, like I'm some kinda perv. Not the first time today. Just kill me.

Let's get it over with. "Are you okay?"

Sam stands up and bats at her skirt all annoyed, like she's slapping me over and over. "You're the one walking around like you got hit by a bus, dude." She reaches into her bag and swipes on her sexy lip gloss. "Man, Luke needs to stop with the easy targets." Her lips smack twice, then the click of the cap startles me I'm so shaken up.

I pinch my legs and—fuck, I'm not dreaming. I touch my throbbing cheek. Ow. "It's...it's nothing. I'm fine."

"Sure, Diamond. You look fucking top-notch." She puts her bag on her shoulder and leans her head back. Tossing her messy hair straight and pulling the blonde ends so she looks all perfect again.

I open my mouth to talk—an apology or maybe, just, like, what happened at least—but nothing comes out. Frozen, back against the lockers, Luke's towel flying.

Sam rolls her eyes and steps closer, looking up at me. She lifts her hand and I close my eyes, bracing for a bitch-slap. Instead, she wipes her thumb against my cheek. It stings like hell, but then my breathing slows down a bit.

"You'll be fine, spaz."

For a second it feels like she's gonna kiss me, but her hand pulls back and whacks against my cheek in a hard slap cross the face.

I *really* needed that. I almost say thank you, but I don't.

Sam heads off, slamming my shoulder like a punk. But then her Reef sandals scratch still.

My stomach drops as she turns to squint right at me. I wait, knowing whatever she's gonna say will slice through me like a hot pink knife.

"And maybe grow some balls next time, Screech."

*Piper*

PINK, puffy, sticky with blood. Like molten cotton candy hand-dipped by Killer Klowns. Yeah, that's my face.

Finally back at home after the most fucked day ever, just standing in the driveway. I'm all Elephant Man in Piper's Lexus window. Bulging, swollen eye. Cartoon villain nose. Totally chunky head. And now I've gotta deal with this woman? Please. Just gimme a hot shower, melt me away like an ice cube.

I'm *so* not in the mood. Piper just showed up one day—total hell ever since. She tricked my dad into a date when they met at his video store. Only one fucking year after my mom died, and now she's playing housewife 24/7 in our kitchen. Too soon, lady. Times like this I wanna crawl into my mom's grave. Just...peace.

My Airwalks squeak on the tile when I try to ninja into the house. Whatever. If I don't play nice with Piper, she'll tattle with some therapy shit like "Asher's isolation is a sign of depression," or "Asher really needs to be more social at home." Living with a therapist blows.

CNN's blaring on about some dead guy and a vigil or something. Like my brain isn't already hammered to death. My face is this mix of, like, throbbing and numb and in outer space. Let's get this over with.

Piper's going full-stop psycho in the kitchen. Smushing tomatoes like the worst Iron Chef of all time.

"Uh, what are you making?" Gotta glue my wrecked face to the wall so this Piper lady won't see the damage.

"Oh, hi, honey. I'm making gazpacho, a cold soup from Spain. Heard of it? It's delish."

*Don't respond. Don't eat shitty cold tomato soup. Just survive.* I look at her, tearing her apart like a paper straw wrapper. She's got this blonde, fake curly hair that sketches me out. What else about her is fake? She might have a drawer of tampons here or whatever, but she'll *never* replace my mom. I dare her to try.

I guess I'm quiet too long, so she turns her head to talk at me. Squinting all confused. "Wait a second...why aren't you at school?"

Ugh.

"Oh my god, Asher. Your eye!" Piper's staring like my head's gone 360, *Exorcist* style. She probably thinks I got jumped. Like I'm gonna admit I did it to *myself*.

She tears through the freezer like *Double Dare* and shoves cold brussels sprouts at me. It stings like hell, but I slap it on anyway. She drags me to the den and hits mute on the clicker, but I lock my eyes on the silent TV. "Talk to me." Her voice is so mushy and annoying, like some baby-talk preschool teacher.

"It's nothing." Yeah right, like that's gonna get Piper off my back. My face is nasty busted and my brain's treading air, and if I think about Luke or Sam or anything for even a second I'll totally lose my shit.

"You know you can tell me anything, right? I think it's important for us...you know, to trust each other."

*Trust*? Seriously delusional. But, I don't know, *can* I keep it together? It's building up, fizzing. Mentos in Coke, gonna blow the cap right the fuck off. Piper's pity face makes me wanna scream, so I stare deeper into the TV. People crying about some tragic whatever. I picture me up there, my shitty school picture and people, like, *missing* me.

My fucking throbbing eye takes me out of it. *Boom. Boom.*

What do I tell Piper? That Luke got me again? That I'm still this weak victim kid? A lit fuse about to blow up some dynamite shitstorm?

This dumb leather couch is squeaking cause my leg's all drumkit. The burning-cold sprouts got my brain frozen, stuck. Lump in my throat, wet eyes. There's my mom's grave again, like my messy, comfy bed.

So I go for it, cracking my neck Holyfield-style, letting it all out. My voice goes all gravelly. This. Fucking. Sucks.

I tell her everything.

Piper's looking at me like she just saw a puppy get tossed into a woodchipper. Crying, I think. God she's so dramatic. "Asher, that's...terrible. I'm so, *so* sorry that happened." She touches my knee.

I flinch. *Don't* touch me. I *don't* need your pity. "No biggie. I'll just...I'll just suck it up this year." *Be strong, Asher.* As annoying as Piper is, she's not an idiot. No way she believes me. Hell, I don't either.

"What that boy did...it's *not* okay. No one should say those things to you. To *anyone*." She stops for a sec and looks at me all new, like a third eye just popped out my forehead. "Is there...something you want to talk about? You can tell me anything, Asher."

Uh, what's this? What's she getting at? Oh, god—is this about what Luke called me? A fag?

Nuh-uh. I bet she'd love to have a gay stepson. Total therapist jackpot.

I squint hard, trying to figure out how to dodge this bullshit, but my mind's blank. "Piper, I can't...I'm fine, I don't need...whatever this is." I shoot up. "I gotta take a shower."

I do a fast-walk to my room and slam the door by accident. It bangs really loud and the sound just hangs in the air a bit. I jump face-down on my bed and—shit. Nokia's digging into my thigh. Five missed calls and a text from Robbie: *Hey, man. Where did you go? Call me back!*

Can't deal with this, just need to crawl in bed. Not wake up tomorrow.

There's a weak knock on my door, but I don't move. Then quiet footsteps.

I roll over and grab the CD player next to my bed. Need to Raid all the bugs infecting my brain. Exterminate it all.

Dashboard Confessional starts up. Chris Carrabba's emo-whine cracks just like mine. Fuck you, Chris. I'm the one lying here with veggies on my face.

Can't stop thinking about Piper. What she meant. What Luke said.

I'm not gay. I'm *not* a fag. And who gives two fucks what Luke thinks?

...Right?

## *No Turning Back*

COULDN'T sleep. That fucking gator again.

Every night it's the same shit—cold yellow eyes, millions of teeth, that fat tail whipping around like a noose. I zigzag as fast as I can, but he's right there. I always bust awake before the kill, but I *know* it's coming.

Maybe today's the day he finally bites.

I roll up to school rocking this pathetic dark purple eye. Like fat Grimace caught me stealing his fries and clocked me. I begged my dad to let me skip. No dice.

We still haven't talked about The Incident. Thank god.

Robbie's leaning on his Civic, trying on his best tough-guy impression. But there's Luke's BMW, sitting like a tank ready to crush me. And Sam's Lexus? Double kill.

Stepping out of my car I snort some fresh air, but it's hot and wet and I almost gag. There's these long palm tree shadows, helping me disappear. I sling my backpack over my shoulder, slouching extra hard.

Then Robbie sees it. "Holy shit, dude."

I can't look at him. "I know it looks bad."

"Worse than bad."

"Thanks, man. Super helpful."

"I called you—"

"Was busy dealing with my dad and Piper. You know, getting grilled and shit."

Robbie kicks my tires like there's more to say that he's not gonna. "So what's the plan?"

"Jump from the belltower."

"No, *Luke*. Chloroform and kidnap? Cut his brakes? Rat poison in his Powerade?"

Thank god for Robbie.

I like picturing Luke's death as much as the next guy, but he never *really* goes away. I zig, he zags. Piper says zigzagging's a myth anyway. He'll bite me eventually. Bloody mess. "Let's be real, though—I'm fucked."

"I'll think of something. Give me till lunch." Robbie has this determined look in his eyes.

"You think everyone knows what happened?"

"They do, but fuck 'em. And fuck Luke. He's gonna peak in high school, anyway."

There's that pressure building in my head again. *Don't cry, Asher.* I fight it back, but kids are staring. A criminal and his accomplice.

"See you, uh, at lunch?" Robbie's all awkward now.

My eyes blur out while I spin my lock from muscle memory. "I really wish I could just stop that evil shithead once and for all." The creaky metal clank of the locker's got me jumping like a cheesy haunted house. *Get it together.*

Nine more months of this shit. Then it's full prison break.

No clue what everyone's thinking as I float up to English. Big, flashing neon sign on my face. But what the hell does it say?

I slink into class and fade low in my chair.

These two lifer guys I've known since pre-K, Danny Fein and Tommy Archer, they're whispering a few desks away. Danny's head turns with this smug, better-than-you look.

"W...what's so funny?" I'm all soft and wussy.

Danny whips around with these dickish eyebrows up like I don't matter. "It's nothing. Just some dumb shit."

I close my eyes tight and try to toughen up my voice. "I said, what's so funny, Danny?" I lunge halfway out my desk and shoot my lids open. "Tell me. *Now.*"

He just stares at me, messing with his gold chain. "Dude. Don't worry about it."

"What are people saying about me?" My long leg shakes like crazy, and my eye's throbbing.

"Uh, well..." Danny looks, like, scared of me. He turns to Tommy for help. It's gotta be bad.

I shout as loud as a whisper lets me get. "Just fucking tell me, Danny!"

Tommy jumps in, mad. "Fine! You asked for it. I heard Silas and some guys talking about it yesterday. That in the locker room, you were looking at the guys and, like, staring at Luke's, uh...dick...or something?"

My head goes weightless on my neck. "I...I don't get it."

"That you tried to grab him, dude." Tommy's voice drops to nothing. "That you...touched him."

Dunno what I look like right now, but it's gotta be crazy. Shaking all over with a busted face and dead-guy eyes.

"Forget it." He goes back to Danny like everything's normal.

*This* is what everyone thinks went down? I'm some kind of psycho sex predator, and *Luke's* the victim?

Suddenly one of the office ladies creaks the door open like a witch and sneers at everyone. "Is there an Asher Diamond in this class?"

Fuck me.

On the walk to Dean Pearson's office, I follow the covered breezy halls, dodging puddles from the morning sprinklers. I watch the sky like TV to turn invisible. The morning's kinda *too* perfect—bright blue with those puffy cotton clouds that always turn dark and mean later on. Like they're just *waiting* to beat me down. Classic Luke.

"There he is."

Why the hell is this Dean Fucking Pearson smiling so big? I think about turning and fleeing, but it's too late. Anyway, he'd just catch up cause he's a jacked ex-Dolphins running back.

"Morning, champ."

His voice is deep and scary. His big Hulk Hogan hand's jabbing toward me, waiting, so I let it squeeze mine like an orange.

Dean Pearson's door swings open, and the office AC hits me like a wall. A surprise guest is waiting.

My dad. Shit.

He's sitting up popsicle-stick straight in his chair, tapping his feet quick. I think he's nervous.

And—duh—me too. I scrunch my forehead so tight I'm gonna pop a migraine. "Uh...hi, Dad."

"Hi, sweetie." His voice is weirdly cheery for a criminal investigation.

Dean Pearson points his thick arm at an empty chair. "Sit."

So I sit like Robbie, folded over with my backpack on. Ready to *run*. I look at the wall, and this framed picture of Dean Pearson's staring right at me. He's in an old Dolphins uniform, clutching a football like a real pro jock. Like a hero or something.

Yeah—a hero. He's gotta fight for the good guy, right? He's basically G.I. Joe.

"Thank you for coming in today, Mr. Diamond." He holds his arm out at me. "Mr. Diamond." Then at my dad. Dean Pearson's pacing around. "We need to talk about yesterday. Coach Henley provided some pertinent information." He towers over me and my dad, ready to tackle.

Oh shit—does G.I. Joe think *I'm* Cobra Commander?

"I also spoke with Mr. Baker." Do *not* call him that. "He admitted he may have overreacted, but he claims he was...disturbed by what he witnessed. What you did."

"What? What did *I* do?"

"We're conducting an investigation—"

"I didn't do anything!" Tight chest, can't breathe. "This...this is *bullshit*."

"Asher." My dad turns at me with a super-scared face like I'm about to lose my shit.

"We need to ensure a safe learning environment here at Palm Reef, and before we jump to any—"

"What'd he say?" My voice cracks loud. "Tell me what he said!"

Dean Pearson's got his game face on. Looking at me all suspicious like my black eye isn't staring right at him. "I can't divulge that information at this time. But please, tell me from your perspective. This is a safe space, Mr. Diamond."

I'm so insanely pissed, but if I blow up? I'll just get fucked even harder. "Fine. It was after PE and I was minding my business in the locker room, changing and stuff. Then all of a sudden Luke comes over and starts saying all this...weird shit. He said I was, like, looking at him?" A cartoon frying pan bangs me over the head with humiliation, even though I didn't do anything wrong. And my dad hearing all this?

"And...were you?" Dean Pearson looks skeptical.

"Of course not! Jesus, *Luke* was the one acting all crazy. He started calling me these really bad names and screaming, trying to get everyone to, like, join in against me." Pressure's trying to bust out my eyes. "It was...it was bad."

I look over at my dad.

He's got this face like I'm so pathetic.

*Don't. Cry.* I close my eyes so no one sees me. "Then he...he ripped my towel off and started...hitting me. You know, rat-tailing or whatever. Then I just...ran. I didn't know what the hell he was gonna do to me. But then I slipped, I guess, and hit my head. That's why I have, you know...this." I point at my bruised eye, damning evidence of Luke's crime.

"I see." Dean Pearson sounds like some shitty detective.

"Asher's telling the truth. He's a good kid. He wouldn't lie about this. And he's not...you know."

What, a pervert?

"Alright, Mr. Diamond. I hear you. We'll look into the matter further and inform you of our findings."

Rage. Building. "No!" Nothing to look into. Nothing nothing nothing. "He attacked me." My voice cracks. "He attacked me!"

My eyes go wet. Backed into a corner. Again. Like the locker room.

Can Dean Pearson even hear me?

Am I nothing?

"I'm sure we can come up with an amicable solution, Mr. Diamond."

Hydraulic press crushing my head. Is he braindead?

I see my dad and Dean Pearson talking like puppets, but they go blurry and I go deaf. *Think, Asher.* How do I get him to listen, to take me seriously? How do I kill Luke fucking Baker?

My mind flashes back to that thing I saw on the news with Piper yesterday, that vigil whatever with all the crying people. Some gay kid got attacked, called a fag and all that. Beat up pretty bad. A hate crime, they called it. My mind spins out.

*You can tell me anything*, she said. She wanted me to tell her I'm gay. I think about what Luke called me. *Fag. Homo.*

Yeah, Luke? What if I was? Would this whole shitstorm get taken more seriously, like the kid on TV? Would Dean Pearson—would everyone—finally *hear* me? Would I be a better victim?

I yank my collar out to breathe. Could...could I pull this shit off?

Or would everyone hate me even more? Become a bigger outcast than I already am. Totally give up on *any* hope of a girlfriend, or sex, or...Sam.

Have I gone completely insane?

Maybe.

Probably.

Definitely.

But hey, when the whole world's trying to screw you over, maybe the only sane option's to just go totally fucking nuts.

Fuck it. I know what I've gotta do, to change things—for myself.

I shoot up from my chair and build a charge like Blanka in *Street Fighter*. "He...he called...he called me a fag."

The room goes dead quiet.

"That's what he called me." *Do it, Asher. Do it.* "And...and...I, uh...I..." I'm glitching out.

"Asher? Are you okay?"

"Yeah, just...um..." *Asher. Don't stop.* "There's something I...I need to say. I'm, um..." My voice is cracking like puberty. Stalling. But then—bam. Luke's evil face screaming at me, whipping me with the wet towel. Pushing that sloppy pizza all over me. What I saw on the news. The right kind of victim, the kind people feel sorry for.

"I'm...I'm gay."

Check fucking mate.

All I see are wide eyes and hanging jaws. I bet they've got no clue what to say. No one's actually said they're gay before at Palm Reef. They'd get eaten alive. Now I'm gonna be the first. Lucky me.

I look at my dad for help, like I'm a little kid again.

He stands up and puts his warm hand on my back. "Okay, listen to me." My dad leans in at Dean Pearson. "You're *going* to fix this. This is *not* acceptable." My dad grabs my chin, pulling it up to point at Dean Pearson. "Do you see my son? Did you hear him? And if you don't do what's right, then...I'll have to get some people involved." My dad's face is stone tough. The most badass I've ever seen him.

Dean Pearson stands up, too. Holding out his big hands, blocking his body from some invisible gun. "Now, let's not get carried away, Mr. Diamond."

"Do you know what this is?" His voice is low and all serious. "This...this is a *hate crime*."

*Boom*. It's like a bomb blasted in the room. Total fiery carnage.

"Come on, Asher, let's go. Clearly this isn't going anywhere." My dad grabs my arm and pulls me toward the door. But then he turns. "You'll be hearing from my lawyer."

Fuck yeah, Dad. Just like that my face dries up.

Outside the office, my dad puts his hands on my shoulders. "You okay?" He pulls me in for a big hug. "I...I love you." He squeezes me super hard. It's nice, but then I notice other kids passing by and looking. I pull away, like instinct.

My dad doesn't notice anything's wrong and grabs his belt-clipped cell. Probably calling a lawyer or something. But I don't want to listen. Can barely think.

I walk around the corner so my dad can't see me. All these kids stampede by, like the wildebeests that killed Simba's dad in *The Lion King*. I'm this nuisance, some perv who tries to peep at naked guys in the locker room.

Am I the creep who attacked Luke, or am I the innocent victim? The fuck's gonna happen now? Did I just pull the dumbest shit I've ever done in my life?

I lift my head and look down the hall, past the wildebeests.

There's Luke. He's leaning his arm over Jackie Kaplan on the science lab door. He's grinning like a real piece of shit, breathing rancid breaths all over her. His last ones, I hope.

Luke turns his head and we lock eyes—cold and yellow. His smile —big, teeth like daggers. A bloodthirsty alligator.

This is when I wake up, but I can't. I pinch myself.

Yep, awake alright.

What in the actual *fuck* did I just do?

# *Buddy*

"YO homo! Hold up."

The fuck?

Tommy barrels over and yanks me into this weird bro hug. Pounding my back like I didn't chew enough. He's smiling like I'm the goddamn president. "Asher! My boy." Tommy messes with his gold chain, all nervous. "Sorry I dumped that shit about Luke on you, dude. Didn't know about...you know..."

I space and forget reality for a sec—what I did—then I go, "Gay?" It hits my ears like Luke's fist.

"Yeah, that. Anyway, respect, man. Luke's always been a d-bag. Def Team Asher. Come smoke a J with us after English!" Tommy jogs away and wraps his arm around Danny's neck like they're dating.

Wait. What? Was Tommy just...*nice*, in his own moronic way? Acting all friendly *because* he thinks I'm a "homo"? What kinda parallel universe is this?

Oh, yeah. The one where I claim I'm capital-G gay and everyone loses their goddamn minds. Gossip buzzing around like bloodthirsty mosquitoes. Dean Pearson, what a dick. I guess *brave kid comes out* beats *kid gets gay-bashed in the locker room.*

Had to hide in my room yesterday, too much thinking and freaking. Like, is this lie gonna have to go forever? Am I gonna be a wrinkly pretend-gay virgin rotting on my deathbed?

No, fuck that. Make it through senior year. Survive Europe with my dad and Piper over the summer. Then jet out of Florida for good. Out of the country, full-on witness protection. Or maybe I can drop out right now. Heard Antarctica's nice this time of year.

Been ducking my dad cause I don't wanna talk about it. And I'll be damned if I'm giving Piper the whole *I'm gay* drama she wants. No, I'll bolt this new monster I created into my comfy little prison with Michelangelo.

On my way to geometry, Silas and his posse walk at me. Great, here it comes. A beatdown for offing their psycho cult leader. But, no, just snickers and nods. What?

Silas passes me, then swivels back. One eye all squinted, tapping his lacrosse stick like a mafia guy with a bat. "Nice bruise."

My eyes go wide like that shower girl's in *Psycho*. "Thanks."

Jackie Kaplan and this girl Allie Alvarez meet up with the guys. They look me over like I'm nothing. Like always.

But then they run up to me. "Where'd you get your jeans, Ashy?" Allie grabs at my pants.

Ashy? Jeans? Seriously? "Uh...Old Navy, I think?" I mumble like it's the most boring thing in the world. "My dad's girlfriend got 'em for me."

The girls giggle—great—but then Allie messes up my hair while Jackie pokes my bruise. "They're cute."

Why the fuck are these hot, bitchy girls finally being nice to me? All I can say is "Thanks," drooling probs.

The bell—geometry time. Even Mr. I is smiling at me in class.

Normally he just glares cause I have a C- and don't try.

Bell—lunch. I grab a chicken patty with rice and gravy and scan the caf for Luke. Where's he at? No way he's in trouble yet, right?

Probably hiding under a table, ready to pounce.

I sit down to eat. My cold chocolate milk's the only thing that feels normal today. All the attention? Definitely *not normal*. My brain needs a control-alt-delete, but I'm scared to reset it and deal with reality.

Robbie slams his butt down so hard and outta nowhere that my chocolate milk drops all over my food. Great. Even worse, what the hell am I gonna say to Robbie?

"So...why didn't you tell me?" Robbie's squinting at me.

I just stare back. My mind wipes clean like an Etch A Sketch. "Tell you what?" *Eject. Eject.*

"Is it true? You're...*gay*?" His whisper sounds like cymbals slamming on my head. A fucking wake-up call.

I have to tell him—don't I? He's the only one who's been there for me, like, for real. All the bullshit? *He* was there.

Fraud, coward. Victim, hero. What the hell am I? Leave Robbie in the dust to fend for himself? Be the biggest asshole ever?

Not yet. Gotta make sure Luke's gone first. Then I'll talk to Robbie. Yeah, that's it. I'll get to the truth one day. "Yeah, I'm...you know..." I can't even say it. Pulsing behind my eyes. Selfish, alone, bad liar.

I guess Robbie thinks I'm gonna cry about it, so he nice-guys me. "It's okay, dude." He picks up my milk carton like *I've* dropped and spilled, too. "Listen, if this is what you want...if this is, you know, who you are...then, I got you."

"You do?"

Robbie's playing with the carton like it's a Rubik's Cube.

Rubbing his scar, trying to solve the rigged *Asher* puzzle, maybe going back through everything, making sense of me and this bombshell. He almost looks sad. "Of course, you dumbfuck. You're Asher."

Gut punch. I feel fucking sick and so amazing. Best friends forever, worst friend ever.

Robbie flips a switch and he's all wide-eyed and hyped. "And I have *so* many questions."

Oh god. I squeeze my eyes shut so tight they'll never open again. Hopefully.

"Any crushes?"

"The fuck, Robbie?" Shit—is this a test?

His hands go up. "Hey, I'm just trying to help. *One* of us has to get laid."

*Laid?*

"Felipe Torres, that theater kid who played Joseph last year? He might be...you know. Got that Elijah Wood thing. You *were* weirdly into *Flipper* in third grade."

I think I'm having a heart attack.

"Well if he's not your type, there's always me." Robbie puckers up and makes this high-pitched squeezy sound that could shatter glass.

"Robbie, fuck." My leg's bouncing outta control. "No crushes, no. I can't...I can't do this." I shake my head and drop it like it's a dead body. *Bang. Bang. Bang.*

"Well, if you ever wanna scope out some guys, I'm covering soccer for the TV station. We can zoom in on those shorts."

"Jesus, Robbie! I'm not a fucking creep."

His face scrunches up like I shoved a lemon in his mouth.

"Shit, sorry...I, uh, didn't mean it like that." *I'm* the creep. *I'm* the crazy one.

"It's fine." Robbie forks his chicken like it's some gnarly science project, checked-out all of a sudden. "I've got some stuff to do before class. I'll see you later, okay?" He gives my shoulder a squeeze, then sulks away to toss his tray in a pile of wet garbage.

"Robbie, I..." Too late.

Just like that, I'm freezing and burning up, fucking terrified. Appetite's gone, so I chuck my trash and float down the hall. Airwalks dragging my body till they drill into the ground right by Dean Pearson's office. Luke comes out the door.

But no smug look. He's totally ghost pale. Eyes all lobotomy. Then his *parents* come out, too, looking *pissed* as fuck. Dean Pearson gives Luke's dad this handshake that looks really final or something.

Luke's eyes shoot up as he walks his droopy face right at me. I'm just...frozen. His eyes get super intense. Death stare. He passes in slow motion, I swear, and he mouths something with these violent lips and teeth. *You're so fucked.*

The whole world goes away and I'm totally alone. Did he get expelled? Is Luke...gone?

Bet *he* can tell I'm full of shit. He knows me better than anyone, in some sick way. I kicked the hornet's nest like an idiot, and they're buzzing around all angry and waiting to sting. I stirred up something...new. Something scary as shit that could ruin my fucking life.

Almost totally dead, I get another jump scare. Sam fucking Coolman's waiting at my locker. *You stare at my tits again and I'll cut your tiny little dick off. Grow some balls.*

Shit.

But something's, like, off. Never seen her like this. Red eyes, baggy sweats, messy ponytail. I think I see an *actual* zit. What's this girl doing here? Where's the pink knife?

I take these baby steps so maybe I'll never get to her.

"Um...can we talk?" Sam's all soft and shy. She tucks this little strand of hair behind her ear with her middle finger. Hot.

Feels like Dracula's at my neck. "Yeah...sure."

"Listen, I just want to say sorry for Luke, and what—"

"No, no." I interrupt like a flinch. "You don't have to—"

"Yes, I do." Suddenly she's all hard. "When I heard what he did, I was like, what the fuck, dude? He's such a vile douchebag, I...I don't know why I put up with him."

"Oh, he's not...that bad."

"Look at your eye, dummy. Luke's a fucking asshole. And...sorry for treating you like shit, too."

I stare at her soft lips. "It's fine. It's...whatever."

"Stop being so nice, freak." Sam tugs at that blonde strand. "I know I'm a raging bitch."

"You're not a bitch, Sam."

She does this cute, scary laugh. "I literally told you I was gonna cut your dick off." She does a head shake like it's something she thinks about a lot. "I don't know what's happening with me and Luke. Things are a mess. I've been thinking about dumping his ass for a while, so maybe now's a good time." Her eyes get redder. "Anyway, I just wanted you to know...I've got your back. For real though, okay buddy?"

*Buddy.* Shattered.

She looks up at me with these flirty eyes. Major mixed signals. Maybe this is just how she is with guys—even gay ones. Like a complete bitch or like she wants to fuck you.

"Thanks, Sam." My heart's racing for a million reasons. If she breaks up with Luke, because of me? What's he *really* capable of? *You're so fucked.*

Sam gets on her tiptoes and pulls me into this warm hug. Her big tits feel awesome against my chest, and her fancy perfume gets me drunk in a split sec. "If you need anything, just lemme know. No one's gonna fuck with you anymore." She freezes up like there's more to say. Awkward, almost. Totally un-Sam. Digging a long, pink nail into her finger so hard she's gonna draw blood. I get a quick smile, then she's off.

Sam Coolman rubbing her hot body all over me? Having my back? Never in a million years.

Maybe this is, like, a sign. That things are gonna get better.

You know what, Luke? Come at me, bro. I dare you.

For once, *you're* the one who's fucked. Not me.

# Sunshine and Rainbows

AFTER school all I can do is sprawl dead on the big brown couch and watch Homer Simpson strangle his son. Brain's too fried to laugh. Stuck spinning on Luke's freaky threat, Robbie's weird new vibe, and...whatever the hell Sam's deal is.

Totally surreal at school today. "New-and-improved gay kid" could help me out, but I can't stop picturing this big, fiery wreck.

Suddenly, my dad busts through the front door like the Kool-Aid Man. "Oh, Asheroooooooonnnny!"

What the hell's this about?

My dad hops into the den like it's a stage. And, Jesus, my jaw drops through the floor. He's got on something so insane my face burns up.

A T-shirt: *Proud Dad of an Awesome Gay Son*, with *Dad* and *Son* in rainbow stripes. He's waving this flimsy little rainbow flag like it's gay Fourth of July.

I wanna jump out a window. Sad for me, my house is only one story.

My dad's arms are out, waiting for applause.

I think I feel chunks jumping up my throat. I grab an ugly pillow

Piper forced on us and press it against my face to pass out. Not working.

My dad pries it off me and chucks it. "What do you think?" Big eyes, all excited.

This shit is next-level cringey, even if I *was* gay. Can't he just strangle me like Homer and Bart? Grab my skinny neck and have at it? Better than whatever *this* is.

I grab the remote and click fast to crank the volume, but my dad walks up to the TV and hits the power button. Damn.

He scrunches his forehead like I failed some secret test.

"So I talked to Dean Pearson today. He called and told me he expelled that kid, that...little P.O.S."

"Wait, are you serious?"

"Yep. You don't have to worry about him anymore." My dad gives the rainbow flag a little wiggle.

My eyes pop open and I float off the ground. Holy fucking shit. It worked! My totally psycho stupid plan worked!

My first thought's to call Robbie, but...uh, too complicated.

"I got you something." He reaches into a plastic bag and hands me a hat. Not like the normal Dolphins or Marlins ones he gives me.

It's black and says *PRIDE* in all caps. Big rainbow over the letters. Red, orange, yellow, green, blue, purple. Burning my retinas. "Put it on, Asher!" My dad yanks the hat from my hands and slams it on my head. I go still.

Maybe it's like *Jurassic Park*. If I don't move a muscle the T-Rex'll leave me alone.

"You look *fabulous*."

I. Want. To. Die.

"Oh! I almost forgot." My dad darts to the kitchen and comes back with a suspicious Dominos box. He opens it at me like it's some expensive champagne. "Hawaiian. Your favorite."

Is this like a bribe or something?

Luke's pizza stunt flashes in my head, and my hand freezes. Fuck. So I glide my hand to the box super slow. Careful, like reaching into an alligator's mouth. Making sure I don't lose a hand. I snatch a piece and try to bolt, but my dad tugs me back by the collar.

"Sit with me." Shit. Dean Pearson's office all over again.

We move to the couch and I shove my face with ham and pineapple. Can't lie with a mouth full of pizza.

My dad gets all serious like he's about to bust into a monologue from "a very special episode" of *Full House* or some shit.

I slam my face with more food.

"Asher, I just want to tell you how proud I am. It takes guts to do what you did." He messes with my hair like I'm a little kid. Is that what I am now? A good kid who gets a prize?

"I love you, and I'm here for you."

My dad hugs me and I get all stiff, clutching my pizza slice like a shield. Awkward as hell, but weirdly okay, too.

I get over myself and give in. Body goes limp, letting my dad hold me up. No guilt, just a nice feeling that catches me off guard. Warm, safe, and for a sec I think I'm hugging my mom. "Thanks, Dad." He went outta his way to do all this shit for me, so I throw him a bone and wave the little flag around. Such a tool.

Thank god he isn't making me talk about what actually happened in the locker room. Maybe we both like avoiding things.

My dad in a nutshell. Focus on the positive. Sunshine and rainbows. Vague support. Just fine for today.

Out of the abyss, Piper walks into the den. Has she been sneaking around the whole time?

She goes in for a hug, but I twist my head around and let my arms hang loose. She squeezes hard anyway, playing the part she wants—mom.

No way. I rip myself out of the hug quick.

"Asher, I was thinking...I read about this cool event in the *Sun Sentinel*." Oh my god, just shut up, Piper. "The LGBT community center is hosting a dance this weekend for gay youth."

I haven't even been fake gay for forty-eight hours, woman. Back off.

That phrase *gay youth* sounds really dramatic. *Don't think about it, Asher.*

"We thought it might be good for you." Piper's smiling like the devil himself. "To get out and meet some other gay kids your age. You know, so you don't feel so...alone in all this? Plus, you might even have some fun."

*Stop. Saying. We.* Blood boiling under my skin. *Don't* talk for my dad, and don't act like you know how *I* feel.

"No way." I bite my tongue cause I have to. Can't freak out at her. Gotta be this new person. New Asher—whoever that is. I swipe the pizza box and dart to my room.

Completely wiped—TV land, here I come. I toss the pie on my bed and crawl behind it, ready to inhale the whole thing. Turn the TV on and it's *Jeopardy*. I don't know the answers but doesn't matter. Slowly, the pizza's tasting better and better. Like victory, like Luke can eat shit.

*Fuck. Luke. Baker.*

I look into my pizza like it's a crystal ball. Tomato sauce—red. I spot Michelangelo in his tank—orange. Number two pencils on my desk—yellow. World civ book on the floor—green. All the *Jeopardy* screens—blue. Alex Trebek's tie—purple.

A goddamn rainbow.

After I scarf down the whole pizza, I head to my bathroom to wipe my nasty grease fingers. As I rub the dirty towel on my hands, my reflection grabs me.

I *think* I recognize that guy. Baggy white T-shirt. Stick arms. Baby face. Too tall for any of it. Huge fucking bruise on my eye.

And now I'm wearing a stupid hat with a dumb rainbow on it. Too big for my head. Stiff, new. Awkward, uncomfortable.

Totally not me, but I feel everything...changing. Like this hat, and how everyone sees me? It's who I *am* now. Who I have to *become*. A better person, I think. If only I was entirely different than who I actually am.

I rip off my hat and see my messed-up wavy hair. Pile of dark curls that won't listen. Dandruff, frizz. There's that boring Asher again. Like nothing happened.

But then I pop the hat back on, and my new alter ego's here. Gay Asher, now in technicolor. I move the hat up and down, off and on. Me, morphing like the new gay Power Ranger.

I picture myself on TV. On *Jeopardy*.

The clue: *This teenage boy pretended to be gay for revenge, and everyone was nicer to him—until they weren't.*

I buzz in. *Beep-beep.*

My voice barely squeezes out: *Who is...Asher Diamond?*

# Eeny, Meeny, Miny, Moe

*SHCCHHHLUUUURRRRPPPP!*

My big Friday night after this batshit week? Stuck in suburbia with Robbie at Barnes & Noble. His lame caramel frap won't shut up, and it's pissing me off.

"You done slurping that girly drink yet?" My eyes pulse laser-shots. Something's up with us.

Barnes & Noble is Boca's big hotspot—fake culture in a bland strip mall, squeezed between Whole Foods and Circuit City. Sure, the pretentious front is fake as hell, but shit—so am I. Anything to catch a break from the Palm Reef petri dish. Too bad I can't shake the monumentally stupid, maybe genius lie holding me hostage.

We're upstairs, hiding in the shelves. Robbie's polishing off three caffeine shots. How the hell does he handle that supercharged buzz? Just one electrocutes my brain.

Fuck—my dumb ass scorches my tongue on molten hot chocolate. I plunge my tongue into whipped cream to cool off the burn. I'm so outta my mind I can't even drink right.

"One more." Robbie takes his last big slurp, staring me right in the eyes. "Ahhh."

"Is that your jerk-off face?"

"Wouldn't you like to know." Robbie shoots up and tosses his sticky plastic cup at me. "BRB." He struts away to who knows where.

So here I am, ditched all pathetic in the self-help section—our favorite spot. Fun to watch the losers creep in and peep the books about being too fat or depressed or divorced or whatever.

And sometimes, if you'd listen hard enough? Grown women just *crying*, trying to hide.

Always felt weirdly good to be reminded I wasn't *that* fucked. But now? Not so sure.

Some random self-help book's pulling me like a magnet. *How to Be Your Most Authentic Self in Five Easy Steps*. Which step is pulling some insane shit on everyone you know, pretending to be gay, and lying to your own best friend?

My finger's up at the book when Robbie jump-scares me. "Holy shit, Asher. I struck gold!" He chucks a shiny magazine my way.

I read it out loud like it's a clue in a scavenger hunt. "*XY Magazine*. Huh."

Now this shit's real crazy. Two guys on the cover, teens with perfect faces like they're CGI or something. One's got frosted boy-band hair and a puka shell necklace, pinned against lockers by some jacked shirtless dude who's staring right at me, like he knows something.

"I figured you'd like it. Hot, right?"

Jesus. Fucking. Christ. "Dude, get that shit away from me." I lob the magazine at Robbie like a grenade.

He slides down a bookshelf, squeezes too close, and flips through the pages like we're in this together—even though I want no part of it. Looking into some weird alternate universe where all the guys are ripped and running around half naked.

*This* is what gay guys look like? *This* is what I'm supposed to be?

It feels like these models and their perfect smiles are mocking me and Robbie—two normal-looking straight guys spying on their weird gay sex world. They're having the time of their lives. Especially locker guy. He knows *exactly* what's coming.

Robbie finds a guy with glasses and a sweater vest, supposed to be a nerd I think. But in the world *I* live in, dorks don't look like Arnold Schwarzenegger.

"What about him?" Robbie circles the fake nerd with his finger. "Hot glasses, like Rivers Cuomo twice the size without any talent."

Is Robbie testing me or am I just paranoid as fuck? Shit, he's like one of those shrinks with those black-and-white ink things, trying to crack my brain open for the truth.

Nope. "Um, he's okay, I guess." My mind's all gunked up with sludge.

"Fine, I get it. Not your type...let me see what I can—" Robbie licks his finger and flips through, then stops on a big two-page spread. Jocks in football uniforms hanging out in a locker room. Half naked, eye-fucking like tigers. Suddenly I'm time-warped back to school, half naked too, rat-tailed by Luke. Frozen. "Maybe you're into these big football guys? Yeah?"

The gay jocks blur up. I'm dizzy and my eyes are all crossed. If I wasn't such a coward, I'd just tell Robbie the truth.

No, too risky. If anyone found out? Shit, I'd be dead. *Stick with the lie, Asher. Play along with this magazine crap.* If I'm gonna pull it off, I gotta figure out how to act like a *real* gay guy or whatever.

"Yeah, uh, sure...they're really...hot." My phony words hit my ears like total bullshit. My lie's coming to life, busting outta my chest like that baby xenomorph thing in *Alien*. A tiny little deadly thing, killing me—slow—from the inside.

"Fine, show me who you like, then." Robbie's rubbing his scar.

Swallowing some of that sludge, I scan the douchey meatheads and do a quiet *eeny, meeny, miny, moe*.

I land on a jock. Wet hair dripping. He's pulling a leg out of Spandex pants, and he's big in the way girls like Sam are addicted to. His face bothers me, though. Eyes too close together.

Oh, shit. He looks like *Luke*.

I dart my shaky finger at him. "This one's nice." I'm gonna pass out and brain myself on some razor-sharp self-help book.

Robbie scrunches his face like he ate too many Warheads. "Eh, I don't know. Looks like he loves jacking off in the mirror."

I chuck *XY*. No clue what to say, so I rip the plastic frap cup lying dead next to me.

Robbie goes all quiet and flops on his side, maybe for a hard reset. "So, how'd your dad take it?"

My eyes shoot open.

"You told him, right? About...everything?" Robbie's voice sounds like me right now. Shaky and weird. We both totally suck at talking about real shit.

Maybe Gay Asher's better at touchy-feely stuff? "Well, Dean Pearson brought him in, and we had a meeting all together. That's where I, uh, you know."

Robbie squints. "Oh...I didn't realize..."

"Uh...yeah. My dad kinda freaked at Dean Pearson and threatened him with lawyers and all that..."

I'm staring at that book while I blab, the one about being your *authentic self*. "But then...you know my dad. Allergic to sad shit. Went all quiet, then got psyched about the whole thing. Threw this cringey pride parade and slapped a rainbow hat on my head. It was all a bit, uh...much."

Robbie looks down and plays with a snag in the carpet. "Well, I think it's nice."

He *loves* my dad. His dad's totally harsh and controlling. That *no-elbows-on-the-table* kinda hardass I see on TV. Why Robbie set up camp at my house all these years.

"Nice? Um...I guess." I stare at the weird green sea witch on my cup. Suddenly I feel ungrateful for my dad. "I don't know. It just felt really...surreal, and, like, awkward."

"Of course it's gonna be awkward." Robbie puts on this nasal, whiny Cartman voice. "Now that's what I call a sticky situation."

What a dork.

"Piper thought I was gonna kill myself or something. She's so fucking dramatic. Trying to have a corny heart-to-heart. I wanted to crawl out of my skin."

"Maybe you shouldn't be so hard on her."

Easy for him to say.

"I haven't even told you the worst part. She told me about some stupid dance for, like, gay—or whatever—teens coming up. Like I'd be caught dead. Probs so fucking lame." I *hate* school dances. Off-the-chart nerves. Some not-hot girls pulling me onto the dance floor to engage in age-old ritual public humiliation—a slow dance.

"Like you have such a busy social calendar." Robbie's almost laughing. "When is it?"

"Uh, tomorrow I think."

Robbie's smile goes deranged. "Oh, we're going."

"Hell no." My face burns up thinking about it. *Real* gay people. Pulled deeper into this bullshit lie. Quicksand swallowing me up for good.

"Tough shit, Asher. We're going. No offense, but there's nothing going on for you at school. Everyone's boring...and straight." Robbie grabs the *XY Magazine* and holds it high, pointing to the two horny guys on the cover about to hook up.

"*This* could be you." He stabs the guys quick with his finger.

Oh shit. This *could* be me if I don't watch it. Like, am I gonna have to make out with *guys* now? Fuck that. Can't even compute.

Maybe I should have thought twice before I screamed I was gay like a fucking idiot.

Robbie's eyes go all psycho-excited. Like he scored front-row seats to watch my life explode into some bloody *WrestleMania* shitshow.

"Get ready for a field trip. Buckle the fuck up, bitch."

## *Oz*

IT'S the night of the dumb dance, premiering Gay Asher 1.0. Kill me.

My closet's all exploded and wrecked. I massacred *XY Magazine* trying to hack an outfit, but my options suck. Just boring tees, school polos, and Macy's clearance-rack junk my dad grabs blind.

I shouldn't care what I look like—it's not like there's gonna be any hot girls there or anything—but to pull this off, I've gotta look the part. Any real gay guy would know I'm a faker in, like, two seconds. So it's Mission: Maybe-Impossible. Keep up the lie and come out alive—or else? *Kaboom.*

Way too much pressure for one dumb outfit.

I close my eyes and grab some shit from a drawer. Yellow Gap polo, dark blue stripe. Fine, I guess. Gotta throw on an undershirt for my nervous pits too.

I jam on my Airwalks, scope *new me* in the mirror—not working yet. I pull at my boring jeans—instant flying squirrel. A really tall skeleton, terminally awkward. My big, fat bruise—a red stop sign. Stay away. Juvenile delinquent.

Oh! Duh.

I jump to my closet and pull out an old brown Members Only jacket. Got it at Salvation Army with Robbie back when us nerds found out thrift stores were cool. Some art girl at school said I was a poser, so I stopped.

I'm covered. Hidden. Might even look kinda cool.

Okay—let's do this shit.

"I'm leaving!" I slam the door behind me and bolt.

Tiny brown lizards freak as I stomp, like I'm Godzilla himself pounding shockwaves in my driveway. The moon's just a sliver, but there's still light. Late-summer sunset.

Gotta pump myself up before I chicken out. So I tune to Y-100, hoping to get hyped by some stupid pop song. Pink's screaming at me to start the party. The Top 40 sludge drowns me while I try to man up—and gay up.

First stop: grabbing my psycho, supportive best friend. Can't believe he's making me go to this dance. Maybe he's plotting with Piper to get me a boyfriend.

Robbie's got no clue he's shoveling my grave. He's trying to help, pushing my limits—new me or whatever. I'd rather hide out in bed till graduation.

Rolling up to his house, I catch him peeping out the window. I stare at his cheesy pelican mailbox as he walks up and hops in. The wood bird's looking at me all cross-eyed and funny, like it knows I'm full of shit. Maybe Robbie knows I'm full of shit, too.

"Cool song, bro. Guess you really are a f—" Suddenly Robbie stops tugging his cheesy yin-yang necklace he got from the Hollywood boardwalk off some guy who offered us drugs. "Shit, man, sorry—"

"You don't know me...*bro*." I hit mute him real quick, pretending Robbie didn't say that word. The steering wheel pulls my skin as I squeeze tight. I give his Hot Topic shirt-of-the-day a dirty look. "You even listen to Nirvana, or just the Weird Al version?"

Robbie just rolls his eyes cause I'm being a prick. "Okay, what's with the PMS?"

"Sorry. I'm just, uh…"

"Nervous? No shit, Sherlock." Robbie spins the volume loud and dances to Pink like a dork. He screams. "Get used to it!"

I'm choking on guilt, so I roll down my window. My car gulps warm, salty air and damp heat sticks to my skin. Glad I wore this undershirt.

We creep up to this real boring office building. We both just sit in the car, staring at sad half-dead palm plants and a huge rainbow balloon arch. Subtle.

Deep breath.

Robbie yanks my ear. "Ready?"

"Fuck no."

Robbie grabs my hand and tugs me hard through the doors like a kid getting dragged to the dentist. My clammy hand slips, almost breaks free. If I ate shit and broke a bone I could skip this whole sham.

Inside, a mean-looking lesbian with a gray crew cut and my exact polo glares us down with the enthusiasm of a DMV worker. "Welcome to Oz."

She shoves a Sharpie and name tag at me.

I think about lying but don't. *A-S-H-E-R* looks like hieroglyphics when I write it.

She slams it on my chest like a brand.

Robbie draws a heart thing over his "i." My life's such a joke.

That new Cher song is playing when we walk in this kinda medium-big meeting room thing. I think I saw on MTV or something that gay people worship Cher.

The room's not empty, but it's not exactly a hotspot. Everything's *Wizard of Oz*. Another gay thing, I think. These big sloppy Emerald City cutouts hang around the room, and some poor guy had to tape down a whole fake yellow brick road across the floor. So. Much. Glitter.

Me and Robbie poke at the decorations like astronauts crash-landed on Mars—foil streamers, saggy balloons, whatever. Two straight guys pretending we belong. I chug a Sprite like it's vodka. Brain freeze.

"Everything you dreamed?" Robbie slurps his Fanta.

"Dream, nightmare, same thing."

As Robbie rolls his eyes, I realize—damn—I can't shit on this forever. What would Gay Asher think? What would he say? Gotta figure it out, and quick.

Robbie bullies me into dancing to that song "I Will Survive" and I feel dumb as shit. I don't know why Robbie's having so much fun. Feels like I'm being forced into a sweaty hora hurricane at one of my cousins' bar mitzvahs or something. I wanna burst into smoke and disappear like the wicked witch.

But no. I'm right here for everyone to see. Can they tell I'm a lying freak?

The song ends and I spring to the snack table to hang with my real friends. Doritos, jelly beans, chocolate chip. I demolish one like Cookie Monster, like a fucking beast.

But, shit, Robbie's talking to some dude on the dance floor. The fuck?

He's cupping this random guy's ear, and his eyes stab at me like a vampire. The two of them walk up.

I almost die choking on my dry cookie. Heart pounding. Faster.

New guy holds out his scary hand at me. "Hi, I'm Ethan." Too chipper, get him away from me. His big smile and white teeth make me feel like a total slob. Robbie's watching us real close.

I mumble out some crumbs. "Asher." I give him a light handshake like I don't care.

He's one of those guys girls probably dream about. Dude's got the whole package—tight green Lacoste polo showing off his gym muscles, jeans that actually fit, and these leather shoes I'd never think to wear in a million years. He's even got that hemp necklace thing and a chunky silver watch, and his dark hair's all frosted like NSYNC. Total pretty boy. The kind of dude Sam would be all over —if he wasn't into guys.

It hits me. He looks straight outta *XY Magazine*.

Let's get this bullshit chit-chat over with quick.

The guy squints at me like I'm some circus freak. Oh yeah, my huge fucking bruise. "Man, I don't want to see the other guy."

"Yeah, that...I, um...it's..." *Don't say a fucking word, Asher.* I shoot Robbie a look like he reads minds. Gotta leave Luke in the past. Fuck Luke.

New guy shakes off his grossed-out look. "I love your jacket! Is it vintage?" He skips the part where you ask and just starts rubbing the polyester on my Members Only. At least I got the jacket right.

He gives me this smile that looks real. "Your first time at one of these things? I haven't seen you before."

Commence the lying Olympics. I sprint to an answer before Robbie can blab. "Yeah, our first time." New guy's got no clue who I *really* am. Damn—neither does my best friend.

"Asher just came out, like, yesterday." Thanks, Robbie. "No, like literally this week."

New guy laughs. "No shit, Asher. Congrats!" He pulls me into a hug and for a sec I think he's gonna give me a noogie.

Feels so fucking weird. One night out and there's gay guys all over me. "Thanks, but uh, no big deal. Not like I cured cancer or anything."

He waves his hand to delete what I said. "It *is* a big deal! You only get your first big coming-out moment once. Live it up, girl!" Fucking cringey. "So, how'd you end up here in Oz?"

"Oh, uh, my dad's girlfriend told me about it. Thought it'd be good for me or whatever." I nod over at Robbie. "Then this guy made me come, trying to pimp me out or some shit."

"And...Robbie, is it? You're gay too?"

"No, no." I blurt quick before Robbie can talk. "He's just, uh, moral support." I slide my fingers through my hair and give it a tug to sting my scalp. I'm kind of a dick to Robbie, glaring like he did something wrong. Even though we both know he didn't.

"Well, he sounds like a really good friend." New guy puts his arm around Robbie and squeezes.

Robbie's all tense, flicking and pulling at his cargo flaps. All this stuff's new to him, too, I guess.

We talk a bit cause I don't know how to get out of it. New guy goes to a different school in Fort Lauderdale, not that far from Palm Reef. He's alright, I guess. For a sec I wonder if I'm jealous of him, which sounds totally insane. Maybe cause he isn't awkward like me. Super weird to see this...better version of fake me, Gay Asher. *No, shut up. You sound crazy.*

Good thing it's the last time I have to see the guy.

Crunch and blood. "Ow! Uh..." Robbie squeezed his empty Sprite too hard and now his palm's bleeding.

"Oh my god, are you okay?" Ethan darts to the snack table and snags a napkin to help, but Robbie pulls away.

"I'm, uh, just...hold on." Robbie slams his eyes shut like he knows he's a spaz and heads to the bathroom.

Shit, now it's just me and new guy. I crack a full set of knuckles with my fist. "This is kinda...normal Robbie behavior."

New guy sticks out his bottom lip. "Aw, he's cute."

Robbie? Cute?

Coma-inducing pop music fills the awkward space between us. The hell do I talk about? He'll probably figure I'm straight in, like, two seconds. Robbie, why do you have to be such a freak? Get back here.

"Has anyone ever told you your eyes are striking?" New guy's tapping his toe and hiding his arms behind his back. "Are they green?"

"Uh, yeah. Green." I always thought they were ugly and kinda boring, but maybe gay guys like them.

"I wish I had green eyes." His eyes shoot up at me and he kinda trails off. Maybe he's awkward, too. I'm Netscaping my brain for an excuse to get the fuck outta here, but then new guy clears his throat. "So...can I get your number?"

My lungs freeze up. Am I getting...hit on? This some kinda joke?

The hell do I do? If I say no I'm a dick, and if I give him my number I'm a dick for leading him on. I'm such a fucking idiot.

I grab new guy's arm and scribble my number with the Sharpie I stole from that lesbian.

Robbie walks back up looking like he's gonna explode. Chill, dude. If anyone's gonna get blown up it should probably be me.

"Let's definitely hang out! I love making new gay friends. We have to stick together."

*Ding.*

New guy pulls out his cell. "Oh, shit. My ride's here."

Thank god. I say I gotta go too, and Robbie nods.

We all head to the lot, super dark. New guy stands in front of me and grabs my shoulders. "Remember my name?"

"Uh—"

"It's Ethan." He gives me this slimy kiss on the cheek. Kissed by a *guy*? Check. "Don't forget." He turns his eyes and body to Robbie a gives him a polite handshake.

A pimped-out silver Mustang with blackout windows rolls up and Ethan slides in. Him and whoever zoom away.

Whew, he's gone.

Me and Robbie just turn our heads at each other, shocked, like we just met a celeb. We head to my Nissan and drive. Gotta get outta Oz.

Windows down, I hear my tires crossing the train tracks by Dixie Highway. Heading toward I-95, buzzing neon signs and harsh floodlights whizzing by. Beaming back through the gay wormhole to reality.

"I don't know about him." Robbie's flicking his nails. "He's, like...too pretty. Suspiciously pretty."

I think about calling him jealous, but what's the point? Gotta forget this night ASAP. Instead I just say a lame, "Whatever."

"Dude, stop being such a downer."

Robbie doesn't get it, what I've done, what I have to deal with now. But, fuck—maybe he's right, even though he doesn't realize why. Keeping up this lie is gonna kill me.

The vibe's weird in the car, and the wind whistles loud through the sunroof. Robbie closes his eyes, slumps down, and melts into the passenger seat. He swipes his forehead back and forth.

I stare at the road, watching the white lines tick by. "Can't everything just...stay the same?"

"Probably not."

Unlike Robbie, I don't get to rest. Fucking wide awake, mind spinning out like a raging category five. My foot on the gas gets heavy, zooming down the highway like a shuttle launch.

I've got two options. Give up the lie, or just charge ahead.

Can't go back to before. Harassed, bullied, fucking assaulted. Luke. Feeling like absolute shit, lower than low. My guts churn, bubbling toxic gas.

Robbie shifts in his seat, rubbing at his eyebrow scar. "So... this is just who you are now, huh?"

He said it better than I ever could. Simple. Final. No rewinds. No exits.

The only way out is through.

I'm Asher Fucking Diamond, and I'm *definitely* gay.

# Good Gay

SAM Coolman's smooth knee is rubbing up on me, and my pair of jeans is fighting for its life to stay dry.

Friday, lunch, another weird-ass week. One week closer to freedom.

I *hate* that Sam thinks I'm gay. Closer than ever, but still no shot in hell.

Sam's lips look hot wrapped around a Nutella sandwich. We're with her alleged best friends—Jackie Kaplan and Allie Alvarez. Disposable goons in short skirts. I've overheard some of the guys talk. Jackie's a butterface and Allie's got lopsided boobs.

"What do you think?" Sam leans forward and juts out her cleavage like Superman. She basically pushes her tits right in my face, knocking me out so hard I might get brain damage. They're squeezed into a skimpy blue shirt. Definite dress code violation, if teachers had the balls. I even see her pink bra.

"Uh, what do I think about...what exactly?" I blink fast, try not to stare—failing.

"My Victoria's Secret, duh. Too slutty? Or hot in a Sarah Michelle Gellar kind of way?"

"Not...*too* slutty." I'm scared as shit and praying my cheeks aren't dorky red. "It...um, they...look good. But, I think I can see your... bra?"

Sam laughs. "No shit, Asher. That's the point." She reaches into her shirt and pushes her boobs up even more. "Guys like it this way. I know Silas does."

Kill me.

She was kinda vague, but she said she broke up with Luke after he got axed from school. Something about him being a "fucking loser." Since then, Silas's stepped in as Luke's replacement. Not much of an upgrade.

Sam's spewing more shit about her bra and I zone out. Can't tell if she *actually* cares about me, or if I'm just a new person to talk at. Like, an accessory or something.

Sam smacks her lips and taps her nails on the table. "So Mr. Asher, how do we get you a boyfriend?"

Sucks I can't scream my guts out without the whole caf thinking I've lost it.

I obviously have nothing to say about dating, other than: *Please Sam, let me put my tongue in your mouth.* But I can't say that. "Uh..."

"Where are all the pathetic closet cases hiding out here?" Sam bites the tip of her finger.

Jackie's eyes get wide. "If I was a gay guy and didn't want anyone to know, maybe...the football team? Slapping each other's little butts."

Sam giggles in this scary way. "Yeah, football's so...*faggy*." Suddenly the air's gunked and awkward, then Sam eye-rolls right through the weirdness. "You know what I mean."

Allie coughs. "Maybe the lacrosse team." She raises her eyebrow at Sam. "There's this guy Silas, super-hot."

"Not funny, Allie." Sam tugs on the ends of her hair. She leans in toward me but talks loud. "Silas isn't gay, Allie just gave him a bad hand job on Space Mountain."

Allie's eyes glaze over. Jackie copies Sam and laughs.

I should shut up. I do not shut up. "Yeah, uh, they probably have, like, secret post-game blowjob orgies or something."

Dead. Silence. Sam tilts her head. "What the actual fuck?"

Abort. Abort. "I—I mean, I just saw this magazine—"

Sam's eyes get sharp like knives. "Oh my god, Asher Diamond looking at gay pornography?" She pokes my chest and scratches me like a dog. "Bring it in. I *need* to see this."

Jackie snorts. Allie scrunches her face. I'm dead.

Brain spirals. Oh god, Sam picturing me lying in bed, hunched over in some lonely gay jerkoff session, fantasizing about Silas and sweaty sports orgies.

I need to fucking launch myself into the sun. "No! Jesus. I mean, it wasn't like—" I rub my forehead. "It was just this thing that Robbie showed me—never mind."

"That guy's so weird." Sam peels apart her sandwich crust. "You can do better."

"*Much* better." Jackie smiles at me, looking pleased with herself.

Then, a long silence, until Allie mutters under her breath. "It...it wasn't Space Mountain."

Sam groans and flicks a crumb off the table. "Oh my god, Allie, nobody cares."

I stare down at my chocolate milk, shake my leg, and focus on not existing.

My eyes wander and I catch Robbie at our corner table, alone, his lame orange Kipling still on. He's chewing on the collar of his Austin Powers *Yeah, baby!* T-shirt, a bad habit since he was, like, seven. Every few minutes he looks over at me and squints. Is he jealous I'm hanging with Sam? Does he want to hook up with her, too? Probably thinks I've lost my mind—not wrong.

Despite all the insanity, there *are* some perks to being a big fat liar.

The guidance counselor pulled me out of bio on Tuesday to lecture me about how hard my life is—or, was. Some closeted sad sack getting bullied. It's like she thinks she knows my life better than I do. Is this what it's like to be gay? All these...assumptions?

So I just nodded along and let her talk, popping jelly beans. She said I can go to her office whenever. A get-out-of-class-free card. I'll fake some TV-movie gay crisis, grab candy, and let her ramble. I'm traumatized, after all.

Also weird? The popular guys stopped calling me a fag and all that. Maybe it's no fun for them since I "came out." Maybe torturing an *actual* gay person takes out the thrill.

But I wonder how long this truce is gonna last. A good reason to keep lying.

Things are weird at home, too. Piper's holding me captive in this re-education camp for gay teens. She made me and my dad watch *The Laramie Project*. She kept glancing at us like we were supposed to, I don't know, bond over hate crimes? Awkward as hell.

My dad made me watch *The Birdcage* for movie night. Funny, but is that what he thinks I'm gonna be? Some flouncy gay cartoon? Is that how I'm supposed to act to be a good gay guy?

I've got a feeling that kids at school wouldn't like me as much if I was, like, flamboyant or whatever. To them, I may be gay, but at least I'm *normal*. People can only take so much before they start seeing me as some freak. And I do *not* want to be a freak anymore.

I've been watching *Queer as Folk* at night in my room. Research.

Damn, gay guys sure like to fuck. And it's everywhere—the club, the bushes, at work even. They make it look so *easy*. Not that I've ever, you know, actually tried to get laid.

Everyone on the show has a six-pack and loves to party. They go to this club every episode. Babylon. Must be nice to have a place like that to go. Escape from reality.

"Asher, you *have* to come over this weekend. We're laying out." Sam's deep, sexy voice yanks me back to reality. "Silas gave me a joint, so we're gonna smoke up by the pool and watch *Freddy Got Fingered*."

"Uh, yeah, maybe...I'll think about it." Half-naked girls? What if I pop a boner? Couldn't lead anywhere good.

Sam yanks a potato chip out of Jackie's hand and shoves it in her mouth. "Don't be lame." She chews big and gives me this flirty smirk. What's with this girl?

When we're done with lunch she gives me a tight hug and I feel her tits smush against me. Allie and Jackie do it too and now I feel like a little perv, tricking them. I don't know what I am anymore.

So, things are better. But also, I'm freaking the fuck out.

Robbie? Guilt.

Sam? Straight-up brain blender.

Home? I feel like a fraud.

Everyone's butting in about who Gay Asher should be, but everyone wants something different. I'm not some puppet. Can't I live my fake life in peace without people shoving their hands up my ass?


After school I'm home, bored as fuck and trying to numb out my thoughts.

I'm half-watching a *Home Improvement* rerun, wishing life could be that easy—all problems solved in a cool half hour. Also playing

*Minesweeper* and eating Cheeto Puffs. Hypnotized by clicking random squares, watching the shapes change and waiting to get bombed.

My cell bleep-bloops. Unknown number. Nobody calls me except Robbie. I think about ignoring the call, but I answer anyway with my sticky Cheeto fingers.

"Hello?" The word flies out between disgusting munches on cheesy puffs.

"Hi, uh, Asher?" The voice sounds familiar.

"Yeah, um, it's me."

I hear a laugh. "It's Ethan, from the dance. I hope it's okay that I called..."

Oh, shit. I forgot. Didn't think he was actually gonna call. Fuck.

I sit up really straight even though I know he can't see me. "Oh yeah, hey. Um...what's up?"

"Not much, just living the dream."

I'm not thinking straight, no clue what to say. "Cool..."

"So, uh, I was wondering if you wanted to...hang out?"

Oh, no. No, no, no. Hanging out with gay guys? Is that really necessary?

And why does he want to hang out with *me*? He seems like a high-functioning, popular guy, and I'm just some rando. And, god, worst of all—does he think it would be a *date*?

I should hang up and throw my phone out the window.

Then, suddenly, a wave of dread. Nine more months of this—the rest of the year—sounds so so boring.

But...is this an opportunity to change? Mix things up? It's risky, yeah, but isn't Gay Asher different? Maybe he takes chances and doesn't act like a pussy all the time.

Gotta keep my cover. Gotta play the part. Maybe I can learn a thing or two about how to act from a real gay guy, not like all the other people butting in.

And, honestly? I have absolutely nothing better to do. Fuck it. "Uh...sure. When were you thinking about..."

"How's tonight?"

"Oh, tonight...uh..."

"You have plans, of course." Ethan backpedals.

"No! I mean...no." I can't tell him I literally never have plans. Only a loser. "Sure, let's do it. What are you thinking?"

"Have any cool hangout spots to show me?'

"Uh...I usually just fuck around at the Barnes & Noble by my house with Robbie...not very exciting."

"Great! I love that place. I need to grab the new *Teen People*." Ethan sounds really enthusiastic to hang out with...me? "Should we invite Robbie?"

"God, no!" I blurt out before I even think. "Uh—I mean, nah. He's, uh...busy."

Ethan's silent for a sec. "...Coolio. See you at eight?"

That was fast. "Okay, cool. I'll, uh...see you then."

I chuck my phone like it's burning a hole in my hand. My tongue licks off the bright orange Cheeto powder caked onto my fingers, and then my weak brain goes back to Minesweeper. Immediately click on a bomb.

Landmines everywhere. Pray for me.

## *Dirtbag*

*TAP-tap-tap. Tap. Tap. Tap. Tap-tap-tap.*

My foot's calling for help in Morse code. SOS.

I'm waiting outside Barnes & Noble, hands stuffed in my shorts pockets. No clue what I'm doing here—or what I'm getting myself into. Ethan slowly creeps out from the almost-dark parking lot, like Ghostface in J. Crew.

But he's not a creepy killer. He's put together all sharp. And super, super gay.

He's got these ripped-up jeans with a tight baseball tee, and a necklace with shiny beads. My beat-up blue-and-white Adidas Slides make me look like a kid, and he could be from The Strokes in his worn-in red Converse. His hair's styled in a way I would *never* try. I'd look so pathetic trying to look cool or suave or whatever. Luke would've had a field day on me.

Ethan gives me a big hug, and his chest against mine feels really weird. Are gay guys just constantly hugging?

We make our way to the Starbucks inside and order. His treat.

*Shit—is this a date?*

I ask for a black coffee cause it sounds sophisticated or adult or whatever, but it tastes like garbage. Ethan orders a hot chocolate. Damn. Jealous.

We sit across from each other at a square table, like a job interview. My paranoid foot taps quick. Can people hear us?

*Do they think we're on a date?*

Ethan's pretty chill so—eventually—I calm down a bit. It seems like he's a decent guy, I guess. He actually wants to hear what I have to say. Asks questions. Listens. The constant eye contact freaks me out, though.

I learn a lot about Ethan Segal. He just turned eighteen and lives with his mom in an apartment in Fort Lauderdale. He's Jewish, too, but his parents are from Venezuela. Maybe that explains his nice tan.

His dad left when Ethan was little. Moved to California to start a new family with some "dowdy" woman from work. Crazy.

Ethan's obsessed with Britney Spears and goes on about seeing her last tour in Miami. His mom took him. He came out when he was fifteen, and he's still the only out gay kid at his school. His mom's fine with it, but he has no idea what his dad thinks about him being gay, because they never talk.

Ethan speaks all confident, just loud enough, like a grown-up. Technically, he is one. "So, how's it been so far?"

"What do you mean?"

"You know, coming out. It can be, uh...kinda nuts." Ethan's eyes get wide. Like something from his past just popped into his mind.

I'm not sure what the hell to say, so I focus on slowly swirling my black coffee around the cup.

Ethan seems to pick up on my cluelessness, so he keeps talking. Nice of him.

"When I came out, everyone at school was talking about it...and I mean *everyone*. Even the teachers gossiped about me. I wouldn't be surprised if the janitors did, too. Not that me being gay was a big surprise."

Ethan laughs at himself. It's probably cause he's kinda girly or whatever. His body and his voice are loose.

"I just couldn't take it anymore, you know? I knew I was gay…I've known forever. But I didn't want to hide it anymore. I mean, what's the point? I was gonna have to come out eventually—why wait? The last thing I wanted was some sad, repressed life. So I just did it. I came out, and the rest is history."

Weird, that's what I did too. Ran away from some sad, boring life. "Did anyone ever, uh, bother you about it?" There's something kind of impressive about his fuck-you attitude.

"Of course they did. You know how straight boys are. When I first came out, they'd talk in the hall, staring at me when I walked by. The jocks would ask me the stupidest questions about gay stuff. Why are straight guys so fascinated by anal sex?"

Uh, anal sex? No. I laugh to cover up what a huge dickhead I am for lying to this nice, innocent guy. My neck swivels as I scan for the nearest exit.

My fake laughter dies down. Now it's too quiet. I try not to twitch my face when I gulp down my bitter coffee.

I decide to ask something real. "Did the guys mess with you… before you came out? I, uh…yeah." I chicken from talking about Luke.

Ethan laughs and waves his hand like it's obvious. "I mean, I'd come up with dances to Janet Jackson with my girlfriends during recess. It's not rocket science…and have you heard my voice?"

His voice isn't a dead giveaway, but I know what he means. It's more the words he uses and the way he phrases things and stuff like that. Never really heard it before except on TV. He's not cursed with a *truly* gay voice. No big lisp or anything—a death sentence as far as high school douchebags are concerned.

"I've been called gay and a fag more times than I can count. Eventually it got old, and I just stopped caring."

I wonder if that's true.

I'm silent for a bit, thinking about how different my situation was. I wasn't running around the playground with girls. I had Robbie. We probably just looked like loners. I mean, we were. My voice doesn't sound gay and girly, either. It's actually kinda deep and masculine. But the volume's low—weak, quiet, like a total pussy.

I *was* still called all those names, though. *Gay. Fag. Homo.* It got kinda whatever eventually. There were other names, too. *Loser. Nerd. Retard.*

Was Ethan called *those* names? Doubt it. He may be gay, but he looks like the popular guys. Biceps that actually fill his sleeves and muscles and stuff. WB hair, like Andrew Keegan. If he acted like a bro, he'd probably fit right in with Luke's posse. Really fucking confusing why he's here with me.

Ethan's looking at me with a raised eyebrow, tearing away at his paper Starbucks cup. What's he waiting for?

Oh yeah, I need to actually say something.

Because he's been so open with me, I guess I can talk about Luke and all that. Gotta keep up the lie. And Ethan's not so bad.

So I go into it. Crash and burn. How that kicked off my big coming out. As I'm talking, I almost forget I'm lying.

Well, lying about some of it. Everything Luke did to me? That really *did* happen.

Suddenly I'm all anxious. Leg's shaking, the toxic lie and the buzzy black coffee getting the best of me.

Ethan's eyes let me know he can tell I'm panicking. I wonder if he gets anxious, too. "That's really horrible, Asher..." Ethan's quiet, then gets bubbly again. It takes the pressure off and lets me chill out.

"But the black eye looks pretty awesome. Very mysterious, that whole bad-boy thing. The boys are gonna love it." Ethan laughs. "And, well, now you know me. Guys like us have to, you know, stick together." He smiles at our bonding moment.

*Guys like us*—shit.

Ethan smacks his dry mouth. "You hungry?"

I feel nauseous from the deception and the gross coffee.

*Is this a date? IS THIS A DATE?*

"Uh..."

"Everything okay?"

"Well, I don't know how to say this, but...is this...is this a..."

Ethan nods his head up and smiles. "A date?" He laughs. "Trust me—you'd know if we were on a date."

*Thank fucking god.*

Ethan reaches his arm around my shoulders, squeezing and pulling me in. "I need some nuggets." He says it all casual, like we're friends already.

I don't tell him I only had Cheetos for dinner. We hop into his yellow RAV4 and drive down the road to McDonald's. We put the seats all the way back and eat fries and nuggets and shakes. They taste fucking great. Better than ever.

He's playing a mix CD with some gay shit. Christina Aguilera. Britney, obviously.

Ethan's a really good talker and a little insane. He quickly figures out how to make me laugh, so I let myself laugh. Letting go of all the bullshit from the past few weeks, like an evil spirit's being lifted right outta me. Feels fucking awesome.

"Teenage Dirtbag" comes on. I love this song, but a surprising choice from Ethan. It's a loser-straight-guy anthem. He sings along, off-key and not giving a shit. Confidence I can't imagine. But I feel weirdly safe in his car, with this gay guy. Drunk off salt and fat and sugar.

So I join in. Quiet, then louder. The lyrics sound totally new. I guess that's always how I saw myself—like a nobody, but secretly wishing everything was different. Hopeful and hopeless at the same time, all tangled in a big knot. A teenage fucking dirtbag.

Then we get to that big climax, and I *really* let go.

Totally surreal. Alone in a car with a gay guy. Singing. Having fun. Not caring about anything or anyone else.

After the noise dies down, Ethan drives me back to my car.

I sit there hoping there's no more hugs.

"Let's definitely do this again." Ethan smiles at me in this way that feels, like, *real*.

"Um, yeah, sure...if you want."

"No doy, cutie."

Before I step out, he hugs me over the center console.

As he drives off, I snap back to reality. Drive home in silence. My focus goes in and out—blurry and clear—and I hear us singing. An echo. The echo gets louder and louder in my head. Too fucking loud.

Then like a fucking tsunami.

Fuck—a dumb suicidal squirrel darts out of nowhere. I swerve and slam the brakes. Miss a stop sign by an inch.

Pitch black. Quiet.

My heart's pumping like crazy. Some scary, intense feeling. I don't know what the fuck is going on, but it's not like *anything* I've felt— ever.

Not Robbie, not Sam, not sad internet porn.

Ethan's not treating me like some new, shiny toy or some fragile, traumatized gay kid. He gets me and actually wants me to feel good about myself. Maybe he wants to feel good, too. Maybe I can even help him.

Feels like I'm being ripped in two. Tonight, was I fake Gay Asher or the real me? Could I be both at once? The ease and warmth of the night turn harsh and cold. Again.

Lyrics barge back. Me, a teenage dirtbag. Lying and lying and lying. Hiding, holding everything in, fantasizing about something better. I wonder if the song means something to Ethan, too. If he has demons, too.

I turn the ignition and my headlights flash on. And of course, there's the motherfucking squirrel, staring me down. He knows I almost killed him.

I almost messed myself up pretty bad, too.

Be careful, Asher. You're fucking dangerous.

# Welcome to the Jungle

MY arms are snapping like pretzel sticks, no match for the empty bar. Pathetic.

It's Monday. Weight training "class" with Robbie. Humiliating as fuck.

After the locker-room incident, Dean Pearson moved me and Robbie to weight training—to "minimize conflict." Regular PE's hell anyway. Too many ways to disappoint everyone. Here, we stay under the radar and pretend to work out.

The jocks blast "Welcome to the Jungle" and the aggro rhythm taunts me: *I wanna watch you bleed*. Weights clank like a warzone. Testosterone hell, but still better than team sports.

It's so weird that "coming out" made this jungle easier. Before, I got some dick-ish comments about how weak I am. But now the guys just check themselves out in the mirror and leave me alone. They love lifting their shirts and flexing their abs. I wonder if they want me to look. Gross.

I really shouldn't be spotting Robbie on the bench right now. One wrong move and the bar will slice his head right off. He's stronger than he looks, actually. Soaked with sweat and I'm totally dry.

"So...how'd it go with Ethan?" Robbie smirks, his yin-yang necklace swinging.

I roll my eyes. *This* is why I haven't told him anything about the hang yet. "It's not like that...I...I'm pretty sure." Robbie's mid-press, probably counting my nose hairs. "Just...fuck off, I don't know."

"Whatever you say, Asher." Robbie punches the heavy metal bar up at me. "So...what if it *was* more than friends?"

"I'm not into Ethan." But how can I explain it without Robbie hating me forever? "He's just...not my type." I tap my foot fast under Robbie's head. "Can we please drop it?"

"Didn't you say before that you don't have a type?"

"I don't, but...I don't know what the hell I'm doing, Robbie. I'm just not interested in him. In anyone." I notice my voice get desperate. "Okay?"

"Fine, Asher. Chill out." I think Robbie's trying to chill out, too. Our friendship's suffocating in the thick, sweaty air. "Was it fun, at least? Hanging out with him?"

I start to pull on my left middle finger. "Uh, yeah...fun. Easy to talk to. Like, not braindead. Cool." I skip the part about how fucked-up it felt to pretend to be gay the whole time.

Robbie sits up and pats down his red, sweaty face with a towel.

Shit. I didn't mean *Robbie's* uncool, even though—duh. But...he's no Ethan.

Robbie tosses his nasty towel at my head. "Maybe we can all hang sometime. You, me, Ethan?"

I yank it off. Gross.

"I want to get to know this guy who's so...*cool*." Robbie does the air quotes thing with his fingers.

Dang, maybe I do sound lame and desperate. Practically sucking

Ethan's dick. Not literally. Why does Robbie care so much? Is he jealous? Am I not allowed to have another friend?

No, gotta dodge that shitshow. Just play it cool—like Ethan would. "Yeah, uh...maybe."

Robbie looks disappointed, but my acting's getting better.

"You wanna come bowling with me and Jax Saturday night?" Robbie's voice cracks a bit. "He's working on his perfect three-hundo."

Ugh, Jax. Sketchy thirty-year-old from Robbie's fire-juggling thing. Wears flame shirts, Oakleys inside. Thinks he's hot shit. He's fucking weird, and it's weird that Robbie hangs out with him. Robbie worships him. I do not.

Maybe I gotta throw Robbie a bone, though. "Sure. You know I can't pass up a good tater tot." I force a smile like he's a stranger.

We move to the mat for sit-ups. The rubber floor's sticky from jock sweat and Monster. I do about eight sit-ups before I drop. I rest back on my elbows like I'm trying to catch an indoor tan under the harsh fluorescent lights.

But Robbie powers through the sit-ups—determined—beyond the pain.

Couldn't be me. Not here, anyway.

His dad's always pushing sports on him, so maybe Robbie's trying to prove something. That he can be a real masculine guy, too. He can get buff, too. Get his dad off his back.

One time in sixth grade, me and Robbie were making these dumb Beanie Baby videos on his dad's camcorder. His dad stormed in and ripped the tape right out—didn't even say anything. Didn't have to.

We knew. Instinct. Boys have to be a certain way, and we can't ever forget that. Robbie's dad doesn't let any of it slide. At least my dad doesn't pull that shit. He lets me do whatever I want, be whoever I want. And now even be...gay.

There's some stuff I think I get a little more, now that I'm gay or whatever. Hearing Ethan talk about his life, I'm learning. Growing. Changing.

Change is good. Right? "Do you think I've changed?"

Did I seriously just say that out loud?

"What do you mean? Of course you've changed." Robbie talks through heavy breaths, still working out. Getting stronger, not letting my stupid insecurities throw him off. From changing himself.

"I mean, sure. Technically I've changed. I'm, you know...whatever. I mean, I always was...I think?"

Robbie stops his sit-ups and sips his water bottle. He's flat on his back, quiet. I search his face for something—anything—and a few seconds feels like torture.

Eventually, he breaks. "I just hope you know what you're doing."

Fucking spooky. To get away from this awkward shit, I start as many sit-ups as I can before I collapse. Pushing my body to its limit, to some unknown place.

Finally, I fold. "I know what I'm doing, thank you very much."

The obvious truth? I definitely don't.

After school I walk back to my car. Another day survived. Barely.

Suddenly—of course—it starts pouring. Totally soaked, like water balloons. Typical Florida weather, but today it feels mean. Some lightning bolt up there. Charging, waiting to zap me.

I scurry to my car for cover like a rat to a pile of garbage. When I hop inside, *bleep-bloop*. A message from Ethan.

*Hey boi. Wanna hang out again?*

For a sec, I'm not paranoid. Not stressed. Not scared my life's about to explode.

*Yes, def.*

A smile hits my face fast, then drops just as quick. Mouth hanging open, frozen. My eyes blur at the windshield as the rain gets louder, heavier, scarier. Raindrops popping off like bullets. Thank god I'm in my car, behind thick glass.

But what happens when the bullets get too strong?

What happens when the glass shatters?

## *Jockey*

ME and Ethan decide to hang at his place tonight. I already regret it.

Piper jizzes her pants when I tell her I met a guy at the dance that *she* suggested. Apparently, they have no problem sending me off to hang out with some random gay guy. Gotta be *really* happy I'm doing something new for a change.

I drive a half hour back down I-95 to Fort Lauderdale, no clue what to expect. Will I still like Ethan tonight? Will I run away? Will he figure me out?

Pulling up to Ethan's apartment building, I notice it's nothing like my neighborhood. No gates, no fake ponds, no golf carts. When I get out of my car, it feels like I stepped into some other universe— messier, more real. The air smells sweet, like flowers and chlorine.

I curve around this glowing blue pool surrounded by little apartments with windows looking out. The sky's pink and orange, and tall messy grass sways under big tropical leaves. As I walk through, I feel like people are watching this sketchy guy creep through their world.

After I climb the staircase, a rainbow flag sticker greets me at Ethan's door. Scratched, worn, like it's been there forever.

Ethan's mom, Raquel, opens the door and gives me a big hug. Her sharp, pitch-black hair makes her look like a bitch maybe, but her smile's warm and the hug feels good. She's youngish and stylish. Hot in that porny MILF kinda way.

Which makes Ethan seem even cooler. No uptight parents or big expectations. Can picture them sitting on their kitchen countertop like in movies. Chilling, laughing, tossing popcorn.

"It's so nice to finally meet you, Asher."

Finally? Didn't I just meet Ethan, like, two minutes ago?

Raquel has a Venezuelan accent. Really exotic. All the other Jews I know are just ordinary.

"Aren't you the most adorable thing? *Muy lindo.*" Raquel reaches out and pushes my scruffy hair to the side. Inspecting my black eye. I wonder if she knows how I got it. "Ethan's told me so much about you. Do you want a snack, *mijo*?"

I do, but Ethan walks up and grabs my arm, dragging me to his room. Maybe he's embarrassed by parents like everyone else.

His room is super cozy and unique. I stand there looking at all his stuff—purple beanbag chair, piles of magazines, green lava lamp. I've always thought beanbag chairs were fancy. I know they're not, but it just feels that way.

There's a big signed Britney Spears poster above Ethan's bed. Just sixteen, sitting on her knees with this innocent smile. A peek of underwear right up her skirt. It doesn't feel pervy here like it would in my room—before I came out.

Britney looks nervous. Exposed.

I get it. But I'll keep my underwear to myself.

I ask Ethan about the poster and he says he got it signed at a meet-and-greet at her Baby One More Time tour. His mom took him. The best day of his life, he says.

The rest of Ethan's wall is…kinda crazy. I'm not trying to be a prude or anything, I swear. Guess I'm just not used to all these… *dudes*.

It's basically a big porn explosion. Shirtless guys, Abercrombie models, cologne ads, the Backstreet Boys, firefighters in their underwear holding big hoses. I even recognize a couple guys from my copy of *XY Magazine*. The one I've been hiding under my bed and studying like I should be for school. Very closeted behavior for someone who just came out.

Everyone's bodies are unreal. Like action figures, but sweaty. I lean in, nodding like I'm appreciating the view. That's what I'm supposed to do, right? Can't look too weirded out. Can't look too into it. I settle on a tiny fake smile. Hope it works.

"I just *love* that Jockey ad. I've been obsessed with it since middle school when I saw it in my mom's *Cosmo*. She must have known something was up when she noticed all the ripped-out pages." Ethan laughs to himself and runs his finger along the firefighters' cartoonishly huge bulges.

"Uh, yeah, me too. They're so…hot." I must sound like a total fucking idiot. I might never get used to this.

Ethan walks over to his stereo and puts on Avril Lavigne "Complicated." I understand her. Completely.

Ethan's singing under his breath. He looks really happy.

"I like your room. It's so unique. Mine's just…boring." I'm embarrassed that I'm putting myself down like this. Ethan would *never*. Get it together.

"It's my sanctuary." Ethan falls back on his beanbag chair for dramatic effect. "It keeps me sane." He grabs a magazine, then hops back up onto his bed. He's facedown with his legs up, kicking over his pillow, like a girl would. I think I'm supposed to do it too. Copy him.

Cause that's what I do now. I fake it.

We're looking at the new *Rolling Stone*. Jennifer Love Hewitt half naked in a guy's button-down. Jerked off to it last night, but can't tell Ethan. When I look close, it feels like Sam, staring right at me.

How many times has Ethan jerked off to those firefighters?

"I loved her in *I Know What You Did Last Summer*." Ethan sounds serious. "Her boobs are huge."

I get an idea. "What are you waiting for!" I do a half-ass impression from the movie. Shit, don't think it landed. Why did I do that?

But then Ethan jumps on the bed. He spins around and around. Fast. Screaming so loud the neighbors might call the cops. "WHAT ARE YOU WAITING FOR!"

I bounce up and down on the bed as he hops. Can't imagine doing something like that. Shouting. Taking up space.

Ethan plops back down on the bed and my body launches up.

"Ryan Phillippe is so fucking hot in that movie. But he's even hotter in *Cruel Intentions*, don't you think? I can't believe he actually showed his butt."

I don't say anything. I don't want to think about Ryan Phillippe's butt, and I'm distracted by a memory. I wanted to see *Cruel Intentions* when it came out back in ninth grade, but it was rated R so I had to see it with my dad. So fucking awkward. Never talked about it since.

Ethan throws down *Rolling Stone* and lays on his side. Staring at me. His arm's propping up his head. He kinda looks like Sarah Michelle Gellar in the movie when she seduces her stepbrother. "So, have a crush on anyone?"

Why is everyone obsessed with crushes? Can't I be a reclusive, celibate, fake gay guy in peace? "Uh, no. And, um, everyone's straight."

Ethan rolls his eyes. "That's never stopped *some* people."

What's he mean by that? Maybe I'll find out eventually.

"It's so boring being the only gay one at school. Well, the only one who's *openly* gay." Ethan grins.

He's got a point. I wonder how many dudes at Palm Reef are gay but haven't come out. There's *gotta* be someone. Luke and his terrorist cell made it so fucked that I was the only one who could come out. A heterosexual liar. Part of me always wondered if that sick fuck Luke is secretly gay himself. He *was* weirdly obsessed with me and dick.

"What about you? Into anyone?"

"Well..." Ethan trails off and grabs a pink stress ball from his desk. He looks at it like it's the most important thing in the world, squeezing it hard, just for a few seconds. "There's this guy I've been kind of seeing. Um...he's a little...older, though."

"Oh, uh, how much older?"

Ethan tosses the ball back and forth, then flips one hand to catch it on the back like a hacky sack trick. "He's...twenty-six."

"Wow." The fuck? What the hell is Ethan up to? Is he doing that *Queer as Folk* shit? It's like he's a full adult instead of a dumb kid like me.

"So, what's he like?"

"He's in law school at Nova. The smartest person I've ever met. You know, he's also breathtakingly handsome. I just about died when he came up to talk to me. His eyes..." Ethan puts the pink stress ball back down on his desk.

This guy sounds shady as hell, but Ethan looks so happy talking about him. What do I say? And what does this creep actually look like? "Can I see a picture?"

Ethan picks at his nails, the first time I've seen him uneasy. He opens his desk drawer and pulls out a photo. A disposable camera pic from the passenger seat of a car, the flash blinding the guy behind the wheel. Covering his face with his arm, hiding. This photo is *not* wall material.

I can barely see him, but Ethan's so excited, it feels like I gotta say something nice. "He's very handsome." I don't want to disappoint him. Lying is good sometimes, right? "So what's Mr. Perfect's name?"

"Uh, let's just call him...John." Ethan rubs the back of his neck.

Damn, another big red flag. Sketchy as fuck. But I try to keep a straight face. "How'd you meet a twenty-six-year-old, anyway?"

"At Pantheon." Ethan says it all casual, like I'm supposed to know what that is.

I just stare at him.

Ethan's mouth drops open. "Wait. You don't know Pantheon?"

"Ummm..."

Ethan grabs my wrists. "It's the *best* gay club." His voice got gayed up a couple octaves. "There's an eighteen-plus night on Saturdays, and they play the *best* music. *Everyone's* there."

Gay club? No. No no no. And who's *everyone*?

"I've been going since sophomore year. And don't worry. I can hook us up with drinks."

Sophomore year? The fuck? Drinks?

"And they do this gay prom thing every year for high schoolers, because, you know, homophobia." Ethan smiles big and stares at me. "It's really cute."

Gay prom? Wasn't even planning on regular prom. I nod like it's all great. Like I wanted this. Like I could ever pull it off.

"We *have* to go to Pantheon soon."

"Well, uh, hate to break it to you, but I'm...not eighteen yet." I pray that'll get him off my back.

"Not a problem, my dear. I know the door guy. He loves me."

Jesus, stop having all the answers, Ethan! Will it be like Babylon in *Queer as Folk*? All that dancing and drinking and fucking? No way, dude.

"Don't worry. It'll be great."

Ethan must be able to read my mind. Or maybe I look scared as shit.

The gears in my head are all snagged. System's failing. Everything's getting...too complicated. Trapped—in my lie, in my body, in this random gay guy's pornographic den of iniquity.

The metal gears crunch hard, loud, sharp. Sparks. I blurt something out before I totally shut down. "Fine."

"Yay!" Ethan gives that big smile again. "This weekend. It's settled."

*This weekend?* When I told my crazy lie to Dean Pearson and my dad, this *wasn't* what I imagined. I just wanted Luke to go away. I'm so dumb.

Oh Fuck, Robbie. Bowling. Should I tell Ethan I can't go out?

Robbie would understand if I canceled, right? He basically pushed me right toward Ethan anyway. Yeah—Robbie will be fine. He has Jax. They'll have a good time without me. Better, even.

Ethan stands up and looks me over.

I'm stuck in place, holding my breath. My body turns stiff and my lungs stop pumping—I'm staring wide like a raccoon who just got caught stealing trash.

"And I'm taking you shopping."

## *Gun*

TODAY'S the day. To start: mall fucking madness. Then my first (and last?) night at a goddamn gay club.

I'm lying by the pool to chill out. Not working. The sun burns my eyes between the low, drifting clouds, and these shitty neon bar mitzvah sunglasses aren't doing shit. Big, gay headache.

Ever since I hung out with Ethan, I've been spiraling. School's been a total blur, and now today's stupid shopping trip is supposed to fix me or something, I guess?

A little brown lizard crawls up the leg of my chair and stares me down, puffing out this bright red fin under his chin. He looks like he wants to fight.

I'm practically sliding off the lounge chair, all this tanning oil. Still pale as hell. I wish I could get a nice tan like Ethan. I *really* need to not look like myself anymore.

Ugh, *shopping*. Ethan hasn't said to my face that my clothes suck, but I can tell that's what he's thinking. I dress to blend in, not to stand out. He's trying to have me go against my instincts, I think. Probably a good idea. Maybe he can tell I'm sick of being me.

I flip over to play *Snake* on my cell. Just as I'm about to crash into a wall, I get a text from Robbie. *Hey man. Am I gonna c u tonite?*

Shit. Still haven't told him I can't go bowling. Avoided it, like a coward. *Can't. Piper fucking it up.*

*K :/ Ttyl I guess.*

I head inside and bury my cell under a pile of clothes.

After my shower, I dig up a pair of elastic basketball shorts and a white T-shirt. Is this really the best I can do?

I dig through my junk drawer and pull out an old shark's tooth necklace—something me and Robbie got at the Seaquarium in fifth grade. I slip it on, check the mirror, and rip it off quick. Looks so dumb. Clearly I have no fucking clue what I'm doing. Guess I do need help.

Michelangelo's sleeping under the little fake log in his tank. His black-and-white tail's poking out. So lucky he doesn't have to wear clothes.

I slip on my Airwalks, head to the mall, and hope for the best.

Me and Ethan said we'd meet at Auntie Anne's, but he's not here yet. The pretzel-wrapped hot dogs in the glass case are making me drool. Maybe I can slam some down before Ethan shows.

Some fed-up mom's screaming at her kid in the background, which echoes really loud in the huge space. I jump when Ethan taps my shoulder from behind, but his hug calms me down.

"Excited?" He's got this devilish energy flying off him. Shit.

Ethan looks at me and my eyes hit the floor. I kick my toes down onto the squeaky marble.

"If I say no, can we leave?"

"No."

I poke at my forehead. "So...what exactly are we trying to accomplish here?"

"We need to make you look presentable for Pantheon. Well, *more* than presentable—we need to make you look *hot*."

That word makes me itchy. I'm pretty sure no one could *ever* call me hot. Right? "And how are we gonna do that?"

"Don't worry, it'll be easy. We've got a great canvas to work with." He's gotta be kidding. He looks me up and down and rubs his chin with his fingers.

Suddenly I'm self-conscious about my lazy basketball shorts.

"God, I love a makeover."

Ethan leads me to our first stop: Abercrombie, where all the conformists shop. Never stepped inside.

The walls are covered with these huge black-and-white photos. Chiseled frat guys playing rugby and hot, skinny white girls with long hair eye-fucking the camera. Ethan's running around like a crazy person. Grabbing shirts, pants, shorts—everything. Feels like I'm on *Supermarket Sweep*.

He pulls me into a dressing room with a huge pile of clothes. Ethan leans back against the door and just looks at me.

I freeze. If he thinks I'm gonna take off my clothes with him in here he's gone insane.

He takes the hint and walks out of the dressing room.

Jimmy Eat World's "The Middle" is playing over the speakers, telling me to be myself.

Right.

I pull off my T-shirt and stare in the mirror. My flat chest is scattered with hair, but not much. It's like my body's half-baked. Clavicles jutting out and ribs pushing up to the surface. The bruise around my eye's jumped to the greenish-yellow phase.

A strong-jawed, pointy-nosed douchebag laughs at me from a framed photo in the changing room. After taking off my shorts, I stare at my skinny legs in baggy yellow smiley-face Joe Boxer underwear. I'm worse off than Ethan realizes.

I try on a million lame t-shirts with meaningless words and graphics. The polos make me look like I'm begging to rush a frat. Fake-worn jeans and striped preppy belts. Barely recognize myself. The little hairs on the back of my neck stand up like static as I stare in this funhouse mirror. None of it feels like me, but I suppose that's the point.

Against my better judgment, I step out. Waiting for the firing squad to spray me with bullets. My eyes refuse to open.

I finally peek, but Ethan's not there. Shit. I tiptoe around this dumb store in my crummy socks till I eventually circle back and find Ethan waiting for me by the dressing room. He's giddy as shit and clapping.

What's he so excited about? I look insane. But I guess there's something he likes. Something I can't see. "I don't know..." My voice trails off as I look down at this unfamiliar version of me.

"What are you talking about? You look great. Basically an Abercrombie model." Ethan steps in front of me and gets really close. He pulls at my shirt collar to straighten it out. "I just love how tall you are."

I thought I was *too* tall, but clearly I don't know shit. My cheeks feel hot and red. "But, um, it's not exactly...me."

"It doesn't matter, Asher. Think of it like a costume—just trying it on. Have fun with it! It's not life or death."

The smell of Ethan's sick A&F Woods cologne starts to piss me off. Can he even hear me? Does he give a shit about what *I* want? Like Sam and Jackie and Allie at school. Like the guidance counselor. Like they know who I should be better than I do.

But maybe Ethan *does* know who I should be. Maybe I'm so far gone I can't even see myself anymore as anything other than who I've always been. *Stop resisting, Asher.* Just let go. It's not life or death.

"You're right. Let's just have fun."

"That's my boy!" Ethan puts his arm around my neck and rubs my chest.

I tug back, spooked. It's something I haven't felt since my mom did Vicks when I got sick. Okay, Ethan. Getting kinda close, bro.

So I buy a bunch of shit I don't want. Put it on my dad's credit card. He's probably thrilled I'm using it for something other than PS2 games and late-night ice cream with Robbie.

I guess I need to man up and trust Ethan. Why the fuck not? If he doesn't transform me, no one will. I sure as hell won't.

We get more stuff at Armani Exchange. A silver V-neck that makes me look so gay and skinny I wanna die. Aviator sunglasses with red lenses, like I'm on Mars—may as well be. Then Hugo Boss. Express Men. Hollister. Stores for braindead sheep.

The last thing I get are these Diesel sneakers. They're okay, I guess.

At this point I'm hypnotized. Under a spell and out of control. Gay Asher's taking shape, one dumb outfit at a time.

I'm starving, so we split up at the food court. I get greasy orange chicken and Ethan gets sushi and a Diet Coke, all sophisticated like. Me? Just a pig with his slop.

We finally call it—thank fucking god. I'm dragging all my shit toward the exit, but Ethan stops in front of Claire's. Big and purple and aggressively girly. Why here?

He pops in but I just stand out front. Can't we be done already? Ethan's spinning the racks of cheap earrings when I notice his virgin ears. Oh shit. He looks over at me, raises an eyebrow, and yells at me from inside. "We're doing it!"

"No fucking way, man." I turn away but he lunges out and grabs one of my shopping bags.

"Why not? It's gonna look gorgeous. You'd look so cute with a little earring. Like, uh...Justin Timberlake. And don't worry. I'll get one too."

Ethan's gotta be out of his fucking mind. Justin Timberlake? Please. He's just buttering me up so I'll go along with his sick plan to turn me into some gay Frankenstein horror show. Suddenly, getting rat-tailed by Luke doesn't sound so bad. "Just not my style."

"Not your type, not your style. Asher, it's time for you to *find* yourself. You're free now. Don't you get it?" Ethan stops and his voice gets low. "You're free."

But I don't *feel* free. I feel *trapped*. And now I'm getting a fucking hole in my ear.

Ethan grabs my shoulders, spins me toward a mirror, and holds up a little rock to my ear. "A diamond for a Diamond." He says it like it's a done deal. His eyes are soft but his lips are dead serious. Despite everything, something about Ethan makes me feel safe. Like when he looks at me, my lie just kind of...disappears.

Our faces next to each other in the mirror look jarring. We're so different, but here we are. Together. An unlikely duo.

I slowly turn my head to offer my left ear for sacrifice. Before I know it, a very out-of-place alt girl in head-to-toe black who can't be older than nineteen holds a nail gun to my head.

Ethan jumps in. "Ah-ah-ah." He twirls his finger around. "Wrong side."

Before I can argue, *click*. Searing pain. Burning flesh. She snaps on the back of the earring and hands me a mirror. My ear's bright red. Sparkly and shit.

Once again, I don't recognize me. But this time it's not, like, only bad. Something about the big, shiny earring makes my face look brighter, more hopeful. Happier. I don't whine about the piercing.

Ethan's turn. And, duh, he keeps it totally cool. Gets a small black stone. Looks good.

Finally we can get the fuck outta here. We leave through Macy's, about to split up.

Ethan nods at me. "Meet at mine at eight o'clock and we'll pregame. Wade's coming, too."

Who the fuck is Wade? More people? Shit.

"Don't worry, he's cool." Ethan smiles. "And you're gonna look like a movie star."

I push my fingers through my oily hair. "Uh, sure...if you say so."

Ethan kisses me on the cheek before jogging to his car.

The nonconsensual permanent ear mutilation feels *huge*, like I can't turn back. The lie isn't just in my head anymore. It's on my body.

I'm Ethan's puppet now. Gave him all the strings and wires keeping me together. I let all my limbs and joints fall slack so Ethan can do all the work. Sounds like a relief, in a way.

I hop into the driver's seat and flip down the visor mirror. The earring, stabbed into me. I think about ripping it out, but it hits me. I'm too far gone. This is me now.

And tonight? The next inevitable step in my idiotic self-inflicted death march to homosexuality.

Only eight hours to go until Pantheon. Suddenly bowling with Robbie and his thirtysomething sketchball doesn't sound too bad. Like the kind of nightmare I could actually survive.

# Perp



CNN's blasting doomsday bullshit at my dad and Piper in the den, so I sneak in through the noise before they can grill me about all these shopping bags.

Maybe some TV will help calm me down.

*Jackass* is on MTV. Johnny Knoxville locked Steve-O in a room with a fucking alligator. He's wandering around in a diaper and a blindfold, waiting to die. Same.

*TRL*'s on next. Vanessa Carlton's at her piano, banging away. Her eyes lock on mine, intense. Wind rushes through her dark brown hair as she flies down a highway. Not as hot as Sam—but who is?

I'm not supposed to like this song, but I do. Something about love or whatever—completely hypothetical for me. What even is love? The closest I've gotten is staring at Sam's tits while she thinks I'm her harmless gay bestie. Still, the song gets to me. I bet Ethan likes it.

Vanessa Carlton's voice fades into the background as my thoughts spiral to tonight. The hell am I doing?

*Stop thinking.* New channel. *Cops.* They're chasing this drug dealer through a residential neighborhood. Running past swimming pools. Jumping over fences from backyard to backyard. Based on the tropical palms, bright blue sky, and low, fluffy clouds—gotta be Florida.

I kinda feel bad for the criminals. I imagine myself running like them. Fleeing, chased by everyone. Robbie. Ethan. My dad. Piper. Luke. Sam. Mr. Pearson. The whole school. When they find out who the fuck I really am.

Two pimps and one crackhead later, I turn off the TV and face-plant onto my bed. I need one final rest before my big night out.

Next thing I know, I'm covered in slimy drool. Half-awake and groggy.

It's pitch black outside my window. I missed the day-to-night transition—so disorienting. *Oh, shit.* Later than I realized. Ethan's waiting.

Quick shower, scrubbing at myself with my ratty loofah, like I can wash the real me right off.

Staring at myself in the mirror, I inspect my stubble. Not much to look at. Can't grow a beard, unlike Luke and Silas. Even Robbie could if he really wanted. My immaturity's right there on my face. Plain as day.

Okay. Now what the fuck do I wear?

It's like some uncrackable code. I mix and match all this new shit till I land on something just good enough. Abercrombie jeans and that shiny V-neck from Armani Exchange.

Still feels like summer in Florida, so no jacket. I fiddle with the laces on my stiff new Diesel shoes for way too long until I finally squeeze my feet in.

As I'm tying my shoes, I notice the pride hat my dad got me poking out from under a pile of clothes on the carpet. I stare in the mirror again and throw the dumb hat on. Then off. On, off, on, off.

Definitely off.

The new earring's shining bright over my ear. The lobe is red and irritated as hell. Hair's still the same. Face, same. Except for the eye bruise. I'm bored just looking at me.

My new shirt sits weird on me. Like I'm seeing my body for the first time. The little bit of chest poking out of the V-neck might as well be a full-blown strip show. The sleeves are short and tight but somehow make my arms look *less* scrawny. Is Ethan a goddamn genius?

Who the fuck am I looking at? I don't hate him, not a *total* douche. But who is he?

*Live a little, Asher.* Like Ethan said. What's the point of resisting? The new clothes might as well be tattooed on my body, and the raw hole in my ear's a permanent brand.

I try to sneak out of the house, but my dad intercepts me. He looks at me like I'm some stranger who wandered in. Eyeing me like one of those criminals on *Cops*. Sizing me up like a perp.

"Wow, Asher." His eyes are wide and dumbfounded.

Can't tell what he's thinking. Maybe he hates how I look. He's gotta see how pathetic and fake I am.

To my relief and horror, my dad's mouth softens into a nice smile. "You look great, honey." He kisses me on the forehead like my mom used to. I feel like a little kid, but maybe that's okay. But is there more he isn't saying? Whatever, it's too late. This is me now.

Thank god I slip out before Piper can see me. I'm sure *she* could tell how fake I am. That's basically her job, right?

I flip on the radio and surf. Pop, rock, hip-hop. Each station feels like a different version of me. Who I am, was, and could be.

None of the music feels right. I leave it on static between stations. Fuzzy, gurgly noise.

Is that me tonight? Blurry, stuck between versions of myself?

I keep the static on as I drive, my brain buzzing with nothingness. This unwritten Asher, heading into who knows what.

And...whoa. For the first time senior year, I get a hint of this hazy, strange feeling. It's hard to pinpoint exactly, but I think I know what it is.

*Excitement.*

It's in there—in me—somewhere. Hiding like those weapons of mass destruction. Shady, waiting to blow, and ready to fuck shit up in a major way.

*Hot*

THIS Mike's lemonade stuff isn't all that bad. Never liked the taste of alcohol. Turns out it's better with a shit ton of sugar. Snuck some Coors from Robbie's dad once, but this is different—my first real social drink.

We're in Ethan's room doing what he calls a "pregame." Seen it in movies, I think. Wade's here. Ethan's okay, but this Wade guy? Fucking scary.

Wade's got that pretty-boy swaggery thing. Instantly annoying. Blond buzz cut, gold hoops, silver chain. Blue eyes like lasers. Baby face, big ears, but not a kid. Kinda short, though.

Orange tank, baggy jeans, silver chain. Serious face. Like some thugged-out gay LensCrafters model who could totally kick my ass. Actually, too easy to picture him laughing with Luke. Like a salivating hyena.

Then there's me. Awkward. Tall. Zero edge.

Wade's a senior at a public school in Miami. Miami kids always seem cooler. Older. More trouble to get into.

They met in the "Pantheon scene"—whatever that means. Fighting over the same guy. Ethan told me Wade's a player. Hooks up a lot and doesn't give a fuck. So far, seems like he doesn't give a fuck about *me*. Maybe I'm not his type.

The guys are a couple drinks in, but I'm lagging like a square. They're blasting a disco-type song called "Can't Get You Out of My Head." Dancing around. They tell me it's someone called Kylie Minogue.

Ethan dances kinda girly, snaking around. Wade just bops—head nod, wrist flick—like Eminem or something. Caught him checking himself out in the mirror, trying to look hot.

Wade's a better straight guy than me. *And* a better gay one.

He stops bopping. "Boy, is that still your first drink?"

"Oh, uh, yeah...it is."

Wade laughs and steals the half-full, room-temp hard lemonade out of my hand and slams it on Ethan's desk. Grabs a red Solo and pours in a shit ton of Smirnoff. Then, like, two drops of Tropicana before taking a swig right from the bottle.

Smells like gasoline and regret. But if Wade says jump...

"Wade! Don't scare him." Ethan swipes the drink.

I yank it back. Not gonna pussy out my first night partying with these gay guys. I close my eyes and chug.

As I wipe my mouth, I start to wonder why Ethan and Wade are friends. So different. Did they just click cause they're both the same age and good-looking and party a lot? Maybe that's all it takes.

Why did me and Robbie click? We both dodged touch football during playground and hung out by the swings. God, we were so totally lame.

"That shirt's...interesting." Wade tilts the red cup over his mouth, just below his staring eyes. Is this guy making fun of me?

"Uh, thanks. Ethan picked it out. I'm not really, um, a *fashion* guy." Air quotes.

No response from Wade, just raises an eyebrow and takes another glug. Dick.

He stands up and I'm alone on Ethan's bed. They're dancing and laughing and drinking. I'm just watching—that's my thing.

But then Ethan drags me up by my arm. "Walk for us." Ethan swipes his finger out.

"Um, what?"

"Show us a runway walk, Naomi."

Oh, no. This is some *real* gay shit.

"Do I have to?" I sound like a kid refusing to take out the trash.

"Loosen up, Asher!" Ethan pushes my shoulders back and forth to relax my muscles. "Have some fun. It won't kill you."

I *hate* when people tell me to have fun. *Smile!* Shut up.

Wade comes at me like an evil stage mom. "Walk, you sexy fuck."

"Fine, fine, Jesus." I ease onto my feet and take short, slow steps like Peter Pan walking the plank.

Before I can think, Wade shoves me forward. I put my hand on my hip and do my best Zoolander like a total tool.

Wade sits backwards in Ethan's desk chair and smirks as he watches this torture.

I should end it all right now.

"You looked sexy, bro."

Total pity-mindfuck for this tragic fake-gay nerd.

"Good try, but you gotta have that *pop*," Ethan juts his hip out. "More Britney, less hostage." He gets up, hands on his waist, hips bobbing—like he practices at home.

My skin crawls from secondhand embarrassment.

Ethan doesn't look embarrassed, though. "Wade, do it."

Wade rolls his eyes, stands up, and shakes himself loose. Slaps my butt as he passes. Perfect.

Ethan did his walk like a girl—all hips and shit—but Wade's got that stiff, cold guy-thing down. Like a predator trying to snag a big meal. Is this what he's gonna look like at Pantheon?

Ethan turns to me, runs his fingers through his hair, and stares at me like he's thinking hard. "Hmmm...give me a minute."

Uh, oh.

Ethan leaves the room and now I feel so fucking awkward alone with Wade. He goes up to the stereo and changes the music to DMX, "Party Up." His body starts grooving toward me to the sound of bright whistles and hard beats. "So, what happened?" Wade nods in my direction, at my bruise.

"Oh, uh...it's nothing." I throw my hand up to block my eye. No way I'm telling. *Wade* would've stood up for himself. Maybe even punched Luke out.

"...Sure. It's kinda hot, actually." He reaches out a finger to tap my hand away from the bruise, exposed. "Very masc. The boys are gonna love it."

Before I can respond, Ethan's back—with his mom. Raquel makes a beeline and picks at my frizzy hair, grabbing little tufts and inspecting my head. I feel like a dog getting judged in *Best in Show*.

"Okay, I know what to do. Come with me, *mijo*."

Ethan pushes me out his door to follow his mom to a bathroom with one of those salon chairs. All the hair products and tools or whatever on the counter look like gnarly lobotomy shit. *Oh fuck.*

Raquel throws one of those black capes over me in a big swoop, snapping it tight around my neck. A pink plastic spray bottle spritzes water all over my head and in my eyes. My coarse, dry hair turns damp and soft. She combs through and tugs the knots—can't remember the last time I used a comb.

"How long have you had this...style?"

I've never thought of my hair as having *any* style. "Ummm... forever?"

"That's what I thought." Raquel plays with my hair. "Do you trust me?"

I lie as fast as I can. "Sure."

"*Chévere.*" Whatever that means. She puts her hands on my shoulders and leans in. "You'll be fine." Her voice is breathy and warm and kinda sexy. My lungs unclench a bit.

Raquel grabs her scissors and gets to work. What gay-ass haircut is she gonna inflict on me? Another adjustment. Another surprise. Another part of my new identity that's changing really fucking fast.

"Ethan tells me you just came out? Good for you. It's a big deal." Raquel sounds chill about it, not annoying and shrill like overeager Piper.

"Um, yeah."

"Ethan didn't have it so easy. *Pobrecito.* Of course, *I* didn't mind. I was so proud of him...he's my baby. Plus, I knew he was gay since he was a little boy trying on my dresses." Snip, snip. "But the boys at school..." She sighs, kinda zoning out on my hair. "Kids can be cruel."

Why hasn't Ethan told me any of this shit yet? What were the douchebags at his school *really* like? Like the ones at Palm Reef?

"Yeah, I just came out a couple weeks ago. It's been okay, I guess." The lies I'm telling this sweet woman make my stomach bubble up.

Raquel looks at my messed-up eye that's clearly the result of a punch in the face or some other fucked-up situation. She raises an eyebrow. "You sure everything's *bueno*?"

"Yeah..." I pause and, for a second, I'm one Asher, not two. "I think all this change might actually be good for me."

"Well, that's wonderful." Absolutely sure she doesn't believe me.

"You should be proud of yourself."

What would my mom have thought if I came out to her? When I was little she'd say things like *I love you no matter what* and stuff. It was confusing, but I guess she was just covering her bases.

"If only his dad could accept him. *Pajúo.*" The snip-snips get bigger. "Ethan's been through so much. But he's a good kid."

Raquel's life revolves around Ethan. My dad's technically a single parent. But with Piper all up in our business? Doesn't feel that way. He probably thinks she fills the Mom-void, but he has no clue how fucking deep that hole actually is.

Raquel puts her scissors down and starts blow-drying. Like I'm trapped in a hot summer hurricane. Hundred-mile-an-hour winds trying to rip me away. There's a jaunty knock on the bathroom door.

Ethan slips in, gives me a once-over, and digs into some fancy hair gunk. He rubs it between his palms, then runs his fingers through my hair—feels kinda nice, weirdly. A minute later, he steps back, smiling. Flips behind me to watch my reaction in the mirror. Another part of my makeover. Another surprise. Here it comes...

Well, *damn*. Barely recognize myself. My hopeless hair's finally... something. Smooth pieces layer on top of each other with softer curls. Who knew this was even possible?

The shine off the hair gunk matches my bright new earring. Even my eyes look different. Like they finally make sense. I might actually look...good? And the bruise—more rebel, less victim. No clue what kind of witchcraft Ethan and his mom pulled, but it worked.

The upgrade makes me feel dizzy. Or maybe it's the vodka.

I wonder what Sam's gonna think.

"Wow, thank you...I...uh..."

Raquel laughs. I must look pretty stunned. She gives me a kiss on the cheek, and Ethan leads me back to his room, steering me from behind with his hands on my shoulders.

Wade raises his eyebrows. "Fuck, dude. Not bad."

Ethan stares me down, dead serious. "Asher Diamond. You. Look. Fucking. *Hot.* I knew you had it in you."

My body goes empty and light and I feel like I'm gonna pass out. Mission accomplished, Ethan. My transformation's complete. Finally ready to go to this stupid club.

We each slam one more drink. Goes down easy. Loose, relaxed, confident...ish.

As we're leaving, Wade stops me from behind. He squeezes my shoulders and invites his mouth to my ear. "You'll be okay."

I must look terrified.

He gives my shoulders another squeeze. There's something about Wade that's really confusing. And maybe dangerous.

Raquel drives us to the club in her white Mercedes SUV. On the short drive, Ethan blasts the volume so loud I can't hear the voices in my head telling me I've made a terrible mistake. Some disco lady's singing, "You've got to show me love..."

Ethan's dancing under his seatbelt as hard as it'll let him. Wade's bopping his head.

It's finally time. *You've got this, Asher. Let's fuck some shit up.*

## How Did You Get Here?

RAQUEL drops us off a couple blocks from the club. Don't blame Ethan for not wanting to be seen getting dropped off by his mommy.

The pre-game drinks Riverdance in my stomach. But the bass, getting louder as we walk, weirdly settles the nausea.

Ethan goes up to the doorman, a gruff older bald guy. They kiss on the cheek, Ethan laughing and playful. He introduces me to Bruno, who slaps a neon-orange band on my wrist.

I smile, trying to keep my face muscles from giving up.

Music blasts through the doors, shaking my eardrums. The space is huge, all around me. Ready to suck me in like a black hole.

Colorful flashing lights and lasers slice through the dim space—like a very gay *Star Wars*. The big, dancing crowd becomes its own thing, like a creature. Massive and alive.

A thought breaks through the blaring sounds and flashing lights: *Can everyone tell I'm a fucking liar? Is it obvious I don't belong?*

Ethan grabs my hand and rushes to the bar. This jacked bartender who forgot his shirt has these annoyingly perfect teeth that glow purple in the blacklight. He leans over the bar and his clenched chest reminds me of Sam and her push-up bras. He probably just wants a big tip.

Purple teeth guy kisses Ethan on the cheek. Free drinks? Awesome. Guess Ethan's a big shot.

He hands me and Wade these clear plastic cups. Looks like fizzy apple juice. I take a sip and, yep—Red Bull. But it tastes like ass so there's gotta be a shit ton of vodka or something. Uh oh. I'm already buzzed from the drinks at Ethan's.

*Keep going. Be cool. Fit in.*

Ethan's giving me this excited smile. "What do you think?"

"Uh, it tastes fine." I take a sip, wondering if there's something I should be noticing.

"No, dummy—Pantheon."

Right. Well, I can't tell him the truth. That it's fucking nuts that I'm here, in a room full of half-naked gay guys. But with the alcohol, another truth creeps in. "It's...incredible." No fucking lie. I'm feeling...*good*.

"Let me take you on the *grand tour*." Ethan grabs my hand and drags me through the club. The drinks blur everything—but where's Wade?

Ethan shows me everything. The main dance floor, the balcony the creeps watch from, and the bathrooms where he tells me sketchy things happen. It's all surreal, like I've slipped into someone else's body. The kid I was just a couple weeks ago is light-years away.

Robbie would never fit here. He'd crack jokes about shirtless bartenders and body glitter. Laugh at my new clothes. He'd hate the crowd, the music—everything.

Wouldn't he be right, though? Have I totally lost my mind? I picture where he is now. Bowling shoes and cargo pants, laughing with weirdo Jax over delicious, gnarly tater tots. A tot sounds pretty good right now.

We jump onto the huge dance floor. I'm loose, and definitely drunk. I shake my body around to "Waiting for Tonight" as green lasers fly over my head. Like I'm right in the music video. The tech is way better than Palm Reef dances. No clue how to move, but I feel oddly safe in this tornado of dudes. I burp and the air smells like Red Bull.

Ethan's mouth, up against my ear. Gossip. "See that guy over there? With the mullet?"

I nod. Too loud to try to talk.

"Well, last year at the big Pride party, he took some bad drugs or something and got stuck dangling off the balcony. They called the fire department to grab him, but everyone started grinding on the firefighters—who were really fucking hot, by the way—before they could get to him. They loved it."

I giggle like crazy. Do I look insane or like I'm just having fun?

"That's amazing!" I yell so loud. Body moving, limbs flying, can't stop. More dancing to weird, gay songs. Beats blending together. Clean, steady rhythm. The crowd can't escape the dance floor, and neither can I, locked in by the music.

*It's not right, but it's okay, I'm gonna make it anyway*

*I'm findin' it hard to believe we're in heaven*

One line stands out: *How did you get here?*

Exactly. *How the fuck did I get here?* My mind, a hurricane, finally catching up. Everything from the past few weeks. Spinning together. Dancing. Dizzy.

Luke and the locker room and Mr. Pearson and my lie? Shame,

sadness, everything. Really fucking far away. Outer space.

Who was that guy? That tall, awkward loser? Was it me? Starting to forget.

Wade appears and pulls me close by my V-neck. Arm over my shoulder. We start grinding. The fuck is this?

I shake my head, but the music's riptide sweeps me out. Brain floating on the pulsing waves. I give in, follow Wade, and let the music take over. I'm a motherfucking gay dance zombie.

Ethan comes up behind me, grinding and holding my waist. Whoa. Now I'm in this weird gay sandwich, like we're Sam and Luke and Silas at Homecoming.

Wade's and Ethan's denim crunch against mine. Arms, hands, skin. Ethan's watch, cold against my chest.

Ethan's body feels less...*scary* than Wade's. Safe, I guess?

But what's in Ethan's head? Turned on? No—Ethan must've been exaggerating. Still awkward, not actually hot.

"You're a good dancer." Ethan shouts, squeezing my waist harder.

I push my body back into his. Totally normal, right?

"I've never seen anything like it." I'm loud, drunk, rambling. "Closest I've been to a club was Rachel Rubenstein's bat mitzvah. She's fucking loaded."

Ethan and Wade catch eyes over me and bust out laughing. I probably sound like a kid—it's not seventh grade anymore. Ethan stumbles away. "I guess Pantheon *is* like a super gay bat mitzvah."

"I gave Shawn Feldman head in the bathroom at his bar mitzvah party." Wade's shouting. Bragging, I think. "Right after he danced with his grandma in front of everyone. Swear to God."

Damn. Is that what's happening behind the scenes?

We all keep dancing in a triangle. "I'm *sure*." Maybe Ethan thinks Wade's full of shit.

"He's the class president now." Wade smiles all evil. "Girlfriend and everything."

Ethan leans into me. "Don't listen to him. Wade's obsessed with straight guys."

"They're obsessed with *me*. I can't help it."

Ethan raises his eyebrows like there's more. Some frenemy shit. He twirls away from the triangle.

More dancing. Minutes, hours, who the fuck knows.

But then—Ethan's gone. Where'd he go? Wade's gone too. I dance alone until the song ends. Drinks are fading, I think. Less blurry. Tired. Need to pee.

The packed bathrooms are really confusing. Boys in the girls' room. Girls in the boys' room. Stalls are all taken. Great.

I go up to a urinal and turn to the corner—no peeking at my dick. A greasy guy with a receding hairline and gold chain creeps up to the urinal next to me. He turns his head, and my body freezes. Goosebumps. I give up and head out, praying I don't pee my pants.

Where's Ethan? Wade's up against the wall talking to some buff dude. Wade's a pro flirt. Kinda like Luke, talking to the hot girls at Palm Reef—when beautiful Sam's not around.

I step outside. Fresh Florida air, warm and cool at the same time. Humid, but the breeze rushing off the coast feels like minty Altoid breath. I love the feeling of the air after midnight. Like there's—finally—enough oxygen.

It's dark, but I think I see Ethan down in the shadows of the parking lot with some guy. I think it's John or whatever, that sleaze he's dating.

Looks like they're arguing. John lunges, clanking his keys over the club's bass. Ethan backs away, hands up, forehead bunched. John grabs for him—Ethan pulls back, again and again. Then John storms off into that dumb silver Mustang, revs like an asshole, and speeds onto Federal Highway.

Ethan can't know I saw them fighting. Gotta get back inside. A woman's voice flows out of the speakers. *Do you think you're better off alone?*

Shit, alone. Where's Wade? I stand around, awkward again. Less drunk. Less loose.

Ethan walks in looking like he saw a ghost. His eyes scan the club, then land on me. He gets a big smile, and my body chills out again. "Let's get outta here." Shouting. Grabbing my hand.

He walks up to Wade and pulls his belt loop, tugging him away from the jock guy's tongue. Wade doesn't look annoyed, though. Just another night at Pantheon, I guess.

I've never seen guys kissing in real life before. Come to think of it, I don't think I've ever met a gay person before Ethan. Now look at me—drowning in them.

I follow Ethan and Wade outside, and he calls his mom to pick us up.

As we wait, Wade sparks a cig. They crack jokes and Ethan says his witty stuff. I laugh. I talk. I'm into it. I feel close to Ethan. Even Wade, this guy I just met. This guy I can't read in the slightest. Don't even mind that my stomach's churning from the drinks.

Something about this world makes you feel like you belong. Like *I* belong. Anyone's welcome. Join in. I'm a fucking chameleon.

Robbie can wait. He's fine. It's my turn to have something for just me.

Get drunk. Fuck Palm Reef. I'm somewhere new. Someone new.

Suddenly my stomach's getting *really* bad, like a rock tumbler inside my gut. My breath stutters, anxiety shoots up, head spins. Shit —it's happening.

Before I can find a hiding place to deal with this like a dying dog, it starts. Tight, squeeze, churn.

Wade squints as he takes a big drag, a bright orange glow staring at me. "Fuck, dude...are you gonna—"

"Aw, Asher, baby." Ethan walks behind me and rubs my back.

Here it comes—bam. Big, watery spray. Booze, Red Bull, no dinner. Feels like a huge fucking relief.

I pull my V-neck to wipe the gnarly chunks off my face. I look up, terrified, and see Wade smirk.

Ethan flips in front of me and grabs my shoulders, his face all worried.

But then this weird chuckle comes out of me, a big burp right in Ethan's face. Great, I'm the biggest spaz ever. Can't handle my shit. But then, something flips. I let go. Can't stop laughing.

Ethan's next, then Wade. We're all cracking up, probably all for different reasons. I don't feel stupid anymore. I feel like I did something big, ran a goddamn marathon.

Just when I thought I'd survived the night, I feel a stream of warm liquid soak my jeans and trickle down my leg. Fuck that creep-o in the bathroom.

The laughs reach their max volume, and Wade lets out this big howl, cig balanced in his mouth, pounding his chest at the stars. He comes up to me and squeezes my face and gives me a big kiss on the cheek. Maybe puking and pissing yourself isn't the worst thing. Maybe I even made Wade proud.

My stomach feels better, so I sit on the curb while we wait for Ethan's mom. I close my eyes and breathe, not really minding that I'm disgustingly covered in my own urine.

A thought creeps up, calm and warm like the night air, my body finally settled.

Maybe I *don't* need to figure out Asher Diamond. Maybe I just need to laugh. Let go. And have some fucking fun.

126

Maybe I *don't* need to figure out Asher Diamond. Maybe I just need to laugh. Let go. And have some fucking fun.

## Set It And Forget It

THE bright stage lights at Velour blast down like radioactive interrogation lamps. Ethan signed me up for karaoke—actual hell.

A string of pink feathers wraps around my neck like a snake, strangling the straight right outta me.

*"I...uh...come home, in the morning light."* The mic's way too loud. Sweat sticks itchy pink feathers to my skin. My voice shakes, flat.

Ethan's voice shouts in a high pitch over the crowd's disinterest. "Wooooo! Yeah, my boy!" He lives for this shit—dragging me into the spotlight, reprogramming my life one chaotic night at a time.

For two months, Ethan's booked my life. Pantheon every Saturday —dancing, meeting people, getting shit-faced. He got me a fake ID, but he knows all the bouncers. Sometimes we drive hours to go out, practically to Lake Okeechobee. I don't mind. He's fun to talk to, and the music's good.

*"My mother says, when you gonna live your...life, uh, right..."* Where's the nearest exit?

Ethan walks up and stands right in front of me, and I feel something heavy over me float away.  I push more air out of my lungs as I sing. *"Oh momma dear, we're not the fortunate ones..."*

Ethan swoops in like a jealous stage mom on caffeine pills, grabbing the mic and hollering. *"And girls, they wanna have fu-un..."* His energy makes it hard to stay mortified. He raises his hands, sipping his vodka cranberry through a super-thin black straw like it's a wizard's wand, bringing the crowd to life with a hex. A few heads bop, then more. Finally, the whole bar joins in and shouts like one big gay fifty-headed monster, *"Oh girls just wanna have fun!"*

Ethan's laughing his ass off, and his face looks like I'm making him proud. I don't feel so humiliated. Guess his project's paying off. Improving Asher Diamond.

And, well, that's Ethan. I don't know what I'd do without him.

On the phone, Ethan helps me pick out my school clothes, making sure I look good. He doesn't let me eat Sour Patch Kids or pretzels or other junk, even though he's a hypocrite and treats us to twenty-piece McNuggets when he's feeling good—or when he's feeling bad.

Ethan drives me to the gym after school a few times a week. He runs into a different friend every time we go. Been teaching me how to do all these exercises and put on muscle. Ethan swears that big biceps and a huge chest make everyone want you. Everyone?

I picture Sam when he says stuff like that.

Sometimes Wade tags along, but he mostly just flirts. We get chocolate peanut butter protein shakes from Jamba Juice after the gym to bulk up. I hope it's working.

Maybe Sam will notice my new body if I do what Ethan says. Maybe she won't be able to resist, and we'll hook up and I can let her think she turned me straight.

I put the mic back in its stand and pull Ethan off stage.

"Aren't you glad I saved you?" He gives me a big, annoying smile.

"Yeah, well...you wouldn't have had to save me if you didn't throw me up there in the first place." I'm mad and grateful and weirdly proud of myself all at the same time.

"Oh, Ashy Ashy, nothing soothes the soul like the stage!"

I don't think that's a famous quote or anything, but Ethan says it like it is. We walk over to a table at the side of the room.

"So where's John?" I lower my head to take a sip from Ethan's drink through the black straw, and I keep this unsettling contact on Ethan's rolling eyes.

Wait, why am I being a dick?

All this time, it's like Ethan's keeping a secret. He never talks about his alleged boyfriend, and he doesn't make out with anyone at Pantheon—unlike Wade, who's hooking up with a different guy every weekend. Sometimes more than one.

Or maybe he's embarrassed...of me?

"I'm not going to dignify the question with an answer, stupid."

"Don't you think it's weird, that...uh, I haven't even met the guy? It's been, like, months."

Ethan's smile goes dark like I flipped a switch, and his eyes get still and wet. *Damn it, Asher. Why can't you just let him have his secret? Like you have yours.*

"I mean...it's just...it's, like, not..." I feel my hand trembling. "Uh, nevermind, sorry...I'm being dumb."

Ethan pushes his hand through my hair, making sure it looks just right. It's both awkward and not at the same time. It's like we can talk without talking.

"What up, fuck-nuggets?" Wade walks up wiping saliva off his mouth and rubbing his earrings with his fingers. A welcome distraction.

I scrunch my forehead real tight. "What the hell's a...a fuck-nugget?"

Wait, Wade's here?

I notice Ethan's eyes get wide.

"Oh, Wade...hi..." Ethan stutters. "Sorry, I would've told you we were coming here, but..."

"Don't even, bro. I'm here with Chad." Wade flings his head back so we notice this jacked guy in a wife beater leaning against the bar.

I pipe up. "Looks like your type."

Wade gets up close to me, menacing. "And he gives the best—"

Ethan pulls Wade onto his lap. "So endearing, my love." He kisses Wade's cheek and digs his knuckles into his buzz cut—trying to piss him off.

"Sit, boy." Wade looks at me and pats his lap.

"No thanks."

Wade rolls his eyes at me for the millionth time and pulls me onto his lap. One, two, three boys stacked up on top of each other.

My brain blue-screens—wait, what the fuck am I doing?

I overhear Wade lean back and say something to Ethan. "I miss you."

Ethan doesn't respond. Just squeezes all of us closer. "Let's bounce."

Wade does this gross little humping thing up at me. "Can I catch a ride?"

"Of course, my love." Neither of us ask why Wade's ditching Chad. Wade pushes me off him and grabs my shoulders, leading me out the front door and into the parking lot. He lets me go and reaches into his back pocket for a cigarette. His lighter snaps, and swirls of gray smoke flow out of his mouth. All of a sudden Wade's quiet.

Whenever he ices me out like this I get freaked, like I'm a nuisance and he can't bear to talk to me. "You coming to the gym tomorrow?"

I'm trying to break my paranoia.

Wade stares ahead, flicking ash into the air. "Maybe. I'm supposed to meet up with Chad, but...you know."

I pretend to know what he's talking about and nod.

Wade takes another drag. He's been bailing on us a lot lately.

"Shotgun!" He shouts to call the front seat. His mood flips too fast—brooding to excited. Fake? Maybe he's pissed I'm in the way.

We all get in Ethan's car and drive. Ethan lowers the windows so Wade can finish his cig. A rush of warm wind whips around me, and I wonder how messy my hair is. With razor-sharp focus on the road, Ethan starts blabbing about some gay-dude drama.

But I tune out, taking deep breaths of late-night air.

How does Ethan have time for all these friends...and *me*? And what do they say when I'm not around? Curious? Judging? Wasting his time? Is Ethan listening to them? Is he gonna drop me?

"You okay?" Ethan's voice cuts through my anxious thoughts. He catches my eyes in the rearview mirror, which settles my mind. "You're quiet."

I sit up and pretend like I've been listening to Ethan's story. "Oh, I'm just...tired, I think. And all these guys, I..."

Ethan laughs. "My boy, you have *no* idea. But don't waste a thought on those petty airheads." He flashes a smile. "You're doing great."

I'm not sure what he means, but it feels good. I nod and smile like I know what's going on.

Wade flicks his cig out the window and blasts Jay-Z. He's rapping all the words in "Can I Get A..." Bouncing in his seat, somehow still full of energy.

The rest of the ride I'm lost in my head until Ethan parks. My legs feel heavy as we climb the stairs to his apartment.

Raquel gives me and Ethan a quick kiss on the cheek as we zoom past her. Wade heads straight to Ethan's bed and flops down on his face.

"Sleepover?" Ethan's on his bed too and starts petting the back of Wade's head.

I really want to, but I've barely been home this week, and my dad and Piper have been guilting me pretty hard. "Uh...that's okay. Gotta be up early to do yoga with the evil stepmother." I walk up to Ethan and give him the usual hug. Feels nice.

Wade startles me by giving me a hard slap on my butt, and I jump up.

Fucking Wade. He lets out this dumb "huh-huh" like he's Butthead or something. I'm out.


After a quiet drive home, I pull into the driveway and walk up to the front door. Shit, the TV's on. *Dateline* or some other garbage Piper likes to watch with my dad. I hold my breath as I walk in.

Before I make it to my room, my dad yells out. "Hey... Asheroony!"

I drag myself to the den, and I find my dad leaned all the way back on the couch so far that his head's upside down. He reaches out to me, motioning me to join them.

"Tell us about your night! Watch anything good with Ethan? A classic? *Gone With the Wind*?"

I step in closer. Another night, another lie. "Um...yeah, this weird movie. *Pink Flamingos*? Uh..." My dad and Piper think I spend my nights with Ethan watching movies or playing dress-up or whatever gay shit they imagine happens.

"When are we going to meet this Ethan boy?" Piper calls out from under my dad's arm. "We'd love to have him over for dinner sometime. I can make my—"

"Uh, he's pretty busy...maybe...soon?" I rudely back away and slip into my bathroom before the inquisition continues.

Safe now, I start my new nightly ritual. The "routine," as Ethan and Raquel call it. Scrubbing my face with exfoliating cleanser, I catch my reflection in the mirror. Something's off.

A digital bloop comes from my computer speakers in the other room. I quickly dry my face and head for it. A message from Robbie: *Yo, you up for some Magic tomorrow? My mom just stocked up on snacks. Let's eat it all then watch each other barf.*

Ah, shit. I stare at the screen, memories of marathon gaming sessions flashing in my mind. When was the last time we even played? Ethan's keeping me busy, so I probably don't have time. Yeah, that's it. *Can't :/ Gym with Ethan.*

I splash my face with ice-cold water. Shocking my skin, shocking myself back to reality. To *before* my lie. Nope, nothing. Why would I wanna go back there, anyway?

Next comes the sticky black charcoal mask. As I smear it on— *bloop*. AIM alert. Robbie: *K.*

Slowly peeling off the mask, I stare at myself in the mirror. I feel like Patrick Bateman in *American Psycho*. Ripping one face off, revealing the stranger underneath. What would Ethan think if he saw the real me unmasked, my real life? No, can't see it. Not ready for those worlds to collide. Not yet.

I dab on this shitty eye serum that doesn't work. Dark circles still there. At least my black eye finally went away. No more traces of Luke.

I smear this fancy vanilla moisturizer Ethan got me from Nordstrom all over my face. A present just because. Makes my face feel soft and shit. I look good.

Maybe I even look gay.

Finally, I drop down for my nightly push-ups. Eighteen in, my arms give out. I'll tell Ethan I did all twenty if he asks.

I grab Michelangelo and give him slow little pets while I try to doze off to TV, even though Wade says it gives you nightmares. I flip the channel to my favorite cheesy late-night infomercial. There's this old tan dude with fake-looking, blinding-white teeth. He's selling an oven that can cook a whole chicken—dead, spinning around and around, bathing in its own bodily fluids, skin exploding with fiery blisters.

The audience chants. "Set it and forget it!"

My new life, the strategy I chose. Full steam ahead. Set it, forget it. Let my whole body burn to a golden crisp, until the pale Old Asher's gone for good. Just blistered gold and flawless.

But if you forget to unplug the goddamn thing? All of it—all of me—turns to ash.

*Bahamas*

BARELY slept last night. Had a dream Robbie was drowning, but I just stood there holding a pool noodle like a moron. Probably means something. I should check in on him.

Walking to my table in the caf, Sam stops me for a VIP invite to sit with her crew. But I force myself to say no. I'm looking for Robbie. Maybe talking will clear my conscience. Lunch, some one-on-one attention. Proof I'm not a total asshole.

So I sit alone, twirling spaghetti. Me and Ethan were gonna hit Miami Subs, but he's busy barfing up a hangover at home.

Then—Robbie appears in his *Respect Mah Authoritah! South Park* T-shirt like it's seventh grade, but I can't help smiling at how dumb and dorky it is. He sits down at the table slow, like he's testing the waters.

"Hey, dude." Why do I sound like Wade?

"You look like shit, Asher."

Harsh, but fair. My stupid eye cream isn't working. "Well *you* look gorgeous." I put on my best, gayest self. Damn I'm good at this.

"Ha ha...but you do look pretty tired." Robbie throws a meatball in his mouth and chews big. "Pantheon?" Robbie's chomping loud.

135

Gross. Ethan would never let me get away with that.

I'm nervous talking about my new life, but Robbie actually likes hearing the gossip and shit. These people he doesn't know? Might as well be kids on *90210*. I tell him stuff so he feels included, not totally shut out. Even though that's exactly what I'm doing.

"Wanna hear what happened to Wade?"

Robbie smiles and leans in, thank god. "No doy. Did Chad find out?"

"Oh yeah. Wade hooked up with some other idiot, and now Chad's spreading bullshit about him. Wade's really pissed—he's got this whole sex-god reputation he's trying to keep. Chad needs to watch out. Who knows what sadist shit Wade's capable of?"

Robbie's smile fades.

Fuck. What's wrong? Something about the story? Gotta turn this around. "What, uh...you okay?"

"It's nothing." Robbie avoids my eyes.

Before I can figure out what went wrong, Sam walks up to our table, hot in her Alicia Silverstone look. Kinda preppy but showing some skin, too. Maybe she's mad I blew her off? She gives Robbie a polite smile, but it's forced—the bare minimum to acknowledge his existence. She's standing stick-straight, just like her ironed hair.

"Asher, babe." Sam's all flirty. "Lacrosse team's having a rager at Silas's tomorrow. This Drunksgiving thing he does every year. His parents are in the Bahamas, so, you know, we're all gonna get fucked up."

Robbie bites his lip, holding back a snicker or a rude comment.

"You *have* to come." Sam's pupils get big like anime. "It won't be fun without you."

No way she means that. But it gets me dizzy. Hanging with Sam at a *real-life* party? Drinking with the bros? It's...interesting. I've heard stories about these lacrosse parties. Or maybe they're just rumors.

There's this one from last year about Sam walking in on Jackie with Mr. Levinson—this young teacher fresh out of college—half-naked at Silas's. Sam blasted it around school, then Mr. Levinson vanished. No warning, just gone.

But then came the counter-rumor that Sam was jealous because she'd been hooking up with Mr. Levinson behind Luke's back. After that, Sam disappeared for a few days too.

Thinking about going to the party short-circuits my brain. Straight Asher wouldn't have been let in the door. Or maybe only cause Luke had some sick plan to humiliate him.

But hell. Things are different. Luke's gone, and Sam's *begging* me to come. Terrifying and tempting.

I wonder if I can bring Ethan?

Fuck it. "Uh, sure...I'm there."

"Yay!" She does a bunch of little claps, then turns and flips her hair to walk away. But she pauses and turns back.

"Oh—and bring Ethan. I've been *dying* to meet him."

Sam runs her fingers through her smooth hair, maybe a nervous tic. Then she walks back to the popular table, where she belongs. Suddenly there's this strong urge to ditch Robbie with his ugly meatballs and join Sam and her short skirt. Can I really go? My shot to—finally—fit in?

No. Too dangerous. School and Pantheon. Sam and Ethan. What would Ethan think of all these preppy airhead girls and ignorant, douchey jocks? He'd probably call it an offensive display of heterosexuality or something. And could they handle big, gay, out-and-proud Ethan? My mind ping-pongs like I'm holding the Hiroshima button.

Okay—I've made up my mind. *Man up, bro.* Go to this dumb,

awesome rager. Bring Ethan. Show them who you are now.

"Well, have fun at the party." Robbie stabs his fork into his tray, flat.

I flinch at his voice—forgot he was here. But, uh, is he waiting for me to...*invite him*?

No, probably just annoyed. He always bitches about Sam acting like an entitled brat in theater. She kinda treats him like shit—which never stopped me from thinking about her naked. A lot. Yeah, that's kinda fucked up of me.

I stay quiet. So much for our reunion.

We pick at our lunch in excruciating, awkward silence. I look over at Sam's table and wonder what they're talking about. I zoom in on her lips and the room goes silent. Shiny with strawberry lip gloss she shoplifted when she dragged me to Walgreens once.

I twirl my spaghetti and the gloopy red sauce reminds me of the fucked-up pizza that ended up on my face. The kind of shit the old Asher had to deal with, when Luke was winning. Out of nowhere, I stab a meatball hard with my fork.

I'm different now. I'm not the kid who's too much of a pussy to go to a party.

I try not to stare, but Jesus Christ, Robbie. That insane bowl cut, straight as a helmet. Making his head look weirdly round like a dodgeball. His Cartman shirt's all stretched out, threads hanging from too much laundry. Clinging to him in a way that's just...like, lay off the tater tots, dude. Got on the same baggy-ass cargo pants he's had since middle school.

And the fucking backpack. Strapped tight like a bulletproof vest. Totally delusional way to protect himself from reality. Then there's the eating. Slurping spaghetti, chewing like a cow, sauce dripping off his chin like a fucking toddler who needs a bib.

I gotta look away. How did I never notice how much of a nightmare he is? How much I must've looked like this too? And here I am, sitting with him like nothing's changed.

Suddenly I feel queasy, embarrassed to be seen with this dork dragging me down. Instead, I focus on my *new* life, my new friends, and way more important shit—like what I'm gonna wear to the party. Denim or chinos?

I should really call Ethan.

## Social Skills

AT first glance it looks like some luxury shit out of a rap video. Fancy pool, tall columns, big-ass yacht on the dock. Stars like bling over everything. But really it's just Mr. and Mrs. Ryker's corny-ass McMansion in Las Olas, packed with drunk, stoned, horny teens ready to rage.

Me and Ethan walk through a dark, narrow path around the side of the house. A jungle of sharp palm fronds slaps my face like it's trying to smack the fear out of me, like it knows Ethan won't fit in. There's a big rectangular pool, an elevated hot tub, and a ton of people.

Ethan doesn't even hesitate for a second—just walks right in. His mouth drops open, giddy. "Holy shit." He must think it's all hilarious. But I'm feeling this weird combo, like anxiety and excitement.

"I'm so ready for this." Ethan rubs his hands together. "We need drinks." He grabs my hand, ready to hunt for booze, but I yank it back and shove it into my Lucky jeans. Too much. Too publicly gay.

The usual Palm Reef A-list is here, plus enough randos to keep the deck from looking empty. Standing around a keg, Sam and her

141

friends look sluttier than they do at school. Caked-on makeup. Shorter skirts. Higher shoes. More cleavage. Tits squeezed in so tight they're about to pop out of their tops. Sam's looking sexy as fuck. Black strappy thing and a short low-rise denim skirt. You can tell she's trying damn hard to hold her throne.

Good Charlotte's "Lifestyles of the Rich and Famous" is playing over the expensive sound system, giving the party an on-point bratty vibe.

The guys are really fucking loud. Bros forcing their voices deeper. Shouting out dumb nicknames and tossing bright neon Nerf footballs. Girls get caught in the crossfire, pretending to look annoyed when really, they just want attention—and maybe to get fucked by one of these Neanderthals. Uh, I mean, these perfectly cool guys who will think I'm totally normal and chill.

I try to picture Robbie here, drinking beer and holding a conversation with one of the bros. No fucking way. He'd probably show up with his backpack on. Not inviting him was *definitely* the right choice.

Gotta shake Robbie outta my head. "Do you get the feeling you're watching some kind of, like, nature documentary?"

"Yes!" Ethan does this funny impression of a British guy. "The graceful egrets swoop down to the swampland as hungry alligators and pythons plan their next meal. The iguanas keep safe watch from the trees."

Thank god me and Ethan are on the same page.

He turns to me, still in character, looking at me like I'm an alien. "But wait! A tortoise approaches, a delicious snack for the gators."

"Oh, god. Is that what I am? A slow turtle?"

"Tortoise, Asher. Tortoise. They're actually really strong." He knocks on my head. "Hard shells."

I scrunch up my face and look around the swamp. The thing about the Everglades? No cover. No escape. Just miles of murder puddles and sawgrass that'll slice your ankles open before an alligator finishes the job. And here I am—the slowest fucking tortoise on the planet, waddling straight into the food chain.

And the predators? They're everywhere. Girls with their Smirnoff Ice, boys with red cups of beer or god knows what.

Sam spots me and rushes over, pulling up a fallen spaghetti strap. She looks pretty drunk. Loose and chatty.

"Asher!" Sam half-hugs me and shouts out to no one in particular, "Asher's here!"

Jesus Christ, this girl is crazy. Hot as hell, but crazy.

"You get drinks yet?" Sam flicks out a strand of hair, and before I know it Allie Alvarez is shoving a red cup in my hand. I sip the mystery liquid—blue, fruity, very strong. Kinda like the drinks at Pantheon. I've gotten pretty used to drinking, so I'm happy. Alcohol chills me out.

Ethan gulps his drink, and his social skills kick into high gear. He introduces himself to Sam, putting on that fake, overexcited voice I've heard a million times—same one he uses at Pantheon when he runs into someone he secretly hates.

"You must be Sam! I've heard so much about you, girl." Ethan's definitely kissing ass. He gives her the side hug she gave me. I recognize that smile he's got. Like he's making fun of you but you've got no idea.

I jab my elbow into Ethan's ribs. Don't fuck with my girl.

"And I've heard all about *you*." Sam's voice makes it sound like me and Ethan are secretly in love. She looks him up and down and reaches out to squeeze his bicep. "You're gorgeous."

What about my bicep?

Shit—just realized: could everyone like Ethan *more* than me? A better version of me. More fun, wittier, a better gay kid to have around. A *real* one.

Ethan takes a step back from drunk Sam. "Um, uh...this is a great house...I love the architecture. The columns...well, they're striking." He's being condescending

But Sam just blinks, clueless, and tugs at the ends of her hair. "Well, Silas's parents are real pieces of shit. Feel free to smash something."

Ethan's voice gets more feminine than normal as he talks to her. What's he doing? Oh, man. Shit. *Too* gay.

If Luke was here, I bet he'd call Ethan a fag.

Sam's eyes uncross and she puts her hand across her head to swoop her hair behind an ear, exposing her long neck. "Silas's parents are fucking loaded. They own half the teams in Florida and they're gone half the year, so we party here and raid their vodka. Only the best for you, Asher." Sam's balance is off. She holds onto me so she doesn't fall on her face.

To my surprise, Silas walks up. "Asher! Dawg!"

He's driven me and Sam around in his obnoxiously wide Hummer—me in the back. Humiliating. I'm happy he hasn't messed with me in a while, but I wonder if he secretly hates me for getting his best friend expelled.

Sam swears he's got the biggest dick she's ever seen. I saw it in the locker room—it's whatever. Sometimes I wonder what Sam would think about mine. If she saw it or touched it or whatever.

I'm lightheaded thinking about Sam and my dick.

Silas reaches out to get me to do one of those scary bro handshakes. Shit. Me and Robbie tried to learn as a joke one time, but we couldn't figure it out.

In my daze, I give him a weak fist bump instead.

Silas moves to Ethan, who nails it like he's been in a frat his whole life. But it looks so ridiculous to see Ethan play bro that I almost bust out laughing. Well, I would if I wasn't so impressed.

"Welcome to my crib." Silas holds out his arm, bragging. What a fucking tool.

There's something dickish about his smirk. Kinda like Wade's. Maybe he's ratting all my moves back to Luke, plotting. Wouldn't be good.

"Sam talks about you all the time, Asher-boy. She wants to take you...shopping."

The thought of Sam talking about me like that to Silas makes me want to *die*. Who does she think I am? Some airhead mallrat?

Wait—is *that* what I am now? Sometimes I forget I'm just this asexual curiosity to her. "Well, uh, thanks for having us." I sound too formal, still no fucking clue how to talk to these guys. Shit—where'd Ethan go?

I spot Ethan and Sam a few feet away, his fingers in her hair. Lord knows what the hell they're up to. Me and Silas stand in painful silence and sip our drinks. About to explode.

"Crazy, man. Didn't know you were such a chill dude. Listen, I can be a dick so, you know, sorry about all that shit from...before."

Silas Ryker, apologizing? His voice is all casual, like he only half gets how messed up Luke and him were.

"Um, thanks. You're...chill, too." I feel a little lighter, more accepted. Or maybe it's the blue alcohol.

Luckily one of the lacrosse boys saves me with a cannonball—fully naked—distracting Silas. The whole party's going crazy.

Ethan rushes back and whispers in my ear. "I'd probably hate every single one of these people if I knew them, but that guy is fucking hot." Ethan's staring at the wet lacrosse player. Water dripping off his toned body. "Maybe Sam can introduce me."

"No fucking way, Ethan."

"You're no fun."

He's right, I'm being lame. No fun, too nervous, and *definitely* not gay enough. Can't be suspicious.

"Fine, you're right. He's really hot." I sip my drink. "Look at those abs." So freaky how easy I can talk like this, been at it so long. "Sam told me Silas's got a huge dick." I think Ethan'll get a kick out of this. "But I don't know why she tells me this shit. What do I care? It's not like I..."

Oh, fuck. Straight Asher almost slipped out. *Shut up, idiot.*

"What do you mean? It's good gossip."

I cover. "Just TMI, you know?"

All of a sudden Sam grabs me by the hand and drags me away from Ethan. Pulls me into a bathroom that opens up onto the pool deck. Pretty sure she didn't hear what I said about Silas's dick.

There's so many gross used cups and bottles all over the fake-marble counter. Everything looks sticky. Sam pulls out a little baggie with two long white rectangles. Pills.

"Uh...what's that?"

Sam laughs. "Xanax, freak." She breaks one in half and holds it in front of me.

I open my mouth but my tongue hides inside.

"Come on, just a little bit." She sticks her finger in my mouth and puts the pill on my tongue.

I might actually drop dead right here on this sticky-ass floor. My whole body catches fire and feels like it's gonna burn itself up. It really feels like she's flirting with me. I try my best not to lick her finger back, but I do. Just a little bit. Her finger's warm and salty and tastes like her perfume. I think I'm actually dead.

She pulls her finger out and laughs. "Dude, your tongue's blue."

I wash down the pill with whatever's in this random cup Sam hands me. I don't know what the hell that pill's gonna do.

Sam hops onto the counter, swings a leg at me, then just kinda... leaves it there. She pushes her hair behind her ear. "So what's happening with you and Ethan?"

Ugh. "We're just, you know...friends." I take another sip of the mystery swill. This whole situation's too fucking weird. "I swear."

"Why haven't you guys hooked up yet? He's *so* hot—for a gay guy, I mean. You should go for it. You'd be *sooo* cute together."

I tap my fingernails in a quick scale on my red Solo cup. "It's not like that. We're just...good friends. He's been really good to me." Okay Asher. Come up with something convincing. Something to keep up the lie. "I can't mess up our friendship. Even if he is...hot."

Sam nods. "I actually *totally* get it. In third grade, Jackie asked me to be her girlfriend, but I was like—Jackie, we're friends. Plus...gross. I'm not a lesbian." Sam cackles like a crazy person. "No offense."

At this point she's slurring her words, all messy.

I'm starting to feel kinda bad for her.

Next thing I know, Sam's holding her red cup with her teeth as she makes her way over to the toilet. She pulls her underwear down from under her tight dress. Pink lacy underwear.

Holy fucking shit. No. No. No. My leg's shaking fast I'm so freaked out.

I look away. Such a gross fucking perv. I hear her pee hit the toilet water and it echoes all around me. She goes on about her breakup with Luke, how she dumped him, and her relationship with Silas. I *hate* hearing Luke's name.

Sam's clearly too oblivious to notice my reaction. Not just cause she's drunk. "What do you think about Silas? So hot, right?"

I feel my chest puff out, angry. She says it like Silas hasn't been fucking with me for years, with Luke. Like everything's fine and I can just tell her he's hot.

"So hot." A sting in my chest.

Sam's done peeing and pulls her underwear back up. "You know… don't tell anyone this, but sometimes Silas can't stay hard…I hate that." She looks me dead in the eyes, biting her nails all cracked out. "Don't you hate when that happens?"

The Xanax is hitting. Starting to feel dizzy. Drunk. I don't respond. Please, god, let this end.

"You'll find a guy soon. Nick fucking Carter with a huge dick." Sam's eyes start to float up to the back of her head. "But why do you hang out with that corny nerd?" She's slurring.

"Who? Robbie?" I know for a fact she knows who Robbie is.

"Yeah, him. Such a desperate weirdo. He *obviously* has a crush on you, too. It's kind of pathetic…like he would have a chance with someone like you."

This girl's totally off, but she confirmed something. Robbie's dragging me the fuck down.

Suddenly there's this loud banging on the bathroom door and a guy's voice is yelling really angry.

I know that voice. Motherfucking Luke.

His voice roars like a lion from a rival pack. "Sam! Sam!" Rattling the doorknob. "I know you're in there! I just want to talk."

Sam yanks the door open. "No one wants you here, Luke. You're embarrassing yourself."

I freeze, my body shrinking behind her. Old Asher. The tortoise. Hiding.

But then something in me unlocks—a bonus level. Surge of

electricity. Ready to fight back and beat the boss. Or maybe it's all the jungle juice.

I jump in front of Sam and reach back to block her from Luke's wrath. Her skin feels nice and soft. Luke's eyes are small, mean, and empty. Like some demented Garbage Pail Kid. He looks, sounds, and smells way too drunk.

"Get away from her, dude. She's...she's with me."

Luke barks out a laugh, all sloppy limbs and chaos. "What the hell are you talking about, Diamond?"

"She's...she...she doesn't want to talk to you right now."

Silas runs up to Luke and grabs one of his arms to stop him, but Luke's fighting back. Then Ethan runs over and grabs Luke's other arm. Luke's fighting like hell, but somehow they manage to stop him from punching me in the face.

I close my eyes and breathe heavy breaths. In the locker room again. Scared. Running. Falling. Pain. *Get that outta your head, Asher.*

"Sam!" Luke shouts. "Sam! I need to talk! I need...I need to see you..." But Luke doesn't look so scary. There's a, like, whimper in his voice and his eyes are glassy.

My breathing slows down. Is he...is Luke about to cry?

Silas and Ethan drag Luke toward the crew of lacrosse guys, who circle him. Luke's shouting gets drowned out by the chaos.

I blow out all the air I've been holding in. Nothing left, light-headed.

I turn around and bump into Sam and she falls on the ground. Fuck.

She's clutching her head in her hands, hair messy all over her face. Her knee's scraped and bleeding and she's trying to grab my legs. I reach to help her up, but Silas jumps in. She stumbles back on her feet. Then, a bright flash and Sam lights up. A camera.

I was just trying to help, but...my clumsy ass fucked it up.

As I watch Silas help Sam stumble inside, she doesn't look as perfect as she wants people to think she is.

The party cyclones around me, blinding me with streaks of light. Blue drinks and perfume and chlorine. Bad pop-punk thumping in my skull. I need to find Ethan. Now.

I push through the crowd, but can't keep my balance. Bumping shoulders, spilling drinks. Luke's voice cuts through everything else —he's still here. Still shouting.

He breaks free from the jocks holding him back and rushes up to me. Pushes me and I stumble back. Luke's breathing hard. Heaving, sweating, messy. "I've got you figured out, you little pervert! You're so fucked, dipshit!"

Hold the fuck up. Does he...*know*? Like, *know it* know it?

Ethan's next to me, holding his arm out to protect me from this beat-down monster. He looks over at me. "What's he talking about? Is this *the* Luke?"

"Oh, uh...yeah. I don't know what the fuck he's talking about. He's a psycho."

Ethan glares at Luke. "That's one word for him."

Luke's right up close to Ethan's face. "Step back, faggot!"

But Ethan just stands there. Doesn't flinch. Fucking brave.

This is all *so* out of control. Luke *can't* tell everyone the truth. Not now.

Ethan starts talking loud, but steady and in control. "Listen, you empty-headed, roid-raging, roofie-slipping, small-dicked piece of shit. You're going to step away from Asher. And leave him. The fuck. Alone."

Holy shit—Ethan *rules*. Handling this all on his own? He's so much stronger than me.

Luke stops throwing his body around and stares at Ethan. Breathing heavy, getting slower. Swear to God, his eyes start to water.

Silas pushes Luke out of the way, backing him out of the party. "Dude, you're such an idiot. I told you not to..." They disappear into that dark jungle.

My stomach flinches all over. I see the dock past the pool and run over, down the wooden slats, up to Silas's yacht bobbing in the black water.

"Asher, what the hell was—"

I'm panting hard. "Can...uh, can you give me...a second?" I force my quick breaths into slow, deep ones. In. Out.

Ethan's hand rubs slow circles on my shoulder. My heart starts to calm, adrenaline fading. That Xanax Sam gave me setting in.

Ethan's voice is soft, steady. "Whatever you need, cutie."

He saved my life tonight. If I was alone, Luke would've *destroyed* me. Exposed me. Thank fucking god Ethan was here.

We sit on the dock for what feels like forever. He lets me rest my head on his shoulder while I recover from all the insanity.

My droopy pupils catch something lurking in the water—or they think they do: two big black eyes and a long, crusty snout, barely breaking the surface. Maybe it's nothing. Maybe it's everything.

But there's only so much Ethan can help. What could he do when a *real* beast comes to devour me?

And Ethan has no fucking clue it's been here the whole time. Circling. Waiting for me to slip.

## *Whipped*

"SHUT...up...you...piece...of..."

"Man up, bitch." Robbie's standing over me, spotting so I don't crush my skull. "Eleven...twelve...come on, princess."

It's a few days later and I'm back in weight training with Robbie. The air reeks of BO and Axe, and Silas's flexing in the wall mirrors like a tool.

Robbie counts my reps as I grunt through my set, pushing past my twenty-five record. A few months ago, I didn't even know what a rep *was*.

Things with Robbie have been *seriously* fucked. No more phone calls, no more weekend hangouts—just lunch, weight training, nods in the hall when I'm walking around with Sam. Ghosts, really. Just going through the motions all empty and far. I've got *no* idea what he's up to. Juggling fire or whatever with Jax and his weirdo crew? Or maybe Jax died. Wouldn't know.

I max out at twenty-six reps and drop the bar onto the rack. The loud *clink* sends a flash of Luke's distorted, screaming face into my head, a sneak attack. I lean back and let my head flop off the bench, letting blood rush into my brain to wash Luke away.

"Someone's been doing their homework." Robbie's being such a sarcastic dick about my gym time with Ethan. Whatever.

"Ehhh..." I fake modesty. "I'll never be, like...huge or anything. Sometimes—I don't know. Like, what's the fucking point?"

But we both know the point: getting people to like us more. And for me, it's working.

I'm noticing some little changes in my body. New double-takes in the mirror when I notice my bigger chest and filled-out sleeves. Who's that guy? I run my fingers over my abs and actually feel bumps, and my neck looks like a stable base for my head. I drink two protein shakes a day. Ethan told me to.

I've noticed at Pantheon that guys check me out more. Sometimes they try to flirt. Being tall with a deep voice helps. Turns out people think I'm attractive after all. Why'd it take seventeen years for me to figure it out? And why now, when I'm playing a part?

But it's all surface. Bullshit. In my head, I'm still stuck: Sam's sidekick, hopeless virgin, friend-zoned and fucked up.

I must be making some kinda face because Robbie throws me a bone. "At least you're tall."

I hate this dynamic between us. Nothing good, no fun, just this blah conversation and hidden resentments.

I think about how Robbie feels about his body. He's strong but pudgy, or—nicer—husky. Kinda short, too, and insecure like the rest of us. Maybe he's ready for a change, like I was.

We move to the mats. Abs. "So...Silas's party. That movie theater real, or just more Silas bullshit?"

What do I even say? He's *for sure* heard the gossip about me, Luke, and Ethan. Everyone has.

I don't say I was happy he wasn't there. I don't say Sam said something shitty about him. And I *definitely* don't say she jammed a pill in my mouth with her finger, and I tasted it on my tongue and jerked off to it. Twice. "Eh. Silas's full of shit. House is whatever."

Robbie raises an eyebrow. He knows *I'm* full of shit, too. He waits for a sec, like he's testing the water. "Maybe one day I can, uh...see it for myself."

I force some crunches and pretend not to hear him.

Coach Henley kills the music. Saved. Time to head to the locker room. A nightmare on repeat. I wish they'd let me change somewhere else.

Me and Robbie slowly shuffle over. Metal lockers slam like gunshots. We find our usual hideout in the back corner—the same one from that day.

As we change, the air between us feels thick and slimy. I'm gunking up our friendship, but I can't stop. I catch Robbie glance at me, confused and disappointed I think. Maybe sad, too.

I *know* he wants to say something about the "new me," about Ethan, about Luke. About everything that's changed.

But he doesn't. And I don't either.

I'm done getting dressed, and I pretend to fidget with my lock until Robbie leaves first.

"See ya."

I nod my chin up, saying nothing.

Robbie's shoulders slump a little as he walks away, slipping back into reality.

Maybe this is—finally—the end.

*Friendship*

STUFFING my face with chocolate gelt, I watch Piper spin through the kitchen like Taz. My dad forced me to invite Ethan for Hanukkah, which could seriously fuck my lie. Too many booby traps in my house of fakery. Plus, my dad's cringey gay rah-rah shit and Piper's nonstop questions could send Ethan running.

Piper's been cooking since the asscrack of dawn, hell-bent on impressing Ethan. She thinks we're dating—I'm too tired to correct her. My dad hovers, sneaking food and pretending to help but getting in the way, exactly like he used to with my mom.

Watching all this has got me super anxious, so I head to my room and dive into *Grand Theft Auto* with Michelangelo, clock ticking until Ethan shows.

I'm carjacking an ambulance when the doorbell rings. "No one get the door!" Shit—my outfit. I yank off my basketball shorts and throw on Express jeans and a Hollister polo. Shoes? You'd have to be deranged to wear shoes in your own house.

I run to the door and make a last-ditch effort to fix my hair in the reflection of a glass-covered painting. I open the door and there's Ethan, holding a massive, crackling gift basket stuffed with cheesy

Jew shit—dreidel cookies, chocolate gelt, a bear in a yarmulke. Total overkill. He greets me with a big smile, ready to charm the pants off everyone.

Of course, my dad's *obsessed* with the gift basket. Hook, line, sinker. They might as well be best friends. Knowing Ethan, he'd probably love that. "Piper! Look what Ethan brought!" My dad disappears to the kitchen.

I whisper low. "Seriously?"

"Chill, it's gonna be fine." Ethan takes a slow, deep breath and I do too, to help the nerves. Ethan knows what to do. *He's* the friend I need.

We walk to the kitchen and Piper's eyes bulge out of her head when she sees Ethan, like he's some catalog boyfriend. She wipes her cruddy palms on her apron to shake Ethan's hand. But he goes in for a hug, not caring if his clothes get dirty.

Piper lights up like a slot machine blasting a jackpot.

"So lovely to meet you, Piper. Is there anything I can help with?"

"Aren't you so sweet. You can grab the Manischewitz from the back." After Ethan turns around, Piper mouths something sick. "*So adorable.*"

I roll my eyes and silently die inside, then push Ethan into the laundry room by his shoulders. I grab the bottle of crap Jewish wine that's probably been sitting here since 1992.

"She seems nice." Ethan sounds scared cause he knows how crazy Piper makes me.

"Trust me. She's nice to your face but who knows what sick shit she's plotting."

"Uh, sure Asher." I know Ethan doesn't believe me. One of his best qualities is that he makes up his mind for himself.

We go back with the wine, and I sit with my dad watching a

boring basketball game while Piper and Ethan get the table ready. When it's finally time, she herds us into the dining room.

The table feels huge for just the four of us, everyone spaced out like a movie family with too many secrets. Did my parents think they'd have more kids? I've always wondered.

Piper isn't Jewish, so she's clueless about the holiday foods. Tonight we have matzo ball soup, brisket, and potato latkes. Piper's food tastes like a dogshit version of the Hanukkah dinners my mom used to make. *Get away from my family shit, woman.*

I think back to being a kid and playing dreidel with my parents. Stuffing my face with chocolate coins. Cutting my fingers grating a million potatoes for the latkes. Ripping open presents I probably didn't deserve.

After a few minutes of bland, safe conversation, my dad digs in. "So, Ethan...you've been spending a lot of time with our Asher. We barely see him anymore. Save some for us!"

Ethan laughs. "I'm taking good care of him. Don't worry."

Piper's eyes dart between me and Ethan. Investigating. "And you're on your best behavior, I hope?" They've got no fucking clue what I'm up to, and I'm sure as hell not gonna tell them.

"Of course, Mrs....um...Piper." Ethan catches himself just in time.

"So, what do you two do on weekends?" Piper's pushing her brisket around. "Asher's so secretive."

Yeah, no shit.

Ethan starts to answer. "You know, we go out to—"

I kick his leg under the table, shutting him up before he spills about Pantheon. "Uh, to the movies...the mall...Starbucks, you know, whatever." I shoot Ethan a death stare to shut him up. My dad and Piper are cool with me being "gay" and making new friends, but I'm pretty sure my dad would be sketched out by his underaged child running around town getting shit-faced with adults.

"Oh—oh yeah, mostly we just spend time at my place, listening to music, watching TV—"

"Gossiping about boys?"

Fuck, Dad. I grab my fork and push the sharp prongs into the back of my hand under the table.

"You know it, Mark." That name, *Mark*, hits me hard, like when Piper says it. Shocking and nauseating.

Piper can't stop herself. "Where are you headed to college next year, dear?" *Shut up.*

"I'm waiting to hear back from NYU, early decision. Should be any day now...wish me luck." Ethan crosses his fingers in the air. Cheeseball.

"Well, *of course* you're going to get in." My dad looks over at Piper. Oh god. "And, you know, it's a crazy coincidence because—"

"Dad, just...drop it, okay?" My voice comes out tight and high, strangled.

Ethan puts his hand on my leg for half a second. Quick flinch, then I'm good. I think.

He smiles big for the audience. "No, it's okay. I've wanted to go to NYU, well, forever. I know it's gonna be better than Florida...oh, uh, no offense."

Piper laughs. "Oh, stop it. Of course you want to get away. And New York—it's just magical." Piper looks at my dad with this sick smile, then at me. "Funny thing—I went to NYU myself."

"What? No way!" Ethan squints at me like I'm Judas or something. "Why didn't you tell me?"

His intense eyes make me nervous, like he's putting the puzzle pieces together. He looks back at Piper and smiles. "My mom took me to Manhattan when I was a kid and it was the best. We saw *Rent* and ice skated and...I just knew that—"

"Yeah." I interrupt his corny memory. "NYU. Great place. Um, so...dessert?"

Ethan looks at me with pity, almost. "And, you know, I've been trying to get Asher to consider—"

"Tell me about it!" My dad just can't help himself, can he? "We've been saying the same thing for years."

I start grinding my teeth to dust. Yeah, Ethan's brought up NYU. He thinks I should apply cause it's easy to be gay there, allegedly. But I'm not gonna be gay next year—I'll be off the grid, Siberia or something, where no one can find me. Luke looming over me like this? No, I have to totally disappear. Become the real me again.

So no, I can't talk about college right now.

We all pick at our food, silently waiting for the next move. My dad tries. "So Ethan, I'm curious. When did you, you know, come out? As a...uh...homosexual."

I smack my face with my palm, but Ethan rolls with it—he's good at that. "I came out a few years ago. I was...fifteen I think? Ninth grade."

"That's very brave of you." Piper sounds like she's in a therapy session with one of her patients.

"Yeah, well, school was tough. But...I survived." Ethan stares hard at nothing. "My mom's been amazing. She went to these meetings for parents with gay kids. Learning and stuff. More supportive than I could have dreamed."

"That's wonderful, dear. Maybe I can talk to her about these meetings?"

"Oh, of course!"

My mind jumps from freaking out to thoughts about my mom. How I wish she was here to support me—instead of Piper—through my fake coming out.

Suddenly I snap back to reality. Piper better not go to any of those fucking meetings. "Uh, no...that's...you don't need to do that."

Piper can't help herself. "Well, no, I just thought that, because of, you know...the *incident* and everything..."

My face burns up. *Get this under control.* "But now I'm out, and I have Ethan, and school's fine, and everything's great." I grab the Manischewitz and take a long swig straight from the bottle.

Piper looks like I just shot up black tar heroin. Everyone's staring at this psycho—me—until my dad jumps in. "I guess that's that."

Ethan bites his bottom lip, then stands up quick. "I've got the plates, Piper. Please sit. Enjoy your wine."

Later, after Ethan helps Piper clean, we all stand around this old menorah the Diamonds have had for generations. My dad sparks a match, and the smell of sulfur hitting wax shocks my brain with memories. The colored candles drip slow, instantly globbing into pools of soft wax when they hit the base of the menorah. We're all saying the prayers—even Piper—and I catch Ethan, glowing, in the candlelight.

He looks really happy. And for the first time tonight, I realize Ethan doesn't have a family like this—like mine.

My dad yells after we finish. "Time for presents!"

We all head to the den, and my dad hands each of us a small package wrapped in cheesy blue Hanukkah paper. I can't believe they got Ethan a present.

My first thought is to light them on fire. Instead, I shred my wrapping paper while Ethan unfolds his all neat.

Inside: rainbow-colored friendship bracelets. Rows of tiny knots that spell out our names, like the ones I made at camp when I'd hide from the asshole boys playing sports. Feels like my dad gave us fucking wedding rings.

The rainbows burn my eyes, and I taste vomit in my throat.

"Aww, what an adorable gift!" Ethan's such a kiss-ass. "Thank you so much, Mark. And you too, Piper." He hugs them like he got a brand-new car. I wonder if they bought these bracelets at the same gay dollar store where my dad found that dumb pride hat.

"Yeah, uh...thanks." I'm too freaked out to fake being excited.

My hand vibrates as Ethan ties my bracelet, and I tie his. No other fucking choice.

Ethan smiles, holding his hand out to pose. Is he for real? Does he actually *like* these cursed bracelets? And what if—oh god—he *likes me*?

I was so busy freaking out about Ethan meeting my family and nuclear destruction that I totally ignored the elephant in the room.

Me and Ethan. The thing everyone's probably been talking about for months, something I didn't take seriously. Something scary.

What the hell *are* we?

Suddenly, with these ugly bracelets, something feels different. Me and Ethan—tied together.

Perfectly aligned, and tangled in a million knots.

Friction

MADONNA'S "Like a Virgin" blares as I bounce my toes off the sandpapery pool floor, trapped in a hot pink inner tube. Winter break's off to a weird start at some creepy dude's pool party. Half-naked gay guys have me surrounded.

This is my life now.

"Asher, come here." Wade, sitting on the edge of the pool, hooks his foot under my floaty. "Take this shit off." He rips away the inner tube, flashing my newly-toned-but-nothing-compared-to-everyone-else body.

"The fuck, Wade! You don't have to be such a dick."

He hops into the pool, squeezing my bicep. "Show off those muscles, boy."

I roll my eyes and let my body go slack like a worn-out Stretch Armstrong action figure.

Ethan walks at us with three beer bottles. "Wade! Stop touching Asher. Asher—you're gorgeous." He gives me a smile and puts a drink down next to me.

I fold my arms to hide my body again, squatting so my head's bobbing on the water.

Ethan's compliments have hit different since Hanukkah. Does he still look at me like a friend—or, dear god, *more*? Gotta be careful with my signals. Gay Asher's been here so long, I don't think twice about what I say or do around him anymore.

Ethan sits on the edge of the pool. "Happy winter break, my dears."

Wade hoists himself out and gives Ethan a big, wet kiss on the cheek.

Ethan just laughs—he's used to this stuff.

"Where's your daddy?" God, Wade. "Busy again? Studying? Saving the world?"

Ethan curls his fingers and focuses on picking at his hangnails. "I don't think it's any of your business."

Wade shoots me this dramatic look like I'm on his side. "Right. Well, give him a kiss for me."

I close my eyes and dunk underwater, drowning out a picture of Ethan and John making out, until I run out of breath and leap up. I flick my hair back so water doesn't drip in my eyes. The tropical winter air chills my wet head.

"Damn, boy. It's like *Wild Things* up in here."

I wonder if Wade's jerked off to that three-way scene, too. "Shut *up*, Wade. Is that all you think about? Sex and dick?"

"Okay nerd, what are you so scared of?" Wade asks like he sees right through me.

"I'm not *scared* of anything. I'm just getting bored with..."

"Dude, you always run away when I try to give you a kiss. You don't kiss *anyone*. What are you, asexual or something?"

Fuck. Is Wade onto me like Luke is, or is he just being a dick? Whatever, I can dodge this.

"Yeah, well, don't be so shocked that someone doesn't wanna

tongue-fuck you.”

Wade gets this villain smile and looks around the pool. “Everyone wants to tongue-fuck me!”

“Hilarious.” Ethan jumps in. “I know for a *fact* that Jacob turned you down at Pantheon last weekend.”

“Jacob’s blind.”

“Well *I’m* not.” I splash Wade, and he splashes me back harder. Chlorine in my eyes. Prick.

Ethan goes full Ethan. “But Asher baby, isn’t it, you know...time?”

Wade butts in. “Time for you to *get some dick*!” He grooves his body around like a huge fucking dork.

Somehow, I’ve stayed out of dating and sex and all that. Ethan’s told me about guys with crushes on me, but I’ve dodged it. Is my time running out? There any way outta this without being forced to fuck some guy just to keep my cover?

No. Fucking. Way.

Ethan looks at me like I’ve got food stuck in my teeth. “You’re fucking hot. And you’ve gotta have your eye on *someone*...right?”

I swallow and pray Ethan doesn’t think that *someone* is him. My head darts around, all these dudes suddenly potential vampires out to feed on my virgin blood. “Uh, I don’t know, man...”

Ethan grabs at the strings hanging off my ratty rainbow bracelet. “Please, Asher. Let me play matchmaker. I’d be *so* good at it.”

Wade surveys the party super focused, then stops and puts his finger to his lips. “I have it! I’m a genius.” He flicks my chest with the back of his hand. “See that guy over there? The one with the glasses?”

I look over and it’s this kid Raj I’ve talked to a couple times at parties, just in passing kind of. He didn’t leave much of an impression.

“Um...yeah? What about him?”

"You guys could play butt pirates." Wade raises an eyebrow and stares me in the eyes.

"Jesus, Wade! No, no." Ethan tries to save me. "Maybe just, you know...a date? Asher's a romantic like me."

Keep up the lie. Bounce it in the air like a hacky sack. *Don't* let it drop.

Maybe one date wouldn't kill me. "Okay! Okay, fine!" I yell at Wade. "If I talk to him will you shut the fuck up?"

"Probably not." He flashes an annoying white smile.

Ethan pulls me out of the pool and pushes me against a tacky stone waterfall thing. Away from Wade so he can't hear. He talks to me close and quiet. "Asher. I know you can do this. Everyone thinks you're such a sweetheart and so handsome—I'm sure Raj will too." He squeezes my shoulder. "Do you want me to feel it out first?"

God, no. I *don't* want to be a pussy about it. I can lie for myself, like a big boy.

"I got it. I'll be...fine."

Ethan grabs a towel and ties it around my waist. Looks me up and down, like our first trip to the mall. His hand grazes my neck before messing with my hair, carefully adjusting every strand.

I wonder what he sees when he looks at me.

"Okay, Mr. Affleck. You're ready." Ethan shoos me off with his hands. "Go, go."

So I start walking. Raj is standing by himself at this food table. He's popping some pineapple chunks into his mouth, maybe so he doesn't have to talk to anyone. Very smart plan.

I take a deep breath and walk up to him. "Good pineapple?" Cool line, Asher.

"Oh, hi." He's awkwardly holding his hand over his face while he chews. "It's, uh, Asher, right?"

Raj's skinny body and outdated glasses aren't doing him any favors. His loose blue-and-red swimsuit screams JCPenney—*a sin*, Ethan would say. He's shorter than me, and, well...not white.

I've noticed that white guys are way more popular in the scene. Kinda messed up, but no one really talks about it.

"Um, yeah, it's Asher. And you're Raj?"

He drops his fruit on the ground and gets this dorky smile that makes me wonder if he already has a crush on me. He pops the five-second-rule pineapple into his mouth, then garbles out some small talk. "So how'd you end up at this party?"

"Ethan made me come...Do you know him? Ethan?"

Raj swallows big and lets out a soft laugh. "Everyone knows Ethan. Well, I mean—I don't *know*-know him. But I know, you know, *about* him."

I can't help but get cringed out by Raj being so up front about the Pantheon social hierarchy. He's absolutely *not* a top-tier cool guy. Just average, hoping to land a date or a kiss or a hand job.

"What about you? Who do you know here?"

"This guy I met online, Victor? It's his party...He invited me, and we talked for a bit, but then he, kind of...you know, disappeared."

"Oh shit, sorry. What a dick...but honestly, you probably dodged a bullet." It's true. These older guys, these...adults, they can be creepy as fuck. If you're young, you have to watch what you're doing in Pantheon, when it's dark and sweaty and foggy and all that.

Wade sneaks up behind Raj like a T. rex. "Ah!" Wade grabs Raj's shoulders and cackles like a hyena. He scares the shit out of this poor kid. Very *Luke* behavior.

Wade's voice pulls me back to my fucked-up reality. "I see you've met Asher."

"Oh, uh, yeah." Raj crosses his arms over his chest like me in the pool and locks his eyes onto some random point in the air. He looks super intimidated by Wade. He *should* be.

Not knowing what to do, I press my fingers into my forehead.

"So are we planning our date?"

What, Wade? *Our?* "Wade! What the fuck! Leave us alone."

"Oh, come on. You two are clearly horny for each other. It's so obvious."

"Sorry, Raj." I wave my arm like I'm apologizing. "This guy's insane."

"Okay." Wade rubs his hands together so you can hear the friction. "Raj, do you want to go on a date with Asher?" Wade stares at him like a bully.

"Um...I...I guess...yeah, sure." Raj looks terrified.

"And Asher, you wanna go on a date with this kid, right?" He doesn't even wait for me to answer, just puts his arm around my neck before giving me that big, cartoony kiss on the cheek he's been threatening me with. "Muuuah! Okay, you freaks figure out the rest." Wade backs away. Cupping his hand around his mouth he yells. "Good luck, boys. Use a condom!" He laughs to himself as he turns and leaps a cannonball into the pool.

Me and Raj awkwardly exchange AIM handles. He says he wants to hang this week. I stall and say I'm really busy over break. Gotta delay this thing as long as possible.

I walk away, stunned and trapped.

This is the realest shit so far. More than grinding with Ethan and Wade at Pantheon—that's just dancing. More than those dumb gay rainbow bracelets my dad got us—just string. More than my new fancy clothes—just a costume.

With Raj, something's *actually* at stake: another guy's feelings.

But if I keep dodging the dating thing? Ethan's gonna get

suspicious like Wade. Plus, going on a date with Raj will make sure Ethan keeps me in the friend zone, right? If I want to keep the lie, keep my new life, and keep Ethan's friendship...

I realize I'm sweating like crazy. Maybe it's the blazing sun, or maybe it's cause I have to face the gayest quest yet.

My first fucking date.

# *The Mall*

SO Ethan blabbed to Piper about my date. Now she wants to take me shopping to find the perfect outfit. Thanks, Ethan.

Piper yanks me from my school-free Thursday TV binge to drag me to the mall. She's in full Christmas mode—chipper, tinsel-obsessed, begging my dad for a tree. Over my mom's dead body.

I *hate* Christmas. Forced happiness, consumerism, empty promises—all of it. Growing up in Florida, I never got that winter wonderland stuff anyway. Though palm trees with the string lights are kinda cool.

The mall's decked out. Santa's house dropped in front of Sears, with scary frozen reindeer guarding some cheapo cottage. Screaming brats and their stressed-out parents line up for a creepy moment with some random fat guy in a fake beard. Yeah, I was that kid—the one who told everyone Santa's not real. No regrets. These kids should be embarrassed.

Piper's trying to put me in a jacket and tie. She's totally nuts. This isn't 1955. That's not what people wear anymore.

I say maybe Abercrombie. She shrugs, but with this big smile. "Whatever you want, honey." She's *so* horny for my gay date.

Just when I'm thinking this mall trip can't get worse—boom. Someone's standing outside the store. *Fuck* to infinity.

Luke Psycho Baker.

My body spins before my brain can catch up.

"Asher? What's wrong?" Piper puts her hand on my back, but I yank away. I'm trying to steady my quick breaths so I look like a normal person.

"Just...uh..." She probably thinks I'm having a panic attack. Maybe I am.

The old Asher would run. Chicken out, stay as far away from Luke as possible.

But New Asher?

Everything blew up at Silas's party—Luke acting crazy, Sam getting hurt, Ethan almost knocking him out. Luke looked super drunk and out of it and...pathetic, really.

Worst of all? He might know the truth. And that's really fucking dangerous.

My body jolts up. *Face your fears, pussy.* Stand up. Fight the fuck back.

I pivot around and march toward him, psyching myself up for another Luke shitshow.

As I get closer, Luke's eyes dart, his fake retail smile wobbling. He looks like he wants to disappear into the ugly Christmas decorations behind him. He's wearing low-rise jeans and a really stupid Santa hat. No shirt, like one of Ethan's wall guys.

But he doesn't look all evil and giddy. There's this weird slump to his shoulders. Tortoise-like. And his tan's faded—from lockup, hopefully.

Luke's eyes catch me before he turns away, shrinking and huddling with another shirtless Santa. The guy looks at me, too—is

Luke talking about me? What bullshit is he spewing now?

I squeeze my hands into fists, knuckle bones almost ripping through my skin. Luke sees me coming—leans back, lifts a hand in front of his face. Is he...scared?

Shit, what do I say? *Wing it. Don't think.*

"You guys talking about me?" I feel like some gangster tough guy in the movies. I don't recognize myself.

Luke rips off his hat and wrings it in his hands. "Uh, no...I mean..." Then he whispers like a secret. "I shouldn't be talking to you...I gotta get back to my job..."

"That's not what it seemed like at Silas's party." My voice is low but sharp. All consonants. "You *really* wanted to talk to me *then*."

The other guy turns to Luke. "Bro, it's okay. Let's just go inside..."

Luke's eyes get glassy again. His jaw muscles twitch and his eyes dart around. Avoiding me.

Fuck confusion—now I'm just pissed. I lean in close. "No. No... Luke...I'm not gonna let you bully me anymore. You can't just—"

"Dude! Please...I..." Luke looks around paranoid, maybe looking for his manager. His shirtless body's shaking like a hairless cat after a tub.

Can't believe I'm seeing him like this. Powerless, freaking the fuck out. I get this weird mix of anger, fear, and...sympathy, I guess? But I'm *over* Luke driving my brain off cliffs.

I lean in even more, almost whispering in his ear. "What you did at the party...no—what you did to me my whole life? It was... *unforgivable*, dude. Unforgivable."

I feel fucking amazing. Fucking powerful. "If you *ever* go near me, or Sam, or Ethan...ever again, then I swear to God, I'll—"

"Just, *stop*...You don't—no one gets it...I lost *everything*."

Piper comes up looking super freaked. "What's going on, Asher?

Is this—?" She pulls my arm back. "Let's go."

But I *don't* go. I need to do this. So I push Piper away. Maybe too hard.

I squint at Luke, not knowing who I'm looking at. "I lost it all, too."

"No, you didn't." He points his finger at me, then to himself. "I *know* I'm a douchebag. I *know* I'm a total fuck-up and treat everyone like shit and push people away. I'm messed up, dude. My life is *fucked*."

Takes a second to sink in, and I can't believe it, but...I think he's right.

I *didn't* lose it all. I gained so much. Didn't really think about *Luke's* feelings, what he's *really* gone through since he got expelled. "Shit, I...didn't...uh..." I fumble my words, caught in my selfish stupidity.

"You've done enough."

No way. *I've* done enough? *Me?*

"Riiight." I draw out the word all sarcastic. "Cause you're the victim here. My bad."

Luke straightens up, bites his lip. "You think you know everything, Diamond, but maybe there's a lot you...you can't understand."

My whole body goes electric. I move closer, my new muscles blocking Luke's escape. He takes these awkward short steps back, trapped between me and the storefront glass. Like I was trapped between Luke and the lockers at the beginning of the year. When this whole mess started. My brain explodes with power.

I feel Luke's hot breath escape his mouth. "But I haven't decided if I'm gonna tell."

"What? What are you talking about?"

"Your secret. I'm not a total idiot, dude." But Luke's voice doesn't sound threatening. "I don't know, I've got too much of my own shit to deal with...and nothing I say will help me, you know, get it all back."

I freeze into a solid block of ice. I just stare at Luke, blank.

Piper tries to pull me away again, but I'm stuck like a statue. She can barely move me an inch.

"What are you saying?"

Luke just shakes his head and sidesteps me, fumbling to slap on his Santa hat but dropping it on the floor like a loser. He turns away quick, tripping over his feet as he stumbles into the store.

I want to yell for him to go fuck himself, but I can't do anything.

Luke knows my secret. *Actually* knows.

Can he destroy me? Does he even want to?

Luke used to be, like, *supernaturally* powerful, totally in charge. Now here he is—working at this stupid store, expelled. Fell from up high with guts splattered over the mall's marble floor.

My breathing's big, but fast. When will my life fall apart like Luke's has? Can I make it to graduation alive? Will I blow up into a million tiny pieces like dumb fake snow?

I feel this black hole open up inside. For the first time, I see it—my life, totally fucked forever. I might not make it out alive.

There's a tug on my hoodie. "Asher! Asher!" Piper's trying to get my attention, but I'm too far gone. Her voice is small, trembling.

This new Hulk version of me? Just another lie. Making threats, shoving people around. It's illusion, fantasy. As real as a plastic reindeer.

Merry fucking Christmas. I'm fucked.

## *Wound*

COULDN'T sleep. Every time I closed my eyes, Luke was there—sweaty, shirtless, in that dumbass Santa hat—clawing into my brain like some chest-waxed demon.

Too fried to function. I tell Ethan I have homework. A lie. I'm sitting out by the pool trying to get a gay-ass tan while half-assing geometry. My eyes might as well be closed.

There's a tiny frog floating in the pool. This happens all the time. Some clueless tadpole grows legs and flops into the water. He tries to jump out, but the liquid's too thick for his little muscles. Eventually, he gives up and boils in the sun. The one in front of me isn't moving. Think he knows he's about to die.

Frog equals Robbie. If I'm gonna self-destruct, shouldn't I at least *try* to get him back? Maybe I *haven't* lost him forever. Tossing and turning on the lounge chair, my mind flip-flops, too. Maybe it wouldn't hurt to check in.

Before I can second-guess myself, my greasy fingers slide to Robbie's contact. That flat ringing suddenly makes it feel way too real. Above me, a red-headed vulture circles like he always does. For a second, I wonder if he'll swoop down and snatch me up with his razor-sharp talons, feast on me, then take a bloody doggy bag home for his chicks.

Honestly, I hope it goes to voicemail.

No luck.

"Hello?"

"Oh, uh, hi. It's Asher."

"I know." His tone's all serious.

Why the hell did I call? Sweat drops prick my skin under the laser-hot sun. "Um…I just wanted to see how you're, you know, doing." My neck hurts from clutching the phone, so I scribble big black spirals on my graph-paper notebook. Hypnotizing myself.

"I'm okay."

I dig my ballpoint pen harder into the page as I study Robbie's voice to hear if it's changed.

"Actually, I've been wanting to…talk. Uh…yeah."

"Oh. Yeah, of course. Um, you wanna come over?" In TV shows and movies, whenever someone says they need to talk it's never good news.

"Yeah, but I can't right now. My dad's holding me hostage for Risk. He's about to reach global domination."

I can picture it easy, and it's not pretty. Robbie's dad is scary cutthroat.

*Do it, Asher.* Don't be an asshole for once. "How about tonight?"

"Sure, sounds good. See ya later."

I toss the phone, and before I know it, my chest is tight and my breaths are weak. It totally catches me off guard.

I think about Robbie. Our past, the sleepovers, the late-night talks, the laughter. Suddenly it all feels rare and special.

Wait. Maybe I *can* have it all. Ethan and Robbie and Sam and everyone. Maybe the lie's fine. Maybe all the shit I've pulled is leading me somewhere great, like fate or something, like I was meant to *win*. Maybe this whole thing was genius!

I draw the spirals bigger and harder, psyching myself up about how perfect it could be—until my pen rips right through the paper.

A huge gash. An open wound.

## *Possessed*

LATER that night, I'm in my room with *SVU* in the background. A detective's arresting some hooker, I think, but it's all white noise under my screaming brain.

Gotta check out with a mindless task, so I scrub Michelangelo's tank. Harder than I need to. Almost shattering the whole damn thing.

Robbie's on his way. My dad and Piper are eating at some overpriced tapas place in Palm Beach, which is for the best.

I keep thinking about what Robbie said. *I want to talk. I want to talk.* What the hell does that even mean?

The doorbell rings and I walk over, my heart thrashing around. I open the door, and Robbie's in black Champion shorts and a tight purple tank top. Nothing like his old Hot Topic shit or washed-out cargos. He's got less body fat and his muscles look bigger. Shoulders and biceps like a goddamn Pantheon guy.

He gives me this nervous half-smile thing and lets himself in.

No clue what to say. "What up, broseph?"

Robbie rolls his eyes and strolls to the living room. He looks around inspecting the details like it's the first time he's come over or something. It *has* been a while, and I hope it's not the last time.

He holds up a Palm Reef gym bag. "I, uh, thought we could go for a swim. You know, like we used to."

We basically grew up in the pool. And right now it sounds pretty nice. "Oh, um…yeah, sure—why not. Just gimme a sec."

Robbie walks through the kitchen to the sliding glass door at the back of my house. Something he's done a million times.

I head to my room and change into a pink gingham Banana Republic bathing suit Ethan picked for me. I check myself out in the mirror and flex my bicep. Smaller than Robbie's. Whatever, good for him.

I grab a couple ratty Mickey beach towels and walk to the kitchen. In the pantry there's a pack of Haribo I left open, so I grab them. We've eaten so many gummy bears together. It's kinda nostalgic, I guess.

I get to the back door and flip on the pool light. It glows bright aqua blue in the dark. I step out and Robbie's wet and shirtless. Wading through the kind of crystal-clear water you can only get from a shit-ton of chlorine. He spots me, dunks his head, and slowly rises up, pushing his hair back. Doing that Denise Richards move from *Wild Things*. Like I did at that pool party, according to Wade. Me and Robbie watched it together so many times. We could never shut up about how hot the girls were.

I lift my shirt and look over at Robbie, nervous about being watched and judged for my skinnier body. The confidence I built this year's suddenly gone. Robbie can see through all my bullshit, anyway. When I catch his eye, he looks away and dunks his head under again.

I step in, bracing for a cold shock—but it's warm, just like the air. Feels nice. I glide in easy and swim to the other side, keeping a safe distance from Robbie. After I freaked out on Luke, who knows what I'm capable of. Gotta keep my shit together. Get my best friend back.

Oh yeah, the gummies. I go back and reach for the pack of semi-stale candy. I hold up a dark red raspberry gummy bear, a game we used to play all the time. "You ready?"

Robbie opens his mouth and I toss it. It lands perfect on his tongue—he's always been good at this. He chews, eyes closed, and a little smile lets me know he's chill.

"Okay, my turn." Robbie smacks the gummy in his mouth and picks up a green with his wet hand.

I open my mouth and he tosses. It's a miss, landing behind me with a little splash. After fishing it out, I think about eating it, but instead throw it onto the grass for the ants.

Robbie raises an eyebrow. "Still great at this, I see."

We're quiet as we wade through the pool, slow under the moonlight. I break the ice. "So, how've you been?"

Robbie squints and runs his fingers over the water. "Uh...I...I'm not really sure."

I wish I could ask what I want to. The *real* things. There's so much I don't know about him and what's happened this year. Why can't I just come out and say what I feel? That I suck and I'm sorry and I don't want to grind our friendship in the garbage disposal.

"You know, just, like...you good?"

"It's been...it's been a rough year." That's all he says, and I don't push. "But how about you? How's your dad? And Piper? And little Michelangelo?"

I chuckle, thinking about all the time we spent playing with my gecko. Making little videos, playing out Jurassic Park like he was a vicious raptor. "Michelangelo's doing great. He just molted."

"Good for him. You think he'll live forever?"

I laugh, imagining myself as an old man feeding him crickets. "Fuck, I hope not."

What do I say about my family? "My dad's, you know, fine. The same. Piper's..." I think about them being on board with the whole gay thing, how they drive me crazy with their support. But Robbie's situation's totally different. Strict dad who doesn't get him, clueless mom. He'd probably *kill* for someone like Piper in his life. "She's annoying...like always."

Robbie looks down at the glowing water, running his hands real light across the surface. "And what about, uh...Ethan? Is it, um, is it okay to ask that?"

My heart sinks to the bottom of the pool. Been such a dick that my best friend is scared to ask me the most basic things about my life. "Oh, yeah, of course. Ethan's good. He's just kinda...Ethan."

"I was wondering, um, if you guys ever became, like...a thing?"

"What? Oh, man." My voice is louder. "No, no, no. He's just my friend. There's never been...anything there." Why does Robbie want to know? Why does he care? And why do I sound like I'm trying to convince myself we're not a thing?

"Have you, like, dated anyone?" Robbie coughs a frog out of his throat. What's he getting at?

"Um...no." I don't mention my upcoming bullshit date with Raj and the dread eating me up.

Robbie doesn't respond and my mind keeps drowning in questions. *Why did he come over? What does he want to talk about?*

I'm scooping a half-alive fly out of the pool when Robbie talks. No frog anymore. "There's something I...um...I, uh...I want to tell you something." He bites his lip and his nerves shoot from his eyes like radiation.

I hope it's nothing serious. Can't take any more guilt.

"Robbie, uh, it's okay. You can tell me...whatever."

We slowly circle each other, bobbing up and down, looking like we're in some weird animal mating ritual. Or gearing up for a bloody fight.

Robbie picks up a gummy bear and glides toward me, stopping a couple inches from my face.

Nerve endings in the bridge of my nose tingle like crazy. He's looking right at me, and I see my warped reflection in his eyes. Two of me. Glowing from the pool light. Icy flames.

Robbie looks demonically possessed. He holds a gummy to my lips, and—I know I shouldn't—but I let him press it onto my tongue.

Then, he leans in.

My body doesn't move. Doesn't think. Just a flash of Sam's perfume in my mouth. Then his lips—hot, slippery, real.

*What the actual fuck?* My first kiss—out of nowhere.

Brain overload. I jerk back, arms thrashing, splashing Robbie. My teeth slam down on the gummy bear—slice my tongue. Fuck. Deserved it.

"The hell was that?" The words come out angrier than I meant, checking my mouth for blood.

Robbie backs away and shakes his head. "Fuck. I'm so dumb. I shouldn't have—"

"No, sorry, I just...I don't know what to say."

"Um...I...I don't know why I did that. I'm not, uh...or..." Robbie pushes his arms down onto the deck to launch out of the pool, and he brings a big splash of water with him. He rushes to his towel and holds it over his face.

Wait. *Robbie Bradford is gay?* And he kissed...me?

This changes *everything*.

I'm such an idiot. Robbie being gay explains so fucking much, but I've got so many questions, too. *What's it been like for you after I ditched you, Robbie? What's it been like seeing your best friend come out as gay? What's it been like feeling that you couldn't come out too?*

Oh god, what's Robbie been thinking about Ethan this *whole* time? Jealous of my new gay friend for reasons I didn't understand? Jealous of *me*?

"Robbie, it's okay." I try to reassure him and save him from too much embarrassment. Guess this is what coming out *really* looks like.

Robbie rips the towel off his face. "I shouldn't have said, or...done anything. I just, I've been feeling so...lonely, I guess. Something's wrong with me."

"There's *nothing* wrong with you." I'm desperate and out of breath as I climb out of the pool.

Robbie holds his towel close to his body like a shield. "Then why do I feel like this? Why did I kiss you like an idiot?" Robbie goes silent for a sec. "Am I...am I too, like, ugly?"

"Oh my god, Robbie, of course not. You, you look great."

"Then...why did you push me away when I...?" Robbie's face is all jumbled up. So scared and ashamed and confused.

I know what it's like to feel unwanted. Rejected. After I came out, he must've felt so alone. What did I do to make him feel like he couldn't tell me?

I totally fucked up. I destroyed my best friend.

My guilt and self-loathing build and build until I hit a breaking point, so I explode, and blurt something out I *never* thought I'd say.

"Because...*because I'm not gay.*"

*I'm.*

*Not.*

*Gay.*

Wow. For a second it feels like a weight's been lifted off my shoulders.

But then it comes crashing back down like one of those Acme anvils dropping onto Wile E. Coyote. Pushing me underground where I belong. *The fuck did I just do?*

Robbie's eyes go wide. "Wait...what? What do you mean, you're not...gay?"

Can't look at him. My hands claw at my wet hair, messing it into knots. This isn't real. This *can't* be real.

But it is. And it's all my fault. "I lied. I lied about *everything*."

"What? What are you talking about?" Robbie backs away like I'm radioactive.

*Just get it out, Asher. Let it the fuck out.* I decide to give myself my own exorcism and release the demon that's been living inside me so I can crawl out of all this alive. Reveal it all.

"Okay, um, shit..." I try to take a deep breath but I mess up and swallow a huge gulp of air. Can't breathe so I rush the words out. "Uh, after Luke did, you know, that thing...and Dean Pearson called my dad in to talk? I was just so pissed off at Luke and embarrassed about everything. I fucking *hated* him. Couldn't *take* it anymore. So I just...I just blurted it out. I didn't...think. I said I was gay so someone would take it seriously. Take *me* seriously."

My breathing's only getting worse. Another gulp of air. Drowning in my own bullshit.

"And then it just...spiraled. Had to keep up this stupid lie. Had to pretend, keep pretending, you know? And then things got...better in this weird way? Like a forcefield, kind of. But now...now I've messed it all up. I ruined our friendship. I ruined...us."

Robbie's quiet, then his face twists. "Us...*us*...I don't see any *us* anymore...I don't even know who you are, who this...bizarro-world Asher even is."

"What...what do you mean?" I stutter, freaked like I'm a kid getting yelled at.

"This person you've become. Hanging out with Silas? BFFs with Sam Coolman? Talking about protein shakes and clubbing? And whatever shit you do with Ethan?" Robbie stops, then comes back with the damning truth. "And it's all been a *lie*?"

Reality smashes into me like a brick to the face. Rage pressuring up, same way it did with Luke.

"So what, Robbie? *So what*?" I stand up straight, towering over him. Water drips from my body, puddles splashing at my feet.

"Is Asher even in there anymore?"

*Fuck this guy*. I need to respond. I need to *defend* myself. I think about Luke. The bench hitting my face. The black eye. Everything.

"Maybe I don't wanna be who I was before." My voice is low and intense. "A weak fucking...victim, or whatever. Is that so wrong? Getting the fuck outta here? Getting away from..."

Robbie's staring right into my eyes. "Me?"

I need to run from the truth, fast. "Fuck, Robbie. No..."

He turns away and I reach out to grab him. "Robbie, c'mon! Stop...that's not what I meant. Please, just stop. Just chill. Please!"

Robbie stops and pulls his arm away. "Whatever, Asher. Go have fun. Go follow Ethan around like his little pet."

My brain's throbbing like crazy. A headache blasts in. Panic. Rage. Even though my blood's boiling, I change my voice to a whisper. Can't make a scene out here where the neighbors might hear.

"You know, you can think I'm being fake all you want. Fuck it, I *am* fake. But at least I'm not, just...waiting around for something to happen to me."

"At least I'm okay with being myself. At least I know who I am."

"You're hiding, just like me."

We lock eyes. His turn glassy, and his jaw's clenched on one side. He *isn't* rubbing his eyebrow. He's serious.

I pause, wondering if I should say what I really want to. It's bubbling up. *Say it.*

"You're fucking *nothing*, dude."

With that, Robbie bites his lip and his eyes turn pink. He just looks at me. Blank. Like I'm a fucking monster.

Silence. Like being smothered with a pillow. He rushes to put on his tank and slides his wet feet into flip-flops. He flees, running into the house. Water flies off him as he sprints to the front door.

I run after, splashing more water on the hardwood floors. Nearly slipping and cracking my head open which right now doesn't sound so bad.

We make it outside to my driveway. I don't know what to say, so I shout what feels like the most important thing in the world.

"Just...just don't tell anyone."

Robbie stops hard and turns. Must think I'm a real piece of shit. He shared *his* secret, and I made it about *me*.

Robbie walks to his car and swings the door open.

"Have your fucking secret, Asher. I'm done."

## Tetris

FOR months, my mind's been stuck on Robbie and Luke like rubber cement. Late-night raging at Pantheon?

Not. Working.

I managed to stall the sham date with Raj week after week. Now I'm finally here, no thanks to Ethan. Threats to turn me over to the gay police if I didn't go. Just arrest me already.

It's Saturday, and we're at a big hot hibachi table. A Japanese chef's flipping shrimp for me, Raj, and some normal-looking family. The place reeks of lighter fluid, sweat, and soy sauce.

They didn't card me, so I got this bright red super-sweet Scorpion thing to chill me out. Raj got a Coke. Makes me feel like I've got a drinking problem. I'm fine. Probably.

Raj's eyes are locked onto the wide metal griddle. I think he's waiting for me to lead the conversation.

"So, uh, tell me about yourself." I talk through my twisty straw, hoping it'll transform my voice into someone who cares.

"I...what do you want to know?" Raj acts stiff in his corporate button-down. Dressing up for me couldn't matter less on this farce of a date. Poor guy.

"Maybe, um, what you do for fun? Who do you hang out with? Any, uh, hobbies?" I realize I'm just piecing together a boring collage of soundbites from MTV dating shows.

"Oh, well, I have three brothers, but I'm not really into sports like them. I'm more of, uh, an indoor kid."

"Sports are lame."

Raj squints like he's doing telepathy. "You play any board games?"

"Used to play *Magic*, but not anymore." Suddenly I feel super guilty about ditching Robbie. How many innocent gay guys can I fuck over? Just gotta survive tonight. Let him down easy, then I'm free.

"Oh, I'm more into D&D..." He's staring at me with this bright face, like I'm a celebrity.

"Nice." I shove a too-hot shrimp in my mouth.

*Clink clink clink.* Loud fried rice saves me. The chef, like me, doesn't want to be here putting on a show. He pumps his spatula, beating a fried rice heart. The guy at our table leans to his wife for a lovey-dovey kiss, and they both smile.

Barf. And I bet *no one* has a clue that me and Raj are on a date.

We sit, stuck, drowning in loud background noise.

Raj stabs chopsticks into his little bowl of chicken fried rice. "Sorry if I'm being...awkward. I've never been on one of these before."

"A date?"

Raj closes his eyes. "Yeah...a date. Well, a good one at least."

"Me either." I'm telling the total truth. "But now I'm curious to hear about the bad one."

"Ugh, oh god." Raj takes a deep breath and slides his plate an inch forward. "So I met up with this guy once, and it wasn't *exactly* a date. We talked online and decided to meet up for a movie. And when I got there he was kind of, um, weird I guess? He didn't look like his pictures *at all*. But we ended up...uh...kissing for a while, but I didn't really like it...Oh god, it was at *The Princess Diaries*." Raj groans and puts his head in his hands. "I don't know. I kinda regret it." He lifts his head and stares at one of the little kids at our table.

"Oh, shit. That fucking sucks." I push out my big tub of alcohol to share. Raj leans in and takes a long sip. "Sorry that happened. Seems like there's a lot of pervy weirdos out there."

"Well, you seem nice so far." Raj wipes his mouth clean of the sticky red drink with the back of his hand.

My eyes drown in the Scorpion bowl. "Am I nice? Not so sure anymore."

Raj narrows his eyes and shifts in his seat.

"Uh, never mind." I give a fake little closed-mouth smile. I need a break. "Excuse me. I'll, uh, be right back." I throw my napkin on the table, scoot back my chair, and lurch toward the bathroom. As I approach the end of the restaurant, I see something *shocking*.

Sam, giggling over teriyaki chicken. With...fucking Luke.

I swallow some air and hold it in, choking me. One glance back.

Sam. Luke. Eyes locked. We're all just...staring at each other. Sam's eyes go wide, but Luke doesn't flinch. Maybe I'm nothing to him. Maybe I spend too much time worrying about people who don't give a shit.

I turn to the bathroom, but footsteps clunk toward me. Get my hand on the bathroom handle when Sam grabs me and flips me around.

"It's not what it looks like." Her eyes have this crazed, manic energy.

My heart's beating double speed. "I don't care, you can do... whatever you want."

"Asher, please don't tell Silas."

I'm more worried about what Luke's been telling Sam about *me*. I jiggle the bathroom handle. Locked, shit. "I'm not gonna tell him, and I, I don't care what you do...it's—"

"No, it's fucked up of me."

My mind jumps straight to the worst thing. Did Luke tell her I'm not gay? Will he?

Sam can *not* know the truth. If anyone would kill me when they find out, it's her. Like full-on *Texas Chainsaw Massacre.*

Sam's fingers tug at her split ends, and her eyes unfocus into thin air. Her top lip curls up, uncertain and scared. For once, she looks real. "I don't know, I just...missed him."

My nails dig into my fingertips, taking the pain away from reality. Why is Sam with Luke? Are they fucking? Is this all bullshit? Does she even care about me?

Sam peeks out into the restaurant, searching. "Wait, what are *you* doing here?"

Fuck. Fuck. Fuck.

"Oh, uh, I'm on this, like...date thing."

Sam grabs both my arms, eyes huge, squeezing hard. "Oh, my god! Is he hot?"

She's trying too hard to act like nothing's wrong, I think. "He's... fine."

Sam smudges her fingers over glossed lips. Then reaches her hand out and pushes back the hair over my ear. Eyes locked. Weirdly, it's the closest we've ever felt.

"Are...are we cool?" Her face looks super freaked out. Shaky and raw. There's so much she isn't saying. But for some reason, I think she knows she's being a fucked-up friend. Do I even have a right to feel betrayed? I've been lying to her all year. She can do whatever she wants.

And maybe, if I'm nice, it'll help deal with Luke.

I nod. "Yeah, we're cool."

She kisses my cheek. Hands on mine. It feels amazing. "Go get fucked, Diamond."

I wait for neon-red Scorpion pee that doesn't come. At the sink, I wash my hands over and over, staring in the mirror. All squiggles and shapes, not even a person.

I brace myself to see Sam and Luke again, but when I head back to Raj, they're gone. Thank fucking God.

As I come up, Raj looks worried. "Everything okay?"

"Oh, yeah...Just had to call my dad. You know how it is."

Raj forces a smile. He doesn't look too happy about this shit date.

After more awkward small talk and me dodging questions, with Robbie, Luke, and Sam haunting the back of my mind, the dinner finally ends.

Raj demands to pay, and it feels like robbery.

We head outside to the parking lot, and he walks me to my car. He stares at the pavement. "So, I had fun."

The fuck do I say? "Me too...it was nice."

We just stare at each other. Total standoff.

He gives in first. "If you ever want to play *Magic* sometime, that could be cool..."

Okay Asher. Can't lead him on anymore. Put him out of his misery. "Um, Raj...think I'm getting more of a friend vibe?"

His shoulders sink forward and he jerks his head away so I can't see whatever shitty emotion's on his face. "Oh, um, that's cool." Raj blurts it out fast. "Yeah, totally fine. Of course. I get it."

All I do is hurt people.

"It's not you. You're cool. It's just that, I...I'm not sure. Maybe

I'm just not ready to date."

"It's okay. I kind of expected this. I'm, you know, kind of surprised you went out with me in the first place. You're...you're very handsome, and you're friends with Ethan and Wade. I...it was a long shot."

Shit. "No, no...that's not..."

"Don't worry about it." Raj puts his hands in his pockets. "Well, um, it was nice meeting you. Maybe I'll see you around."

"Yeah, for sure." I really, really hope I don't run into him.

I go in for a hug, cause that's what gay guys do, but it's awkward. His disappointment's a magnetic field.

I'm a total, utter, *dick*.

On the drive home I blast "Motorcycle Drive By." Third Eye Blind.

The night feels extra quiet. As I wind over the fresh asphalt, I notice how black and dead all the fake ponds look. Who lives under there? Where do the turtles go when they disappear into the dark?

Sam's secret meetup with Luke digs into me like a big-ass splinter. My paranoia's got me so spaced out, I almost swerve straight into the water.

Then—*thwack*. A spray of heavy sprinkler water crashes onto my windshield.

Jolted back to reality. My thoughts slide down like the water on my windshield, getting all drippy and warping reality.

I finally get home, and all I wanna do is watch infomercials in bed with Michelangelo until my eyes bleed.

When I head inside, there's my dad and Piper watching *American Idol* in the den. They're cuddled up on the brown couch eating Sun Chips. Truly the worst kind of chip. Bet Piper thinks they're healthy or something.

"Asheroony, honey, come join us."

"Oh, uh, that's okay. I think I'm just gonna go to my room."

"Come on. Spend some time with your old man."

Piper butts in. "It would be so nice to see the elusive Asher."

Don't want to fight this battle, so I give in. "Okay. Fine. Gimme a sec."

I rip off my date clothes like they're crawling with spiders. I slip into my comfy blue Umbros and a soft white No Fear T-shirt with a bite-stretched collar. I grab my old Game Boy that I dug up the other day and snap *Tetris* into the slot. In the den, I tune out my dad and Piper by lining up blocks till each row disappears. Something I can control. Something I can win.

My dad asks if I think Clay Aiken is *you know,* and I just roll my eyes.

My landline rings—thank god—and I bolt to my room to answer. Caller ID says it's Ethan.

I pick up. All I hear is Ethan breathing heavy. Shit, this can't be good. I sit down on my bed to focus and flip my black Uniball pen around my fingers. "Ethan...hi. You, uh, you alright?"

More breathing, then Ethan finally speaks up. "Hi, um, yeah. Well, no actually. Can I...come over maybe?"

My throat tightens up. The last time a friend showed up like this, everything fell apart.

I cough to force open my throat.

"Of course. I'll see you soon."

# Halo

"THEY can't see me like this"

"Who?"

"Your dad, Piper. I look bloated."

"Oh, it doesn't—"

"Asher, I *can't*."

Shit. Has he figured me out? I bite my nails for the first time in my life.

Ethan's in my driveway leaning against his yellow RAV4. Even in the dark, I can see his eyes are all red and puffy under the thick black-framed glasses he only wears when no one's around.

"Of course, let me just—" I crack the front door, yell some shit about going for a walk. I step outside and the door clicks shut.

Ethan's already halfway down the driveway. We head down the dark street. Silent. I shuffle next to him in my Adidas Slides—ironically, the least athletic shoes in existence.

Ethan's mind is far away.

I do something weird. Put my arm around his shoulder.

His breathing slows down.

My fingers find the back of his neck, playing with the soft hair above it. Whoa.

Even though I'm kinda confused about us, it's nice to feel connected. To Ethan. To someone. Helping, for once, instead of just taking, mooching, leading on.

His body loosens up. *Such* a relief. Thank god this isn't about *me*.

We walk through a narrow path between two houses, leading us to a huge open space with perfectly trimmed grass. A golf course.

The moon lights up the rolling green and sand pits like some *Lord of the Rings* fantasy world. We disappear into the dark and lie back in the middle of the grass. Ethan puts his hands behind his head, staring at the stars.

Feels like I'm Freud with a patient, which feels weird, so I lean back too. Copying him, even when he's at his lowest. "So...you okay?"

"I'm so pathetic."

Wait, how could he *ever* think that? "Ethan, trust me, you're *not* pathetic. Just...talk to me, okay?"

"It's about John." Ethan tries to laugh but it gets all mixed up with tears as he wipes his face. "God, I can't believe I'm crying over this asshole. I'm such a cliché."

*Of course. John.* Mysterious, obviously bad news. Ethan's kept him hidden for a reason.

"We've all cried over some dumb guy." Probably stole that from a rom-com.

Ethan snorts. "No, you haven't." He lets out a big sigh. "So, we were at his place, cuddling on the couch, you know...normal. Then we started making out, and all that. That's good, right? I like that stuff...kissing, blowjobs, whatever. But then..." Ethan stops, staring up at the stars like he's trying to draw a new constellation. "I could tell he wanted more." He swallows hard. "Uh...is it weird? Me telling you this?"

"No, no, not at all." I say it quick, even though it *is* weird.

Ethan exhales. "Okay, well...you might be surprised, but I haven't, you know...actually done it yet...*all the way.*"

Hold up. Ethan? A virgin? He's always talking about hot guys and dates—I just assumed. How were John and him not fucking?

"Seriously?" My voice comes out louder than I meant.

Ethan nods. "Yeah, seriously. Anyway, John wanted more, and I didn't. I told him no, but he just kept pushing. I pulled away—then he *shoved* me. Hard. I hit the floor, and it fucking hurt. Then..." Ethan lets out a bitter laugh. "He just grabbed his Xbox controller and started playing *Halo*. Like I wasn't even there."

"What the fuck?" I suddenly want to punch John in the face. "That's *actually* insane."

Ethan shrugs. "I mean, yeah. But it just...messed me up, you know? I feel stupid. Like...what's wrong with me that I didn't want to have sex?"

"There's *nothing* wrong with you, Ethan. If you don't want to fuck John, then, you know, fuck him."

Ethan groans. "Then we got into a big fight. He told me I'm immature, and all his friends think he's crazy for dating a high school kid. How I'm a tease, how I'm fake. He made me feel like such *shit*. Then I called him an asshole, got dressed, and ran outta there. I felt like I was having a panic attack or something, so I called you. No clue where to go. I couldn't go home and have my mom see me...like this."

"You did the right thing. I'm glad you called."

"But maybe John *was* right." Ethan keeps picking a bald patch on the green. "Maybe I *am* fake. Maybe I deserved it."

"What? Ethan..."

"Am I a fraud? Is it all just, like, an act? Am I just pretending to be this big fun character when really I'm just some...scared little kid?"

It's like Ethan pulled those exact words outta my brain and made them his own. I pull at the loose strings on my rainbow bracelet. "You know, I feel that way sometimes, too. I think it's probably... normal." But I leave out the most important part. That our entire relationship is based on a lie.

We stare at the stars, quiet. I'm faker than ever. And somehow closer to my new best friend than ever.

"There's another thing...some stuff, from, uh, school, I kind of left out...It's embarrassing. I've never told *anyone* the whole story..."

Ethan's always been sketchy about what happened at school. *Kids can be cruel*, his mom told me. I never wanted to pry. But now, finally, I'll hear the truth.

"Oh, man. Okay." Ethan lets out a big deep breath, crosses his legs, and sits up. "So, after I came out freshman year things were, like, fine. Nothing terrible, no big surprise. Everyone just kind of, you know, tolerated it, I guess. People stopping calling me a fag, too, for whatever reason."

Ethan rips tiny green blades like they've done something to him.

"It all started with this stupid AIM message. From this guy on my soccer team—Ronaldo Abreu." The name comes out like a killer in a campfire story. "He was popular and *soul-crushingly* handsome. He *never* talked to me before."

Ethan scatters his little pile of torn-up grass. His voice shakes.

"So, in that message, he actually *came out* to me. I was like, what the fuck? He told me this whole thing about how he couldn't tell anyone, how his parents and everyone at school would freak out. And then...he told me he had a...crush...on *me*. I pretty much died. We kept chatting, like, flirty and stuff."

Holy shit. I can't believe Ethan's never told me this before.

For a second he smiles, but it goes away as fast as it came. "He avoided me at school because he said he didn't want anyone to find out, which...is pretty dumb now that I think about it. I was so desperate, you know? This hot guy giving me attention, and just feeling less...alone. Then—oh god—he wanted dirty pictures or whatever, and because I'm a desperate moron, I emailed some...not, like, totally naked or anything, just...that's what he wanted, right?"

Oh fuck. My heart pounds like I'm watching Michael Myers creep up on Laurie Strode. Gore and death, right around the corner. I start to get that guilty gut-punch feeling.

"Then he just...vanished. No more messages, nothing. Cut me off like I didn't exist. A few days later at practice, I walked into the locker room and saw my pictures everywhere. Printed out. Taped to every fucking locker." Ethan presses his wrists to his eyes. "Everyone was watching. Laughing. I wanted to disappear."

I want to throw up.

"Turns out the whole thing was a prank. A joke. Ronaldo, the whole team—messaging me together. Fucking sick."

Ethan goes quiet.

*Why Ethan? Why me?*

"That was the end of my soccer career." He lets out a weak laugh, trying to lighten the horror. "At least the photos didn't get around school. I don't even know what would've happened."

"That's the worst thing I've ever heard, Ethan."

But no—it's not. The worst thing I've heard is what *I* did.

Locker rooms. Jocks. Humiliation. A twisted mirror of my life, both of us left feeling like absolute shit. The worst part? I'm no better than those guys. My lie is just another betrayal. Manipulation. Cruelty.

"So, what did you do? Did you tell your mom, or the school or whatever? Did the guys get in trouble?"

"No way. Telling anyone would've made it worse. I'd have been a tattletale *and* a fag. So I said screw them all and became the hottest, funniest, most fabulous version of myself. I realized—if I wanted to find happiness, I'd have to get it...make it...for myself. So I did."

Me and Ethan are more alike than I ever imagined. Both of us just making shit up to escape feeling like garbage.

"So when John was pressuring me to have sex, it really messed me up, like the whole situation with the team. Getting taken advantage of. Feeling so powerless and scared. I told myself I'd never let that happen again...that *I'd* be in control. But then here I was with John, and...maybe I'm not so strong after all."

"Ethan, you're the strongest person I know."

"Thanks, Asher. You've been such a good friend this year. I don't know how I'd have survived without you."

I'm ready to dig my grave right here. Bury myself under pounds of dirt and grass and sand. It's what I deserve.

I always thought Ethan's so confident, that his life is perfect. But it turns out I'm too self-involved to realize he's struggling too. I just took and took. The worst part? He doesn't have a clue how bad a friend I'm *actually* being. How bad a person I've become.

I think about sprinting away, never coming back. Why should I keep putting Ethan through my bullshit? Maybe Ethan—and everyone—would be better off without me.

But no, I can't bail. *Gotta keep going, play the part, wait it out.* Just a few months until I can run away for real.

"You know, Ethan, I think it's okay for things to be fucked up sometimes...maybe they'll always be." I brush my hands together quick to let the sand and grass bits fly off, then slap my hands against my Umbros. "Maybe it's good, even."

I reach a hand out to pull Ethan onto his feet. I give him a hug, and he squeezes me back extra hard.

His voice is quiet, with his cheek against my shoulder, close to my ear. "I can't decide if you're wise beyond your years or totally full of shit."

I give a tiny laugh and his head bounces on my shoulder.

We stay like that for a while. The longest hug of my life, longer than any with my mom. While we're hugging, I feel all my fear and anxiety and shame just melt away. Hadn't realized how good it could feel to be held tight by someone. Comforting and relieving.

Ethan pulls away and grabs my hand, then starts playing with my bracelet. We walk back to my house, and Ethan holds my hand the whole way.

I'm too afraid to let go, worried it'll come off like rejection, but I also don't *want* to let go, and I have no idea why.

Suddenly I feel this...charge shoot up my body, my stomach goes tight and weightless like on a roller coaster.

Ethan pulls away and puts on a shy smile. "Thanks for being here for me. I needed this."

We do one last goodbye hug, and I feel Ethan exhale all the sadness out of his lungs. His body's this limp, empty balloon, his head resting on my shoulder.

After the hug, he gives me a kiss on the cheek. Nothing new, but tonight it feels different. More honest and true.

Ethan gets in his car and drives away.

I stand there shocked, watching his tail lights disappear. I sneak back inside. My dad and Piper are still in the den watching TV. *Lethal Weapon* on HBO, I think. Piper's asleep, resting her head on my dad's shoulder.

I just hang back, silent, watching them. They look so close. So comfortable. So safe together. For the first time ever, I think I want that too. Like, really want it.

My cheek tingles. My hand feels empty. What the hell's happening to me?

Then it hits me—*Tetris*. The right block, finally falling into place. The line clears. Everything resets.

Boom. New level unlocked.

*Oxygen*

FOR the first time in months, I feel almost normal. Pointless TV, sugar highs, jerking off. Spring fucking break.

It's 11:42 a.m. on a Tuesday in April, a couple months after that night with Ethan.

I'm in bed. Lucky Charms float in chocolate milk, an ice cube bobbing around—my mom's trick to keep it cold. *The Price Is Right* ding-dings in the background. I'm dunking marshmallow rainbows under the brown milk with my spoon. How long can they hold their breath down there?

Something cold touches my wrist. Bracelet's soaked. Milk creeping toward my skin like a lit fuse. I suck the strings and taste gnarly chemicals, snapping out of my spring break bliss. Ethan, the bracelet, us. Linked.

Bet *his* bracelet's clean and perfect. I've been skipping the gym and all of Ethan's lifestyle rules. Everything just feels kinda pointless now.

Countdown ticking. College decisions drop any day now. Ethan got into NYU back in December, keeps telling me to dream bigger. My dad and Piper piled on the pressure, so I caved and applied.

The college counselor and Dean Pearson wrote a rec about me as some brave, out-and-proud gay teen. Complete bullshit. But none of it matters. Can't go to NYU. After graduation, I need to disappear. Dig myself to China.

Well, only if I make it to graduation alive. Hope to god Robbie and Luke have kept their traps shut. When's it all gonna end? How? Everything's unraveling, messy as hell, like a ball of string.

On TV, some fat woman with a thick Minnesota accent wins big on the Showcase Showdown. African safari, furniture, lifetime supply of vitamins. She's losing her shit, jumping and screaming. Her excitement? Can't relate.

This dumb fucking bracelet killing my vibe.

The woman reminds me of guys at Pantheon who climb on the platforms, rip off their shirts, and grind against nothing. Attracting a crowd. I'm jealous of people like that, who aren't scared of being seen.

I was almost there.

So here I am. Bingeing TV under the covers, watching other people win big while I rot.

My sugar high crashes. OD'd on *Maury* paternity tests. Time for my dreaded daily ritual. Checking the mailbox for that purple NYU logo.

My fingers stick to the latch. A rejection letter would be clean. No NYU, no Ethan. No mess. Eyes closed, I reach in like some *Fear Factor* guy sacrificing his arm to a tub of worms. I hit a thick packet. Fuck.

The purple logo stares like gator eyes in a swamp. Meaty. Dense. Anyone else at Palm Reef would be flipping their shit, but not me. I take it inside and shove it under a pile of socks in my dresser. Can't have my dad and Piper obsessing over it, screwing up my plan. Out of sight, out of mind.

I sit on my bed, staring at the dresser. The envelope's a stone in my gut, sinking deeper, heavier by the second. My fingers find the wet bracelet. I pull, tighter and tighter, cutting off circulation until my hand's red and numb.

Ethan. The bracelet. Getting tighter.

Cutting off my oxygen.

Suffocating. Drowning. Chocolate milk in my lungs.

And maybe...this time for good.

## No Offense

GEOMETRY class. Mr. I's droning on about cosines and Pythagorean crap while I zone out to *Space Invaders* on my TI-83. Overachieving sophomores all around me, calculating their futures. Me? I'm stuck on Robbie, Ethan, Sam, and how the hell I'll make it out alive.

The bell.

Lunch sucks now. Just floating between tables, making shallow chit-chat with people who don't know me, or care. Not really.

I brace myself to see Sam. She's been stressing me the fuck out. We haven't talked about when I saw her with Luke at the restaurant. So now it's just, like, awkward. I guess we're friends. I've grown to like her as an actual person, not just some empty-headed sex icon. But I'm still her little gay virgin sidekick, and I haven't figured her out yet. I definitely haven't figured out what I saw. So I bury all my sexy Sam fantasies deep, deep down—so deep I forget they exist. If I think about them, if I let myself go there, I'll jump across the table and kiss her like a goddamn idiot. And that cannot happen.

I walk out of the lunch line with hard tacos and look over the crowd. I see Sam sitting with Jackie and Allie, and she waves me over.

Okay Asher, *don't stare at her tits. And don't think about Luke groping them.*

As I go up slow, I hear Sam shutting Allie down. "Allie, no offense, but you have *no* idea what you're talking about." Sam pushes her hair behind her ear. "Saddam Hussein didn't even have anything to do with 9/11."

"Why are we even talking about this?" Sam's in charge, duh, but Jackie's trying to keep the peace.

"I don't know, Jackie." Sam's so annoyed. "Maybe some of us care about what's going on in, you know...the world."

When I reach the table, Sam taps the bench for me to sit next to her. "What do you think, Asher?"

"Um..." What the fuck are these girls talking about? Whatever. "Didn't they say those weapons of mass destruction or whatever didn't even exist? But I don't really follow the—"

"Thank you!" Sam yells like a dick at Allie. "Asher knows what he's talking about. He's a genius."

"Uh, thanks."

Sam flips into her fake-ditzy voice. "So what's new with you? Tell us *everything*."

I stare into Sam's eyes, away from her cleavage, and try to keep my face normal. Can't let them know what's really going on in my head, so I talk about the first thing that comes to mind. "It's my birthday this weekend. Finally turning eighteen."

"Happy birthday!" Allie tells me before Sam interrupts.

"It's not his birthday yet. God." Sam looks at me like only I can understand. "You see what I have to deal with?"

Jackie fake-smiles at me. "What are you doing for your birthday? Having a party?"

"Well, uh, actually...yeah, I am...kinda. Ethan's organizing it. It's dumb. We're getting this party bus thing to drive us around, get dinner, and go to that place, uh, Pantheon."

"Oh my god!" Sam sounds *way* too excited. "I've been *dying* to go with you guys. It sounds like so much fun. I wanna hang out with Ethan again. Such a sweetie."

I black out.

Sam holds her Diet Coke straw to her lips, sipping slow. "Please?" She gives me this pout. Flirty *fuck-me* eyes.

Having Sam at my birthday would be a total head trip. An SAT-level test of my bullshitting skills. My brain's screaming *no*, but my chest is tight and my skin's tingling. Her face and hair and lips short-circuit everything. My mouth hijacks my brain before I can stop it.

"Um, sure. Why not."

"Fuck yes!" Sam raises an eyebrow at her friends. "And you guys aren't invited. Right, Asher?"

Allie and Jackie look at me, faces falling, disappointed that their supposed friend is treating them so bad.

"Oh yeah, sorry. There's, um, not enough room in the party bus." Great. Now *I* feel like a dick.

But as my fantasy of Sam in a skin-tight dress sears into my retinas, my mental math shifts.

I erase the geometry proof in my brain—the one keeping her at a safe distance. Can't deal with all these angles anymore. Screw logic. The proof's going in the garbage, along with any sense I have left.

What's the harm in letting Sam come along for my birthday? How messed up could one night get?

Math's bullshit anyway.

## Playboy

IT'S my eighteenth birthday, and there's a thirty-something dude's dick basically in my mouth. Well, almost. There's a tiny Cuban flag thong in the way. While Lil' Kim's "How Many Licks" blasts, Ricardo the exotic dancer flips me around and I try to escape my body, hoping to float out the sunroof.

*Be chill.* If I say it enough in my head, maybe it'll come true.

Ethan and Wade are here, along with some of our Pantheon friends. Our creepy party bus driver keeps swerving to stare at me and my slutty lap dance.

And then there's Sam. Jesus Christ, I can't believe Sam Coolman's seeing all this.

She's cackling like crazy, butting in for a turn on the stripper pole. She instantly becomes best friends with Wade, because of course. They look like they could be boyfriend and girlfriend. Ethan's friendly to Sam, but he doesn't trust her. I think he's protective of me, which I really don't deserve.

Ricardo moves to Ethan, who expertly handles the attention. Smiling, laughing, slapping the guy's ass. I guess the stripper's straight, cause he puts his smiling face into Sam's cleavage and motorboats the fuck out of her, which makes everyone go apeshit.

Usher's "Nice & Slow" comes on, and Ricardo's gyrating slows down. I back into a hiding spot in the corner of the bus. Washed out by the tacky neon lights, I'm lost in the mirrored counters and fake black leather seats.

*You can do it, Asher. You can be normal.*

Dread comes and goes as the night marches on. We drive down I-95, across the palm-lined causeway onto South Beach for dinner. Nobu. Everything's fancy and shiny with Japanese writing all over. Wade swears he sees P. Diddy walk by, but no one buys it.

I shove pretentious tuna in my mouth for dopamine hits, chewing instead of talking. Sam's laughing way too hard next to Wade, and Ethan gives me these worried looks I dart away from. We're all drinking lots of fizzy champagne, which helps chill me out.

After dinner we head to Pantheon. The party bus glides up to the entrance, and the driver winks at me as I walk off. Bruno waves us all in and gives me a birthday kiss on the cheek. I'm pulled inside by a surreal, skittish beat. "Gotta Get Thru This."

"No shit." Sam's eyes get wide, taking it all in. The music, the lights, the huge crowd letting loose. The heat, the warmth, the vibe.

"Stay with me." Wade grabs Sam's well-lotioned hand and they run off to flirt with the bartender.

Ethan puts his hand on my back. I must look frozen. "You okay?"

"Oh, yeah. I'm okay."

"You don't really seem like it." He squints one eye and looks at me like Piper does. "Birthday blues?"

"No, I'm good!" I force a huge smile that'll hopefully work backwards. "Never been better." I pat Ethan's chest while I scan my surroundings. "I need a fucking drink."

We head to the bar, but Wade and Sam intercept us.

Wade yells over the music. "Party favors!" He takes out a little plastic baggie, like the one Sam had at the lacrosse party, and nabs four pills. Pink and shaped like the Playboy Bunny.

"Uh…" The fuck is this, now?

"Don't be a party pooper, Asher. It's your birthday. Loosen up, bitch." Wade shakes me around by the shoulders. "Open wide."

As I scream, "I'm loose! I'm loose!" Wade pries open my mouth and shoves a pill onto my tongue. Tastes bitter, like chemicals. I need what's inside.

"Wade! Be nice to the birthday boy. Asher, you don't have to do this if you don't want to."

"Shut up, Mom. It's my birthday." Don't protect me, not now. I swallow the pill dry and keep my eyes away from Ethan's. "I don't wanna see straight."

After everyone pops their pills, Wade pulls Sam and Ethan onto the dance floor. I follow, not sure if Wade left me out on purpose.

So we dance, waiting for the ecstasy to kick in. Slowly, the lights get brighter, the music hits harder. Reality isn't feeling so bad. Then I realize…it's working.

The music digs inside me, rewiring my DNA. In my brain, in my veins, in my fucking eyelashes. I'm floating. Everything's good. *I'm* good. Fuck, I'm *great*.

The colorful lasers and flashing lights have me zooming through space. Fucking heaven. I could dance *literally* forever.

Nothing bad has *ever* happened to me. Never an anxious day in my life. Just music. Electricity. Movement.

I look over at the others having a blast. Wade and Sam are grinding extra hard, which makes her look *crazy* hot. Ethan pulls me closer, and his hand is soft and sparks in mine. Everything's comfortable with Ethan. But now it's just, like, more.

"Drink this!" Ethan shouts over the noise, handing me a bottle of water.

I chug it, because he said so.

Suddenly Wade grabs me by the waist and pulls me in. He puts his butt against my crotch and Sam goes in front of him. They're grinding hard while he pushes back into me. He leans in and starts kissing Sam. They're making out. Whoa.

Wade pulls out from between me and Sam, and pushes us together. My heart rumbles inside like an earthquake.

Sam leans in, high out of her mind. Shouting in my ear. "Don't worry about Luke. It's over."

I pull back and just stare, never so confused by anyone.

"You're safe." She pushes her body against mine. *What does she know?*

Wade leans in and yells into my ear. "Kiss her, you idiot!"

Sam gives me this horny look, like she wants to make out—*with me.*

*Fuck it.* I lean in. My first kiss with a girl. Holy shit.

Her lips feel super soft like pillows, and she slowly opens her mouth. She pushes her tongue against mine, and it's like nothing I've ever felt. Fucking fireworks. There's a buzzing rush through my whole body, and I *pray* I don't get hard. Our mouths close a bit then open again, and we're pushing our tongues deeper together.

I feel fused to her, molecular-level shit. I put my right hand behind Sam's head and hold it up to my face so she doesn't back away. Her hair feels smooth. I press my dick up against her and now I'm pretty sure I'm hard. Our slick, wet tongues pulse slow. Forward, back. In, out. Her lips taste like watermelon and her breath smells like Red Bull. Fucking delicious.

I'm holding Sam's waist, and my fingers crawl down to her butt. I squeeze it, nice and full. Firm but just soft enough. My hand goes down her leg a bit and her skin feels amazing. My fingers feel like they're burning right off. I pull Sam even closer and play with the bottom of her short dress.

She swats my hand away and stumbles back. Starts cackling like a witch or something. Like she did something as crazy as me.

I stand there dizzy, trying to keep my balance so I don't get trampled. I look over at Wade and his face is frozen and wide-eyed. His dropped jaw slowly turns to a devilish smirk.

"Holy shit, Asher." Wade gives me a big kiss on the cheek. "You *horndog*."

I just made out with Sam *motherfucking* Coolman.

But all of a sudden—I'm freaked. Did I look *too* into it? Did I fuck up? Did Straight Asher and the alcohol and the ecstasy take over my body like a demon, unable to resist hot fucking Sam?

Was this whole night a huge mistake?

Gotta pee. Good time to catch my breath and solve what the fuck is going on.

I stumble into a bathroom stall and the bright fluorescent lights sting my eyes. After unzipping I realize I'm still half-hard, but manage to pee. I stuff my dick back into my pants and open the door.

Wade's here, waiting for me.

He pushes me back into the stall, walks in, and locks the door behind him. Twists me around and backs me up against the door, giving me that crazy look he gets right before a Pantheon make-out. He's on his toes, mouth to my neck. Kissing, working up to my face. The drugs makes it intense and *almost* good, but I turn to the side so he can't kiss my mouth. He grabs my head and jerks it toward him, but I push away again.

"Asher, chill out." Wade's mouth goes back to my neck, and his fingers touch my stomach under my shirt. He starts pulling at my belt, undoing it.

I'm frozen, overwhelmed. His skin on mine feels crazy, sensitive, but I'm trapped. Can't breathe.

I hear my zipper shoot down. Wade's hand brushes over my boxers, probably figuring out that Sam turned me on.

I push him hard into the stall door.

"Come on. Don't you want this?"

"Uh, what? No...fucking hell, Wade. Get off me."

"I know you've wanted me since we met. I see how you look at me."

I push him off harder. "Well I fucking don't." I run my hand through my hair and it feels amazing, even though I'm going insane.

Wade squints and suddenly he's super serious. Aggressive like Luke. "Or maybe there's someone else you want."

Fuck. "What? No..."

"Is there something you want to tell me? Something you don't want Ethan to know? Or...Sam?"

"Um...what? No...no."

"I think you have a secret."

Can't speak. Brain glitch.

"I *just* saw you out there with Sam! That guy wanted to fuck her."

The hell's he talking about? Wait.

Wait.

No. No. Oh god.

I'm such a dense motherfucker. Wade isn't trying to hook up with me—*he's trying to out me*. Detonate my entire fucking life.

"I think you've been a bad boy, Asher." Wade gets up close to my face again. Not for a kiss, but to slit my throat. "You've been lying to us."

I'm waiting to burst into flames. Feels like it did right before telling Robbie the truth. Overwhelming panic. Giving in is the only way out.

"Just...it's not...just shut up about it."

"So it's true!" Wade laughs with this evil smile. "I knew it. I fucking knew it." He stops and just looks at me. "Do you have any idea how psycho that is?"

"Of course, I didn't...want—"

"Honestly, I'm impressed you pulled it off so long." Wade smiles, proud. "You sneaky little shit."

Pressure behind my eyes. The room spinning. "Don't...don't tell Ethan."

Wade thinks for a sec, then comes back confident. "I'm not gonna tell him." He licks his bottom lip. "You are."

He crosses his arms and leans into the stall. "Don't you think Ethan deserves to hear it from you?"

"I can't...there's no way..."

Wade rubs his lips with his fingers. "How about this? I'll give you till gay prom to tell him. A month's plenty of time, right? Unless, you know, you're too much of a pussy." Wade puts his hand on my shoulder and squeezes. "I believe in you, bro."

My eyes roll back into my skull. Not in my body anymore.

Wade grabs my face and smacks a big kiss on my mouth. Fucking mind games. He heads out of the stall, and I stumble out, too. He washes his hands like nothing happened. The bathroom attendant gives him a paper towel, and he dries his hands as he stares at his reflection. He gives a sexy pout and runs his hands over his prickly fresh buzz. Walks out and I just stand there, catching my breath.

But suddenly my stomach tightens, then lets go. In and out. Shit.

I run back into the stall, fall to my knees, and push the toilet seat up. I vomit it all out—flying chunks of sushi, champagne, mistakes. And the truth.

Spicy Listerine swishes around my mouth. How often does this attendant have to deal with dumb barfing kids who can't handle their shit?

Can't run away, can't be suspicious. Fuck me.

I head back to the dance floor and find Ethan and Sam. Ethan grabs me, pulls me in, and puts one of his legs under my crotch. He yanks my chest up against his, and rests his head on my shoulder as we dance. My head's next to his, and all I see over his shoulder are Wade and Sam. Laughing and grinding and having the time of their lives.

What a sick fuck.

Or, no.

Is it me? Am I the real monster?

*Barney*

MY dad checks his clipboard. "How many *Maid in Manhattans*?"

"Too many." I flip through a spreadsheet, mumbling through a Twizzler dangling off my lips like a sad red cigarette.

My dad shoots me a look, seeing through my brat thing.

"Fine…fifteen."

He grabs the stack of Jennifer Lopez DVDs and heads into the maze of shelves.

A few weeks post-birthday-insanity, it's inventory night at Diamond Video—my dad's yearly bonding tradition. The only perk? Unlimited candy.

Ethan's blowing up my phone with a live feed of Pantheon's latest bullshit. The usual gay drama that's gotten really, *really* old. Going to that place, that club, where everything went down with Wade and Sam? No fucking way.

Except tomorrow I *have* to go. That fuckwad Wade's deadline. Gay prom. Me and Ethan—"dates." Whatever the hell that means. Just imagining Wade, lurking, smirking, setting up booby traps, has me clawing at my skin. And Robbie and Luke? Who the hell knows. Can't ask.

"So, how's school going?" My dad comes back with a new stack of DVDs. "I can't believe my only son is about to graduate high school."

"Yeah, uh, time flies."

"I haven't heard about my boy Robbie in a while."

"Oh, Robbie...yeah. He's good, he's just been, uh...busy with theater and stuff."

"Did he find out about college yet?"

I realize I've got no idea what's going on with Robbie, so I have to make some shit up. "Uh, he's not sure yet, I don't think."

My dad looks at me like I've got food stuck in my teeth. "You better hold onto him, Asher. I've been watching you boys play since you were little. I see more than you think. He's a good kid."

"Don't worry, Dad. I...I will."

Now he's looking more curious, raising an eyebrow. "And Ethan?"

"We're not dating." I shoot it down dead.

"I'm just asking!" He holds his hands up like I've got a gun.

My face scrunches, realizing how defensive I sound. My dad's just interested, and here I am, snapping at him like he's interrogating me.

The truth about Ethan? I've been wondering if he sees me as *more* than a friend. As a potential *boyfriend*. That night on the golf course, rolling at Pantheon—Ethan felt different. Like maybe I wasn't just his friend anymore.

But now *I'm* the one pulling away, and he's the one chasing me. He deserves more, but can I give it to him?

"What if it seems like...nothing makes sense?"

"Then you keep moving." My dad karate chops the air. "Forward."

The way he says it makes it sound so *easy*. "But what if I can't... move on?"

"You'll work it out, Asher. You always have."

I want to believe him, but it doesn't compute. When have I ever worked anything out? "I...I don't get it."

My dad puts down his clipboard and squats onto a plastic video crate. "Let me tell you something you probably don't remember. When you were a kid, you had this...strange ability. Somehow you could sense whenever Mom or I were feeling, you know, sad." My dad looks up and holds a finger to his chin.

"When you were in first grade, I think, you did the most amazing thing. Grandma was sick, and Mom was really struggling. She tried her best to hold it all together, for you. We both did." He holds a stare, then shakes it free.

"So one day, after getting some bad news from the doctors, Mom went to our room and locked the door. You and I were in the den watching *Barney* together." My dad glances at me and smirks. "You remember, that creepy dinosaur?"

I chuckle. "Duh."

My dad's smile fades and he stares at the ground or somewhere invisible. "Well, she cried for a while, then came out to make you dinner. She had to hold them back...the tears. She didn't want you to see her upset. When you saw her you got so excited and ran up to her. Gave her a big hug. Then you took her hand and walked her to the den next to me. Right where you were sitting before." He lifts his eyes and focuses on mine.

"Then you went back to the kitchen, got on your tiptoes, and made her a peanut butter and jelly sandwich. No one asked you to. No one even suggested it. But somehow, you just... knew. Right then. She needed someone to take care of her, and *you* did that. *You* made the sandwich." My dad's eyes get shiny, and he pivots with a joke.

"Well, honestly it was a bit of a mess, but...you *did* it. You brought it down and sat between us, and you just...watched the show. You let her eat the whole sandwich, even though you must have been hungry too. She always said it was the best thing she'd ever eaten."

I'm quiet, trying to swallow the growing lump in my throat. It doesn't sound like me. Who was that kid?

"You've always had this...knack for understanding people. You seem to know what they need, and you're there for them. You're a great friend, Asher. A really great friend."

"Right, well, I'm not sure about much these days."

My dad walks over and takes a knee, like I'm a kid again. "You know, I'm really proud of you. Look how far you've come, since, you know. I've wanted this for so long. For you to just be...happy."

I think he's out of words so he gives me a big hug, and I hug back. I squeeze extra hard,  thinking about my mom and the way her body felt wrapped around me.

My dad looks at me like I'm still that innocent, wide-eyed kid making sandwiches. Like I'm someone worth rooting for.

He's got no clue about the master criminal underneath. And I don't have the guts to tell him. Not yet.

If he knew half the shit I've done this year, he wouldn't be saying *any* of this. Somehow, I even tricked him into thinking I'm still that good kid.

I think about my mom and that alleged sandwich. The whole story must have been a misunderstanding. Maybe I wanted the sandwich all along but was too scared to ask. Maybe I was just pretending to be the kind of person who gives.

But that's not me. The Asher I know *takes*.

We don't finish inventory until really late. I push my thoughts aside and play the role my dad wants me to. The good friend. The good son. The good person. I smile and laugh, even though it hurts, to give him what he wants.

On the quiet drive home, I can't stop thinking about tomorrow.

Is Wade for real about telling Ethan? If he does, can I take that trip to Europe, run away, start a new life eating baguettes and shit?

Or what if I give in and just...tell the truth? Maybe I *can* fix everything. Maybe I *won't* be shunned by everyone I know.

Maybe my dad's right. Maybe I'm not all bad. Maybe I can even be good.

Good Asher? He'd tell Ethan the truth. Ethan deserves it.

Okay. *That's it.* I'll tell him tonight. Drive over to his place right now and bang on the door. Tell him I'm straight and pray.

Or maybe I'll shoot him an AIM message tomorrow, when I'm getting ready for gay prom. *Hi QT! One thing. I'm not gay...whoops! My bad.* Or how about when we pregame at his? Whisper to him in the limo! Scream it out on the Pantheon dance floor! Yell it through the speakers from the DJ booth! Fucking explode!

At least I won't have to keep this killer secret anymore. And if I'm super fucking lucky? I'll still have Ethan.

Or maybe I'll pussy out entirely.

If only fixing shit was as easy as making a PB&J. But everything's way messier. I close my eyes and picture Pantheon tomorrow night. Strobing lights, pulsing bodies, Ethan's trusting smile. And me, decked out in my fake gay bullshit.

One way or another, this joke of a costume comes off tomorrow.

Just hope I'm not standing there, naked, pissing myself.

## Red Light

SIX hours until everything goes to shit. Six hours until I lose Ethan. Maybe forever. Six hours until I have to face the truth myself—or have Wade blow it all up for me.

Meanwhile, I'm standing here in my skanky Calvin Klein boxer briefs like a wannabe Marky Mark, trying to figure out how to wear this leprechaun-ass green velvet suit to gay prom without looking like a total fraud. Staring at the suit like it's a Magic Eye, hoping some other version of me will pop out. I wonder if once-confident Asher's already evaporated.

Thank god Ethan let me get a clip-on bowtie so I don't have another riddle to solve.

Ethan wanted us to match cause he nominated us for "prom queens" or whatever. Which is some kind of ironic joke I guess? No clue how serious Ethan's taking it, or how seriously he's taking our "date."

My dad and Piper are volunteering at gay prom tonight. Fucking kill me. Thinking about them stepping foot into sticky, scuzzy Pantheon—it makes my head explode.

Gotta hurry up so I'm on time for Ethan's. We're going in a limo with Wade and some other Pantheon kids. People who—to be honest—I couldn't give less shits about.

Shower's up. Waiting for hot water, I stare at this guy in the mirror —smooth hair, clear skin. A total stranger who *way* overstayed his welcome.

Shower. Skincare. Hair—even though I know Ethan's gonna fix it later. Buttoning, tucking my shirt in. None of it pumping me up to tell Ethan the truth tonight. I've still got a few hours to get it together.

Another thing that's gonna make tonight totally nuts is that Wade invited Sam.

*Sam. Coolman*. At gay prom. With me, Ethan, these ugly suits.

No, can't have her here. Not tonight. Not after…everything.

Even crazier? She's bringing *Silas* as her date. The Palm Reef lacrosse captain does not belong at Pantheon. Sam better watch out for Silas and Wade before she walks in on some fucked-up, drunk bro-on-bro coercion blowjobs. Wouldn't be the first time Wade pulled that shit.

I wonder if Sam told him we kissed. I wonder if she told Luke.

I'm finally dressed and styled. Don't look like *full* shit. I give myself a little wink in the mirror—what a tool—and pull at my clip-on bowtie. The clasp is cheap, flimsy, so it snaps right off, exposing the horrible truth that it's—that I'm—a total fake.

I creep down the hall to make a clean exit, but my dad stops me by the door.

His eyes are all cold and serious like someone died. Can't be good.

"Asher, we need to talk."

"Um…yeah? Is it about…tonight or something? It's okay if you don't want to, uh, chaperone…anymore."

"No, that's not it." My dad's voice is low and heavy—not his usual chipper vibe. "Piper found something in your room, when she was putting away your laundry..." He pulls out that dumb thick envelope. The one I stashed under my socks, apparently not good enough. The one I should've lit on fire.

Why the *fuck* was Piper snooping around my drawers? Once again, trying to ruin my life.

My palms get damp. Mouth bone-dry. Walls closing in. Jumbo-jet explosion in my gut. Scrambled egg brain. *Skin. On. Fire.*

"Oh, um...yeah, that. I was gonna tell you, but..."

"You got in? I don't understand. Why did you tell us you got rejected? Why would you hide this?" He slips out the acceptance letter and looks it over, again I assume. His eyebrows scrunch together like it's bright out. His eyes scan quick back and forth before flipping it toward me all aggressive, like he's serving me papers or whatever from TV.

"Can...can we talk about this later?"

"What's going on with you?" His voice sounds like I really let him down. And, like, sad.

I swallow and almost choke. "No, it's not...I don't know, I just didn't want all this...pressure."

"I thought you wanted to go to NYU. Did something happen with Ethan?"

I *don't* want to go to NYU, but I *can't* tell my dad the real reason why. *Fuuuck.*

"I *did* want to, but...I'm not sure. Things are kinda messed up right now."

My dad looks at me like I shredded a winning lottery ticket. "Why not? It's a great oppor—"

"Can we not talk about it?" My voice is getting louder. Angrier. "Just...not now?"

I reach for the door, but my dad steps into me and holds his hands on my shoulders.

"Asher, I'm your dad. I know when something's wrong—you're my kid, I can feel it. You don't have to keep shutting me out. I'm... I'm here."

Piper's voice gets closer like a bulldozer a mile away. Soft and pretending to give a shit, annoyingly therapist. "Yes, you can talk to us. Let us help you. I'm sure we can—"

I jerk away from my dad, free. Losing my patience. Pissed. "I said I don't want to talk about it! Jesus, Piper, just leave me the fuck alone!"

My dad gets this new face—eyes all big and lips clamped tight. Rage. "You know, I let a lot of things slide, but you absolutely *cannot* talk to Piper that way. I won't let you do that in my house. Show some respect, kid."

*Kid.*

Just a kid. Fuck him.

"You don't understand! I don't know what I want next year. I don't know where I wanna be. I don't even know who I *am*. I...I just...things are really out of control right now."

"I don't like these secrets. It's not...you."

"Maybe I'm not who you think I am!"

My dad gets this deer-in-a-headlight look. "What are you talking about, Asher? What's going on with you?" Voice like mush.

Now's my chance. Tell them. *End this.*

"You don't...get it. I don't *need* your help. Just let me go to this stupid dance."

I turn around and see Piper's face.

Horrified. At me, being a little bitch and freaking the fuck out.

"I'm late. Ethan's gonna be mad at me."

"You're not going anywhere until we figure this out." My dad blocks the door.

Fuck. Trapped. "Move! I have to go!" I slam my hands against his chest, trying to shove him out of the way. He barely moves.

*He won't let me go. He won't let me go. He won't let me go.*

"You're scaring me!" Piper sounds so hysterical. "Asher, please! Just stop!" Her breathing's all over the place. "We love you, and we just want to help."

Feels like my head's big and purple and about to explode, like that *Willy Wonka* blueberry girl.

"Shut the fuck up!" I try to hoover a breath but it doesn't work. "I don't need your help!" But part of me wants to grab onto my dad's shoulders and scream for it. Instead, I push him away, because letting him see the real me—the shitstorm—feels even worse.

"Just go." Now my dad's *really* pissed. His voice isn't mad, just small—broken. It's the worst sound I've ever heard, but I can't bring myself to stop.

I bolt out the door, car keys jangling in my shaky hand. As I speed away, I can't look back.

Sweaty palms on the wheel—no music. Thick velvet squeezing my lungs, cheap bowtie choking me out. I rip it off and yank my collar.

I pull up to a red light, my fingers gripping the wheel way too hard. I peek up at my reflection in the rearview mirror—and flinch.

Who the fuck—?

The fuck is he?

It's a *New*-New Asher. Some shitty *RoboCop 3* copy of a copy of a copy.

Shock-eyed, sweat-stained, ghost pale and messy as hell.

The light turns green.

I slam the gas.

Let's go to this stupid fucking prom.

## Unforgettable

*BANG-bang-bang!*

My body jolts up to see Ethan with this cheesy, innocent smile. Pounding my window like gunfire. Been sitting here with my eyes closed, trying to chill out from my psycho tantrum. It's been hard to breathe.

For a split second, I'm actually glad to see him. Then I remember I'm about to squeeze our friendship into potato chip dust. This dude's got no clue what's coming.

Ethan tugs me out of the car by my collar, yanking me into his orbit. No escape. No gravity but him. "Where's your tie?"

"Uh, it's...in there, somewhere." I knock my head back.

Ethan pokes at my shirt to straighten it out. "Asher, you're soaking wet, and...Are you okay?"

No simple answer for that one. I grab his hand and drag him toward the rest of the kids. *Thud, thud, thud* loud in my chest.

My eyes dart around for Wade—there he is. Just standing there, looking like a totally normal non-sociopath.

Everyone's in a line along Ethan's apartment pool. Big orange hibiscus like a blue screen for the photo shoot. The guys are in crazy outfits—leopard print suits, leather pants, wigs and shit—doing ironic impressions of corny prom poses. I bust into the middle of the group with Ethan, trying to squeeze all the demons outta my mind with my biggest *say cheese* face.

*Don't think, Asher.*

And *especially* don't think about the imminent, inevitable, or maybe totally avoidable destruction of the most amazing, brain-melting, *Sixth-Sense*-level plot twist to come out of this insane senior year—me and Ethan.

Raquel's playing art director, fixing hair and makeup like we're on a TV set. Her face is intense. Senior prom's once in a lifetime—super important, they say. For me? The stakes are *extra* high.

Me and Ethan's matching velvet suits—green and magenta—really bum me out. We look like super-gay grooms about to tie the knot in Europe. I wanna crawl right out of my suit and slither away.

Wade's decked out in a shiny black T-shirt, blazer, gold chain, and Nike Dunk high tops. His lucky, sharp jawline makes him look like a GQ model, with a shitty attitude to match. He's posing with one hand under his chin, and it fucking terrifies me.

*Don't think.*

There's guys in Whitney Houston and Britney drag, a lesbian in a tux, and some really slutty high heels. Everyone's drinking Hawaiian Punch spiked with cheap vodka, but the parents probably know. Like it's just another night at Pantheon, but also entirely different.

Raquel pulls me and Ethan away for a private shoot. She makes us do that dumb prom pose, with Ethan in front of me and my arms around his waist.

I feel crazy. My cheeks burn from holding a fake smile. The Florida humidity, velvet suit, and impending doom bust out a lonely bead of sweat that creeps down my sideburn.

She finally lets us go, but stops me by grabbing my arm. "You look beautiful, *mijo*."

For some reason, I believe her. Raquel *only* tells the truth.

My collar's chafing my neck raw, so I sneak inside to breathe some AC. I grab Oreos from the pantry—if my mouth's full, I can't say anything stupid.

Suddenly Wade comes into the kitchen and snatches an Oreo right outta my hand. He lifts himself up to sit on the counter. "So tonight's the night, big man." Wade chomps into the crumbly cookie. His eyes are bright and sick, a rodent with rabies. "You ready for it?"

Feels like a big bucket of squirming cockroaches dumped over my head, like in *Fear Factor*. Freaky little pricks all over my body. Skin, spine, lungs. "Uh...what do you mean?"

"Oh, come on. You know exactly what I mean." Wade sounds annoyed at my incompetence at being his victim. "The night you finally come out—for real. Just like the rest of us." Wade takes a big, deep breath and does this showy exhale. "Bet it'll feel good."

This fucking guy. His words hit like another *bang-bang-bang*.

*Don't talk about Ethan, dude.*

Rage builds to pressure. It's everywhere.

Wade's mindfuck threat about telling Ethan, my dad and Piper closing in about NYU, and Ethan himself. Our friendship's like toxic gas making my head all loopy—fucking fun and really scary both at once.

Everything's getting blurry. "Just...don't do anything, Wade. I'm gonna figure it out, I'm gonna—"

"Good boy." Wade hits me with a big toxic smile. "I can't fucking wait. I'm sure Ethan's gonna be very proud."

Just then, Ethan walks into the kitchen. "Did I hear my name?"

I jump in, my teeth chattering. "Oh, uh...yeah. Wade was just saying that you, um, look good in that suit."

Ethan looks down at himself and flexes his hands out. "Aww."

Wade rolls his eyes and hops down from the counter, then gives Ethan a gross lick on the cheek. "Gorgeous, dear." Before he walks away, he gives me a nice big slap on the butt. "Save me a dance."

Ethan looks confused as hell. "What was *that* all about?"

"Nothing. Don't worry about it."

Ethan just kinda shakes his head quick. "Anyway, no one's telling Britney over there that her wig's crooked. Should I?"

I don't respond. Just force another cookie down my gullet.

"Hey, uh, are you sure you're alright? That's a lot of Oreos, Miss Piggy..."

"Yeah, I'm great." I hold back a scream and reach into the fridge to pour some milk into my mouth. Swishing it around like Listerine to get the black Oreo gunk out from my teeth.

"Sure..." Ethan definitely does not believe me. He comes an inch away and fixes my hair. "We're gonna have fun tonight. I'll stay close." Ethan puts his hand on my shoulder, but I pull my body away so it slides off.

"Let's get this show on the road." I try to switch gears and talk like a regular person. Doubt Ethan buys it.

We pack into the limo, parents waving like we're going to Afghanistan. Not far off.

Whitney pulls out champagne and everyone goes crazy—more booze, more fun. And alcohol's a truth serum or whatever? Maybe it'll loosen me up so I can *finally* be honest with Ethan.

"I'm a Slave 4 U" blasts over the limo speakers. Britney dances but falls whenever the limo jerks. Speaking of jerks, I watch Wade take a swig from a flask he's hiding in his jacket. Our eyes zap each other.

He gives me this evil smile and holds the flask up like he's saying *cheers*. Like we're buds, like everything's normal.

Everyone's chatting and shit, but I'm like a corpse at the end of the limo. Ethan puts his hand on my leg, squeezing. Showing off the corsage Piper forced me to give him. The feeling of his hand on my leg calms me down, and for the first time I picture myself saying those two words.

*I lied.*

The limo circles Fort Lauderdale aimlessly for an hour, like we're trying to outrun the inevitable. Finally, we're at Pantheon.

Everyone jumps out all psyched, bouncing into the club—except me.

I'm sitting in the limo alone, hoping the driver'll peel off with me still inside. A getaway car, the open door flapping and smashing in the wind.

Instead, Ethan reaches an arm in for me to take. He grabs my hand, and I let him pull me out of the limo. Into the...who knows.

I freeze at the door to Pantheon like it's that first time. It's done up like the Moulin Rouge—streamers and fabric hanging deep red, like my blood racing a hundred miles an hour.

Each slow-motion step feels like I'm dragging my legs closer to my execution, my heart pounding louder than the techno beats.

Like that selfish Marie Antoinette girl about to get her head chopped off in front of everyone. At least an extra-sharp guillotine's quick and painless.

This? A rusty saw, slow, jagged. This is gonna fucking *hurt*.

*Butterflies*

AS I walk in, red streamers slide up my face—*Carrie*'s pig blood in rewind—and Pantheon hits me like a semi. I wish this loud-ass monster would swallow me whole and shit me out already.

Pantheon's *packed*, music blasting so hard my teeth buzz. Everyone's dancing like crazy, and they've all got this look, like they finally belong.

Not me though—I'm frozen, waiting to get crushed. I don't belong here.

Music hammering, lights hypnotizing. Freedom all around me. Dancing like no one gives two fucks, growling like some gay death metal band.

I watch. Hairless skinny boys with rainbow bracelets and fuck-you body glitter, butch girls in Miami Heat jerseys, sweaty hipsters with skinny ties. One night without the bullshit.

Not me. I dragged the bullshit in with me.

I get it now. Like, survival, to make it here, tonight. Fucking brave shit.

And cause I'm a self-centered dick, I weaseled in and ransacked the place. Their, like, church or whatever. But *none* of it was mine to take. *They* earned it, not me. Right?

Then there's Ethan—he actually went through hell. Got tortured for sending some soccer jock shirtless pics or whatever. Just cause he wanted...something. Dick? Love? Both? But he survived. Manned the fuck up. And now my bullshit might mess it all up—for him, for us.

No big self-discovery moment for me. Just piggybacked. Hijacked. These guys are better off without me—they've got each other. Let the disco ball fall and shred me up already.

I zone, trying to breathe steady. Everyone's grinding to "Get Low" by Lil Jon—just like regular prom. But I'm so spaced out I totally miss Ethan walk up to me.

"Come on, wallflower." Ethan pulls me into the crowd and switches behind me, grabbing my waist and pushing his body against mine—nothing new. But tonight, my body's limp. Distracted. Am I leading him on? How fast is he gonna kill me when he finds out the truth?

Then I see my dad and Piper, and my stomach goes Big Bang. They're behind a table with punch and pamphlets and stuff. My dad leans in and whispers something to Piper, who's staring right at me. Can't believe they saw us dancing like little gay sluts.

Ethan spots them and waves, all excited. He grabs my hand and pulls me closer to Piper's nervous smile. But my dad can't even look at me. I snatch a Sprite, crack it open, and gulp to shut me up.

"Well, don't you two look handsome." This sick woman's fucking with me.

Ethan curtsies.

Mortified. After all this time as a fake gay guy, I still cringe at some of this girly stuff. Maybe that's normal for real gay guys, too.

My dad whispers something to Ethan, then pulls him into a big hug. Ethan's smile makes it look like he's posing for his funeral photo, like the perfect Ethan he wants people to see. My dad goes back to Piper, grabs her hand—still won't look at me. Hope Ethan doesn't notice.

"Go have fun, boys." Piper holds this freaky eye contact until I run away to the dance floor with Ethan.

I look up at the balcony to check for snipers. There's Raj, alone, fumbling with a flimsy cup. Something about his lonely eyes zaps me with guilt—until some older guy walks up and hands him a fresh drink. Better not be spiked or I'll kill him. Raj lights up. I hope he gets what he's looking for, whatever that is.

Suddenly I hear the familiar, distinct grunt of a stereotypical high-school jock. Shit.

Silas is on the dance floor, sloshing punch—probably 99 percent vodka. He's soaked in sweat and cocky, bro-y energy. His wrinkled button-down's half tucked, splattered in red stains. Looks like he's having the time of his douchebag life.

Then I see her—Sam, bent over in front of Silas. Perfect, like ballet. She's shoved into this tight black dress that shows off her nice legs. Extra-high cleavage, long blonde hair, ironed and fresh. They both look like Martians.

Things have been mega-awkward with Sam since we made out on my birthday. Been kinda avoiding her. Why does she think I kissed her? And what's going on with Luke?

Sam looks up as she's grinding on Silas and spots me.

*Run.*

"Asher, baby!" She hops over and throws her arms around my neck, hanging off like heavy bling. I guess, uh, nothing's wrong? Sam screams. "You look great!"

But her face says something new. Like she actually sees me—gets me. Hard to explain. She makes my brain mushy.

"No kisses tonight, though." She lets out this deep, wild laugh, then leans in and cups her hand over my ear. "I'm really glad I got to know you this year—you fucking nerd."

50 Cent's "In da Club" hits like an earthquake. Sam throws her arms up, shimmies wild. Wade hands her a drink—Silas snatches it like a pro. Wade drains his and chucks the cup onto the dance floor. Gets crushed in seconds. Figures.

Sam does these full-body laughs while Wade grins like the devil. He tries to grind on Silas, but even Wade can't pull that off.

Some guy taps Ethan's shoulder—boom, exposed.

Wade slides up. Fuck.

"Hey, boy." He grabs my shirt and yanks me in—too close, way too close—grinding on me just to piss me off. A boa constrictor, squeezing me dead. This sick fuck.

"What do you want, Wade?"

He pushes his burning cheek against mine, right in my ear. "Ya gotta do what's right, dude."

"I...I'm trying."

His knee wedges between mine—no way out, bouncing with the music, some fucked-up yin yang. "Try harder."

I suck in a deep breath and roll my eyes at the air. "Ethan's *literally* gonna kill me."

"Don't you kinda deserve it, dude?"

Ethan spots us across the dance floor and chuckles. Just me and my best friend Wade grinding up on each other. No fucking clue what's up with us.

My eyes latch on Ethan's. "Why...why do you have it out for me, Wade? You always have."

"Believe it or not, Asher, I actually liked you."

"Oh, uh...really? I...I couldn't tell."

Wade pulls back, gives me that look like I'm the dumbest kid alive. "No shit. You were too far up your ass to notice."

"How...how'd you figure it out?"

He rolls his eyes and yanks me in again, alcohol breath hot against my ear. "Oh, come on, dude. You're...Asher. You're not like us. I can just...see it." He pulls back and stares me in the eyes. Like, really looks. "I can see it."

There it is. Plain as day, right on my face, this whole time. So surreal, hearing someone say the truth so casually.

My eyes get big. Shiny, fragile, sharp like glass.

Wade shakes my shoulders. "Lighten up! Life isn't that serious."

Deep down, I know he's right. But I can't help it. Things feel so heavy for me. They hit so hard. Something's wrong with me.

Wade pulls me in. "And then, of course, when I saw you basically swallowing Sam whole...then I *definitely* knew."

"Fuck, I'm such an idiot."

"Listen, man. I talk a big game or whatever, but shit was hard for me. I wasn't always like...this. I went through a lot, and I think you get it." Wade leans back just enough to grab my shoulders and look me dead in the eyes. "It might sound kinda gay, but I, you know... *earned it*. Ethan did, too. And he deserves someone *real*."

*Brutal.*

No clue why, but I grab Wade tight—like I need to hold onto something, anything. This busted little growl rips out of me. "Grraargh...Wade, I...I can't. I can't do it."

He leans in, one last whisper in my ear. "You can. You'll see."

Ethan waltzes up like nothing's wrong. My chest throbs. Wade and him dance, both smiling really big, Wade's arms hanging around Ethan's neck.

Can't watch this shit. I spin and dart my eyes around the dance floor, like some pathetic victim instinct. Then I see something fucking shocking—*Robbie*.

Whoa.

He's smiling and dancing like he belongs here. Polo shirt, wrinkled khakis, old Sketchers—unmistakably Robbie. Spinning some Palm Reef theater girl around, doing that dorky fishing pole move. Robbie's gotta feel so awkward.

Staring at him, my whole body turns cold.

He looks at me and drops his smile dead. Staring at each other, frozen. Maybe he's waiting for me to smile first, but I can't. He turns back to the girl and changes back to normal. Fucking harsh.

Don't know jack about his life, who he is, how he got here. He's gotta be *so* over my shit.

Psychedelic lights spin all around me. Fog machine, spooky mist. Everyone in my life, all in one place. A true fucking nightmare.

I realize I'm not breathing, so I bolt off the dance floor before I pass out. Need to chug water. Need out.

I'm halfway to the bathroom when a voice stops me.

"Voted yet?" It's Bruno the door guy at a janky folding table. Stack of papers and a shoebox.

*Shit*. Prom queen.

Bruno holds out a slip and shoves a pen in my hand.

Still breathing heavy. I scan for my name, but it's spelled wrong. *D-I-M-O-N-D*. Great. The other nominees are these quirky lesbians everyone likes, a trans girl with some jock-looking dude Wade's always after, and this overly perfect gay couple who've always rubbed me the wrong way.

Pray to god we don't win. *Cannot* be the center of attention.

So I do what I can, short of punching Bruno out, stealing the ballot box, and flushing all the papers down the toilet. I put a check mark next to the lesbians.

The bass drops out—then, goddamn Celine Dion. "Because You Loved Me." The crowd *woooos* like they've been waiting their whole lives for this. The ultimate gay prom fantasy.

Fuck me.

*"You were my strength when I was weak…"*

Ethan appears out of the monster's mouth like he's Prince Charming or whatever and holds out a scary hand.

Slow breaths, woozy—drugged? I wish.

He pulls me to the middle of the dance floor. My hiding spot.

Last time I slow danced? Some frumpy girl at homecoming last year. Still no clue if it was a dare. But this? Ethan? His arms, heavy on me. Eyes locked in. No joke, no dare—dead serious.

Slow dancing's easy math. Boy's hands on girl's waist. Girl's arms around the neck. Adam and Eve and all that.

But now? Where do *my* arms go? Where do *I* go?

Ethan's all confident and drops his forearms over my shoulders. Guess that makes him the girl. So I put my hands on his waist, and we sway, slow, back and forth. Starting to get seasick.

My heart's beating so fucking fast. Pumping, pumping. Like my blood flows right through Ethan and back into me. One closed-circuit thing, not two.

Why do I feel so crazy? Wade's threat? My secret? Trying to figure out how to say it? Trying to figure out *if* I'll say it?

Or maybe…it's something I've never let myself feel before.

Our eyes snap together like magnets. His are soft and puppy-dog, with a smile like he wants me to pet him.

No one's *ever* looked at me like this. Like they actually see me. Like, *all* of me. Even the garbage parts. I don't even see myself like that.

And the way he's staring into my skull? Can't even bullshit what it feels like. Like, butterflies or some other cheesy shit? Never actually *felt* them before. Not with Sam, or any other girl. *Definitely* not with a guy.

But with Ethan, there's this new thing. Sharp, raw. He let me into his world, into himself. Something I had no fucking clue I needed so bad. That night on the golf course, hearing him spill his guts, showing me his scrapes and scabs, something between us split open. *Bam*. I opened up, too. Let someone—him—in for the first time.

Touching his neck, him playing with my bracelet, what the hell did it all mean? Why did it feel amazing and horrible and scary all at the same time?

I shake my head and let the butterflies do their thing. This feeling, I don't want to give it up yet. I can't. Not right now. It'll ruin us. Just a few more minutes.

Ethan looks up at me, swaying to this corny song that's got me feeling. "We made it."

"Uh, to prom?"

He lets out a little laugh. "Senior year. It's finally over."

"Oh yeah...we survived high school, I guess."

"Barely..." Ethan trails off. "Hey, I've been wanting to ask, but... did you ever...hear back? From NYU?"

Shit. Haven't told him yet. Seasick. "Well, uh...I got in."

"Asher! That's amazing!" His fingers dig deep into my neck. Wonder if he's feeling butterflies, too.

But mine start to rage. Now they're not butterflies at all—they're fucking hornets with razor wings, tearing up my insides.

Ethan's eyes hit mine deep. "I can't believe we'll be in the same place next year. God, I can't wait to get the hell out of Florida."

I stay quiet because I can't lie. Not out loud. Not anymore.

Ethan pulls me closer, eyes drifting toward me. "I'm glad I met you."

"Me too."

"I needed this." I feel Ethan play with my hair as we dance. "I've never had a best friend before. Well, not like this anyway."

Crazy. Someone could need me and I could show up for them. I think about the story my dad told me, with my mom and the sandwich. Maybe I'm not total garbage after all. Someone actually needs me—Ethan needs me. And fuck, maybe it's okay for me to need him too.

"Neither have I." My heart's just a big vibrating ball of flesh.

Then, it happens.

Ethan leans in. Kisses me. Soft lips. Warm.

I don't pull away. I don't flinch. I need to know.

It's weird, but part of me *wants* to feel something. That thing everyone's always talking about. It'd be easier if it ends like that—me kissing Ethan, realizing I'm into him. Maybe I'm not so straight after all. We'd fall in love, and I wouldn't be alone anymore. Simple, right? I'd finally have that missing thing. The one I never let myself dream about. Like it could actually happen. What a great fucking ending.

But that's not how it goes. That's not how I feel. That's not how my story ends.

The kiss feels... fine, I guess. Maybe more than fine. I don't know. I don't know shit. It was different with Sam—that wild hunger thing. But this? It's all so confusing.

The fuck does any of this mean? What about the lie? I knew I wasn't gay—never really thought about it. Luke's been calling me a fag forever. I just assumed whatever he said about me was bad. So being gay was bad.

Labels. Fucking labels. That's what started this whole mess. Gay. Straight. Maybe it's all bullshit. Maybe it's just about who you care about. Who you can't stand to lose.

What is this thing I'm feeling? Something from a movie? Maybe even...love? Close, maybe. But not the real thing. Not all of it.

Is that what love is? Some random feeling you're supposed to trust? I'm not ready to trust myself. I'm no good. And I've got no clue what's going on in Ethan's head.

Does he feel it too? Is love messy for him, too? The thought of it —leading him on, not knowing what I am—it makes me sick.

My heart's pounding too fast, exploding. I push Ethan off. Panic. Dizzy.

"I...I can't."

Ethan runs his fingers through his hair all nervous. Not breathing, I don't think. "Oh, uh...sorry, I..."

*SAY SOMETHING, ASHER. TELL HIM THE TRUTH.*

I'm so cruel. Such an idiot. He doesn't deserve me, or my bullshit, or my lies. I'm a fucking basket case. "There's something I...I need to tell you..."

Ethan gets close again, arms folded over his chest. "What is it? Are you okay?"

"Not...not really. Um, uh..." Feels like it did right before I told Mr. Pearson and my dad I was gay. Like I'm gonna say something huge, something that'll change everything.

But before I can say it, Celine Dion suddenly cuts out. It's Bruno, in his weird Moulin Rouge costume, standing on stage where the go-go boys usually gyrate. Can't tell if I'm annoyed or relieved. Distraction or sabotage. I was so. Fucking. Close.

"I hope everyone's having fun at the Moulin Rouge!" Bruno growls into the microphone, the bass rattling my whole skeleton.

The crowd goes crazy. "Time to crown the queens who'll rule us all!"

Oh, no. If there is a god, keep my name out of his mouth.

"Drumroll, please." Someone hands Bruno a slip. His face does this fake shocked thing. So annoying.

*Don't say it. Don't say it.*

"Ethan Segal and Asher Diamond!"

*Fuck. No. Can't be happening.*

"Beautiful" by Christina Aguilera starts blasting. Everyone turns to stare. Hollering, excited, like it's some fairy tale. Caught up in the fun of the moment. Playing out this prom fantasy. Their dream night.

My waking nightmare.

Ethan's scared, disappointed look flips the second he's in the spotlight. He flashes that same charming smile I've seen a thousand times—the one that sucked me in from day one.

I try to smile back, but my face won't do it. Never learned how to fake it right.

Ethan grabs my hand, leads me behind him as we walk to the stage. His hand zaps mine all the way up the steps—full-on electrocution. Pain. Punishment. I deserve it.

On stage, I forget how to hold my body. Every cell feels awkward.

Bruno places a cheap tiara on Ethan's head, and he gives a big cheeseball smile. Bruno slaps a king crown on me.

No clue how I'm still a living, breathing person.

The crowd cheers while this cheesy-ass song keeps screaming. Bruno holds out the mic, and Ethan grabs it after this weird pause. He won't fully look at me—the kiss is still there, heavy, weighing us down.

"This isn't the first time I've had a crown on my head." Ethan jokes like a pro. "Thanks for the Princess Diana costume in first grade, Mom!" He folds one arm over his front and coughs into the mic, awkward.

I can't stop thinking—what's he gonna say? What's he thinking about me?

"Okay, so...bear with me. I've got something important to say. I used to think I knew who I was. Where I fit. But eight months ago, I met this queen right here." He laughs. "Oh god, he couldn't dress for shit, but there was something about him, something I knew I needed. Some kind of, um..." He trails off, searching for words I think. "Wise stupidity? Okay, that sounds wrong, but it makes sense to me. He was so... *him,* because he didn't know who he was." He pauses. "I missed that—being lost. Then we started hanging out, and for the first time in forever, I felt like I had permission to be..." Another pause. "Stupid. Real. Just be."

The crowd laughs.

"Oh god, Asher's gonna kill me." He glances at me, then away. "But no—I wouldn't change a thing. Two teenage dirtbags. Clueless as all hell. Not trying to figure anything out." He runs his fingers behind his ears, staring off into nothing.

My heart hammers against my ribs. If he only knew.

"To being total..." He searches again. "Basket cases. Hot ones, obviously." He lifts his plastic crown and finally locks eyes with me. "And to whatever the hell comes next."

The crowd claps, picking up on some kinda weirdness between us but not understanding it. Ethan shoves the mic at Bruno and whispers in my ear. "We need to talk."

Can't speak. Can't breathe.

That's when I see someone lurch up the steps, swaying toward us.

Fucking Wade.

He's wrecked, jacket hanging off a shoulder. He puts his arm around my neck and grabs the mic from Bruno, who doesn't even try to stop him. Wade shouts into the mic. "Let's give another hand to these fucking queens, am I right?" He lets me go and pushes his hands up in the air to egg on the crowd. "Man, these guys..."

Wade starts pacing the stage. "You all know Asher, right? We love little Asher, don't we?"

There's some weak and pathetic *whoops* and slow claps from the crowd. I think people are confused about why the hell Wade's up here.

"Asher-boy here's been holding out on us, huh?" Wade steps up to me and pushes my cheeks together with his hand like I'm a little kid. "Enough from me. Let's hear from him."

He pushes the mic into my hand and it slams my chest, making a high-pitched feedback screech.

Ethan whispers loud behind me to Wade. "What the fuck are you doing?"

Wade just shrugs.

I just stand there. Mic in hand. Total idiot. "Uh...I...um..." Fully paralyzed, except for my whole body shaking. My voice booms out. Too big. Too loud. Too much. My breaths go short and fast, and play loud in the huge space.

"Yes?" Wade raises his eyebrows at me and the crowd. "No? Not gonna tell them?" He looks at me and his face changes one last time. It's that pity again, and almost...hopeful that I'll do the right thing? Like he isn't exactly trying to ruin my life, but to help me?

But I just freeze.

Eventually Wade's eyes roll. He grabs the mic out of my hand and cracks his neck. Suddenly he's blaring on the speakers again, staring into my eyes, his voice flat, serious, disappointed. "Okay, then."

Wade stands back and displays me like I'm a set of Siamese twins at a freak show. "So this kid, this one right here...he did something pretty wild. Turns out, he's, uh, got this big secret. Get ready for this. This one's really good."

Ethan runs up to Wade and tries to grab the mic, but Wade jerks it away hard. So Ethan comes over and puts his hand on my shoulder, trying to reassure me I think.

Wade looks like he's doing a stand-up set. But none of this is funny.

"So...it turns out...this guy, our little Asher-boy...He's...he's not even really gay. He's *straight*. Totally hetero." Wade lets out this big, drunk cackle. "Can you fucking believe it?"

The crowd shifts like one organism—whispers spreading, laughs breaking out. I watch the news travel from person to person like a virus.

Ethan's hand drops. He steps back. "What?" Ethan's voice cracks. His eyes search mine, begging me to say it's all bullshit. "What are you talking about? What's...what's going on?"

I turn to Ethan. "Let me explain...I can—"

"He lied!" Wade screams into the mic through big laughs. "He thought it would make him...cool or popular or something. Fucking crazy, man." Wade rubs his hand into my chest and raises my hand up in the air. "Let's give it up for Asher, the world's straightest gay guy!"

He starts clapping and tries to get the crowd to join.

But there's nothing. Who the fuck knows what people think is going on right now? Probably doesn't make sense to anyone.

Ethan squints at me. I see his mind try to make sense of something it can't.

I just stand there, frozen. The hot spotlight feels extra harsh in my eyes. I think about everyone I know, looking at me. My dad, Piper,

Sam, Silas, Robbie, and all these random Pantheon people. Staring. What the hell do they think about me, now that my secret's out? Now that everyone knows the truth?

Suddenly, Ethan rips off his tiara and slams it into Wade—right into the mic. *CRACK*. Then he bolts, off the stage and through the crowd.

I freeze—then chase. I jump off the stage, push toward the door, shoving past everyone. Eyes stab like needles. Voices slash past my ears.

Then, as I'm leaving, I crash into this big cardboard windmill outside the door. Eat shit onto the concrete, landing hard on my hand, palm scraping open on the rough surface.

Everything's wobbly like Tilt-A-Whirl, trying to pull myself off the ground. I finally stand up and spot Ethan walking away from the club, into the parking lot.

I could flee right now. Never look back.

But something pulls me toward Ethan. To confront this. Finally.

"Ethan! Stop! Just...just wait." I stumble after him like a bloody zombie into the dark lot. Everything's harsh out here—hot asphalt, metal, none of that cozy Pantheon haze.

Ethan stops walking and swivels around. "Fine. What do you want, Asher?"

"I, uh...I need to explain. You need to understand—"

"I don't think I really want to hear it right now."

"No, you have to...you have to listen to me."

"Actually, I don't." Ethan folds his arms in front of him. "I don't have to do anything."

"Just...just let me explain. Please!" I'm panting, losing my breath. My hand fucking stings.

Ethan starts walking backwards through the parking lot. He stares at me, waiting. Walking.

"So, um, you know...all that stuff that happened that I told you about? The stuff at my school with the locker room, and, uh...my black eye and all that?" I stop to see if Ethan's gonna say something, but he doesn't.

He turns a corner in the parking lot, one foot back, then the other.

I look like a mess. Stumbling after him. Can't catch up. Can't think.

"Well, uh, yeah, so all that, that...it happened. It's true...and it fucked me up. Really bad. I just felt...trapped, and like...like there was no way out." I slide my hands down my cheeks. "I know it's totally insane but...I got this idea that if I said I was, you know, then...then they'd finally believe me."

"Believe what?" Ethan's face looks like he's trying to solve an impossible SAT problem.

"That it was real. All the shit that Luke gave me. That it was fucking killing me."

"Do you realize how fucked up that is? To lie about that?"

So shaky, my body and my words, trying to convince myself of what's right as I talk. "Yeah, I do...I know now...I just wasn't—"

"You don't get it, Asher. You can't...you can't get it."

"But I do!"

"It's not the same." Ethan's voice is harsh. "It's just not."

"It was real...what I felt...I couldn't do it anymore...It's not fair."

Ethan laughs. "Not fair? Are you kidding me, dude? None of it's *fair*. All the shit that's happened to me wasn't fair. The shit you went through wasn't fair. We just have to, you know, suck it up and deal with it. It's not my fault you couldn't handle it."

"I tried. I thought I did."

"You fucked up." Ethan's just shaking his head.

"You think I don't know that? I know better than *anyone* how bad I fucked up." I worry my legs might give. "Just, another chance... please."

"I've given you enough, haven't I? I gave you everything."

"I know, and that was....you changed me. You made everything better."

"I did."

Tears build over my eyes. "Maybe we can still—"

"Still what? Be friends?"

"Um, yeah...next year...at...at NYU. Maybe we can—"

Ethan stops walking and whips around, closing the distance between us in three quick steps. "Are you out of your fucking mind? I'm not going to college with you. You're not my friend. I don't know who the fuck you are."

"You do. I'm still me."

Ethan's pupils get big, like everything finally makes sense. "You're nothing."

His words sting like fire-ant bites. "What...what do you mean?"

"Listen. There's a lot I could say to you right now. I could tear you down and make you feel like shit. But you know what? I don't need to. I don't need this. I've been through too much to deal with your bullshit." Ethan starts walking away, then turns around and takes a step toward me. "I should have known you were a lost cause."

More fire ants, right where it hurts. Me, the lost cause. I can't believe I thought I could pull this off. Be something more. Luke was right. Ethan's right. I'm nothing.

"Ethan...I don't know what to say—"

"You don't have to say anything. Just stay the fuck out of my life." Ethan turns and heads back toward the club. He looks like he's got his shit together.

I probably look like hell.

I spin around. There's a crowd outside—my dad, Piper, Robbie, Silas. And Wade, lurking in the shadows.

Someone starts coming at me. All I see is, like, a spooky shape in the dark lot, strobes peeking out from the door behind this person's head. I see long hair. Bouncing as they...she...runs up to me. It's Sam.

"Are you kidding me, dude? Are you *fucking* kidding me?"

"Fuck, Sam, I—"

"I actually thought we were friends." She shoves me hard in the chest.

I stumble back. "We *are* friends."

"Turns out you're just another horny fucking loser creep."

Before I can respond, I see a blur—an arm, I think—then *pain*. My face, throbbing, dull. I hit the ground *hard*, landing on my right arm. My head cracks against the pavement.

When I open my eyes, Sam's walking away sideways, flipping her hair, tugging her mini-dress back into place. Heels clicking like gunshots. She reaches Silas. "Let's get out of this shithole."

He gives her a high five.

Piper screams and my dad rushes over, pulling me. "Oh my god, Asher...get up. Come with us."

"No! I can't. I'm not...I'm not going with you!"

"Don't be silly. I'm taking you home." My dad tries to hug me close to help me walk, but I shove him off.

"I don't need your help." I start to hobble away. "I don't need anyone. Just leave me alone."

I ignore everything—my face, my hand, my bloody palm—and run. Through the parking lot, down the road, all the way to Ethan's house. Eventually it hits. Everything hurts. My brain's just flopping around in there, full of pain and shit thoughts.

Finally, I make it to my getaway car. Gotta get the fuck outta here, before everything—and everyone—catches up to me.

261

## Imitation

I speed up A1A like a crazy person. Shit parking job, my mind's racing. Honestly, probably worse than driving drunk.

Me and Robbie used to sneak out to this beach spot at night. To get away and just, like, hang out. Dark, alone. Felt good. Epic nothingness.

Guess my brain dragged me here on autopilot.

I follow this sandy path to the beach, past some sea grape plants. They've got these big flat leaves like cards. Can't tell if they're welcoming me hello or waving bye cause I fucked up my life.

These dumb Prada shoes kick up sand as I walk. Body heat catching up with me. Too much running, thinking. I rip the ugly green jacket off and tear open my shirt. The night beach breeze cools me down.

Face fucking hurts. I touch my cheekbone and it stings bad. Slide my fingers through the sides of my hair, and I feel a snag at my right ear. Ow.

The stupid rainbow friendship bracelet, the one I thought would never go away and that means absolutely nothing, gets caught on my earring. Flash in my brain—Ethan brushing my ear, helping with the earring at the mall. That weird, woozy, first-time feeling.

Gotta collapse. My scraped hand lands on coarse sand that digs into the torn skin. That string—strong as rope—still wrapped tight around the earring. Can't get it off. I wanna rip off my whole fucking ear.

I manage to pull my earring out and fish it from the tangled string. Feels light and cheap. Fake stone. Shitty knockoff of a real diamond. An imitation of something—someone—better. Brighter. Worth more.

It burns in my hand like hot coal. Rage. I hurl it at the ocean before it scars me. The jewelry disappears into the black air. Good fucking riddance. Wish I could throw me in the dark water too.

Bet Ethan would be disappointed in me for tossing the earring away. *Dammit, Asher.* Stop caring so much what he thinks.

I can't help it. What he thinks still matters. But why can't I just be my own person for once?

I plop back on the sand. Waves crashing in my ears, dark sky like I don't exist—feeling like a kid under a blanket. This safe feeling slows my heart. Big, long breath. Exhale.

So, it finally happened. It caught up to me. All my idiotic decisions blew up in my face. Worse off than ever. Lower than I ever thought could happen.

Boom, back to day one of senior year. Luke, pizza, standing up for myself for the first time ever. Robbie had my back. Dreaming up revenge plots.

Locker room. Fucked-up accusation, towel, humiliation. Robbie taking care of me. Last straw.

"Coming out." My big lie. Changing everything forever. Selfish, didn't stop to think. Only thought about myself. Didn't think about anyone else. Everyone else, collateral damage. And I didn't give two shits.

Hypnotized by Ethan, shoving Robbie away. Turning on my best friend in a flash, like he was nothing. He was hurting, too, and I couldn't, wouldn't see it. Tossed him in the fucking garbage.

Whole new life—explosive, exciting, confusing. Couldn't get enough of Ethan and the new me. Addicted, kinda. We changed each other. For better? Worse? No clue. But led him on, pushed him away too.

Sam being nice to me, opening up. Trusting I wasn't a perv trying to get in her pants. Turns out I am. I deserved that punch. Sam's kiss set me on fire, Ethan's safe hugs. How could all this shit feel so right in such messed-up, opposite ways?

What's Ethan doing right now? Thinking about me too? Or did he just wipe me from his brain like a hard drive? No room for this junk, me. I can't, won't, reformat him. Not like I have a choice. He's burned deep into me. Ethan-shaped scar.

Me, such an ungrateful little bitch. Secrets, punking out on Piper. Pushing away my own dad, hurting too, only wanting the best for me. Forever, since Mom.

I even fucked over Wade. He was struggling in his own messed-up way. Probably didn't even wanna be an asshole to me, and I'm the one who sent him over the edge.

Robbie's gone. I'm blacklisted from Pantheon—banished from the place that let me in. I'll miss the dancing, the freedom. Ethan's body against me.

What the fuck am I saying? I've lost my mind.

Maybe I'll be grounded for life without parole, stocking DVDs till I'm old and gray. Piper analyzing me—perfect case study in how to fuck up your life. Out of control. Trust—gone. How can I ever fix this shitstorm I got myself into?

Then it hits me. Something I really don't like thinking about.

After my mom got really sick, I guess I was thirteen, she had to stay in the hospital for a few months. I'd visit every single day after school. She'd help me with homework, or we'd just talk, or watch *Cheers* reruns on the fuzzy hospital TV. *Cheers* kinda sucks.

Then she took a nosedive. Stressed me out so much to see her like that. Looking less and less like my mom. Visits slowed down. Too scary, too sad. Big fights with my dad about it.

One time, me and my dad really got into it, but he dragged me into the car to visit her in that bleak, stale, hospital room. Walked in and my mom wouldn't look at me. My dad went over to her, and she whispered something in his ear. I guess I lost my grip on my Yoo-hoo and the bottle smashed, glass shattered in a million shards on the floor. My mom snapped, so loud. "Asher! What's wrong with you?"

In a flash, my dad yanked me out and went back in.

I peeked in that little window in the door, saw them talking for a while. Wondered the whole time if she hated me. Why she couldn't even have me in the room.

After a while my dad came back out. We walked to the car, no words the entire way home.

All these years, I couldn't figure out why she yelled at me like that. Why she couldn't even look at me. Why no one told me shit.

I was used to it, wondering if there was something wrong with me. Luke's cruelty, making me question myself every single day. But this was different. My own mom. Thinking I'm not enough. Broken garbage.

The rest of the time she was alive, there was something confusing about her. How she saw me, how I saw myself. If I was good enough. What I was really worth. The diamond—fake or real.

Who the fuck am I gonna be now? I'm everything and nothing.

Can I tie my life up in a bow like some *7th Heaven* episode? Fix it all just in time for the credits? Or is that only on TV?

More than anything, I can't get Ethan outta my head. So fucking confused. What even were we? From stranger I wanted nothing to do with, to friend, to best friend, to maybe-more-than-friend, to guy who fucking hates my guts.

How do I even like him? In what...way? I started all this as a hopeless virgin straight guy, but what the hell am I now? I'm not in love with Ethan, not exactly, but something's different. Is it okay to not know? Maybe. But it's definitely a dick move to string him along.

Can I even change? Go back to being Good Asher?

Doubt it. Keep lying, selfish, learning nothing from my year from hell. Life on the run, stirring shit up wherever I land. Maybe that's easier.

Or maybe it all just goes back to bland, unremarkable life. Hopeless and alone.

Not sure which sounds worse. Not sure which I deserve.

But—maybe this is nuts—but what if I didn't do anything wrong? What if I did what I had to? To survive? Maybe that's all there is. Every man for himself. Maybe that's how the world works.

Maybe I deserved to feel good. Like somebody, for once. Why shouldn't I get that? Doesn't feel fair.

There's that word again.

I dig myself deeper into the sand, alone, and close my eyes. Listen to the waves, wondering if the tide'll creep up and pull me under. Save me from facing the consequences. Facing everyone. Facing myself. The real me.

But it's all so terrifying. Like a python slithered up to me, wrapped me tight, squeezing the life out. How the hell am I supposed to face Ethan after everything I did? Or Robbie? Sam?

Everyone at school?

Maybe it's easier to just stay here buried in the sand, let the waves slowly wash me away.

Because the other option? Going back to school, trying to fix my life? Fucking impossible.

The stars blur as I stare up. Picturing myself on some doomed space walk—drifting, alone, stranded in the black void. No clue who I am, what I want, or how to unfuck my life.

Maybe I never will.

Maybe this is the end of Asher Fucking Diamond.

*Piper 2*

BEEN a week since all the shit went down at Pantheon. Barely left my room. Just spend all day on TV and eating junk food, the stuff Ethan said makes my skin break out. Fuck my skin. I'm invisible anyway. The air's stale and dead. I hope dirty-clothes stench and Cool Ranch pollution don't kill little Michelangelo.

I've been MIA from school. Can't face it. Kids and teachers. Sam, Silas, Robbie, everyone. Probably all celebrating my demolition.

But I think Dean Pearson's been calling my dad, trying to get me to come back. Sometimes I hear my dad and Piper argue. My dad knocks on my door every day. Soft, then harder, then nothing. I never answer.

So for now, I'm just rotting away in my bedroom. Then, after my dad and Piper go to bed, I sneak out and eat whatever's left over from dinner. There's always a plate waiting in the fridge.

I've watched so much *The Price Is Right* I could win it all. *Fear Factor* doesn't gross me out anymore. Scarfing down worms? Easy. Mr. Burns is my new hero on *The Simpsons*—bitter, isolated, everyone hates him. Just like me. Put me on *The Real World* and let me loose. I'll be a dick. I'll play the villain. Why not? Got enough practice.

Michelangelo's been keeping me company while I ice my new black eye. Souvenir from Sam. At least this time I earned it.

I wonder if my gecko knows what's up with me. Sometimes when he blinks really big, it looks like he's silently judging.

It's late Sunday night and I creep out to the kitchen like a street rat. Bowl of gazpacho in the fridge, so I grab it and head to the den. Fresh air feels good.

Fuck—Piper's here. Doing her therapy notes on a big yellow legal pad. First time I've seen her since I ran away at gay prom.

"Oh. You're out." She sounds too nice to be talking to a criminal. "Come sit with me."

I'm *so* not in the mood to get lectured by the morality police. Trust me, woman, I get how bad I fucked up. But to get back my life? Gotta play nice.

I sit on the couch and balance my soup in my lap. Not sure what to say. "Uh...any interesting patient stuff this week?"

Piper squints, then her eyes get wide. "I have this one woman who got detained by security while trying to shoplift bananas from Publix. I wasn't surprised, actually. She called me from the store phone and asked for an emergency session."

Honestly, I can barely follow. Too nervous.

I think Piper knows I'm not all here. She reaches out and swipes my messy hair to the side. "Hi."

"Hi." I put the cold soup to my lips and slurp.

"How are you feeling, honey?"

Here we go. Therapy.

No point in putting up a fight, so I don't. "Not good. Like my whole world got nuked."

Piper looks at me like I'm real pathetic. "That makes sense."

My leg's shaking the soup up and down. What does she want? You know what, I'll try something out. A test-run apology. Low stakes, cause I don't really care what she thinks. "I'm sorry."

Piper scrunches her forehead. "What are you sorry for?"

"For...for everything. For what I did."

"Well, what did you do?"

Annoyed, I set down my soup hard on the coffee table. A little pink drop splashes in the air. "I'm not really in the mood to list all the terrible shit I've done. It's pretty obvious."

Piper stares at me, still, like she's taking an X-ray in her head. "Asher, I've been doing a lot of thinking this week. About you, about us."

Shit, here it comes. Telling me off. "Us?"

"It's been four years, hasn't it? I know I came into your life pretty soon after your mom passed."

"She didn't *pass*. She died."

Piper shakes her head. "Of course, I'm...so sorry. Well, that must have been hard for you. A new person, so soon."

Thanks, Piper, for this tired summary of that shitty time in my life.

"I know how your father can be. Not the most...emotionally open guy. Just you and him, such a difficult time. So young, not knowing how to move on. Him, clueless how to parent on his own. I felt for you so much, Asher. I knew how it felt. When I was about your age, my grandmother died. I know it's not the same, but we were close. My favorite person in the world. Then, I got sad. Like, *really* sad. I realized I was depressed, and it took a long time to heal. I still deal with it off and on. I think that's why I became a therapist. And sometimes I wonder..." She looks right at me. "Was it like that for you? Were you...depressed?"

My eyes won't roll even though I'm trying. They're locked to Piper, starting to feel sharp. I've never thought of her as, like, a real person with feelings. And that word...depressed. It feels foreign and familiar at the same time. Like a long-lost twin brother I've never met.

Is that what I was? Depressed? Is that what I am...now?

"I...I'm not sure. Maybe. I haven't really thought about it. I thought depression was just for, like, sad crazy people."

Piper laughs. "There's nothing wrong with being sad and crazy."

I laugh, even though I wish I wasn't.

"So, back then, I approached carefully. I was so nervous, and I wanted you to like me so badly. I didn't know if I'd ever have kids, but I loved your father, so I knew it would be worth it. To be part of your life. I loved you the best I could. I still do."

She pauses and puts her hand to her mouth, thinking. "I know I'm not your favorite person, and I know you're not going to think of me as your new mom. To be loved the same way. And you shouldn't. I don't want to replace her. But I do want to love you, to fill in some...gaps, I guess. That were left...empty."

Piper's never told me she loves me. Maybe she was scared of me. I wonder how many times she's wanted to say it but stopped herself. Maybe she thought I'd get sad or blow up like a nutjob or something. Just from, like, love or whatever.

What a fucking absolute monster I am. Treating her like a villain when all she wants is to love me, and maybe be loved back.

"I've been thinking about everything that happened this year, and I've been trying to see it from *your* perspective. The bullying, what he did. Such cruelty, so young. When you came out? I was thrilled for you. Really was. I kept thinking, 'How can I support him?' Even when you kept...pushing me away."

Hearing this, how I treated her like trash, just laid out right here. Fucking terrible. So embarrassed, exposed, immature.

She puts her hand on mine. "But I don't blame you at all. I tried not to be too bothersome, but I was waiting—hoping—you would come around." Piper takes a pause and lowers her chin, looking into my eyes. "Now, I bet you're pretty mad at yourself?"

I *hate* that she's right. And I'm holding back these fucking tears like the Hoover Dam.

"Um, yeah. I fucked up so bad, and now everyone hates me. I'm such an idiot, like...why would I do that? Say I'm gay? It's so insane." I look down and pick at my fingernails. "What's the point of even trying, you know, to get my life back?"

Piper's damn eyes are getting wet, too. "That's the thing, Asher. Nobody hates you, not even close. It's not hopeless."

I roll my eyes and push my head back into the couch.

"Asher, let me tell you what I saw this year. You came out, and that took *guts*. The bullying stopped. You didn't dread school. Then— Ethan. It was like you turned into a different person. Happier. I wasn't sure if he was just a friend or more than a friend, but it didn't matter. I was happy you were happy."

"Well, I guess I *was*...for a little. But then everything got so complicated, and I started fucking things up. I felt so guilty, like, *all* the time. Like this huge liar and a fraud and—"

"I didn't see a fraud. I saw a damn good friend. Confident. Risk-taker."

"Uh, that's great and all, but...it's over."

"Just stay with me for a second. You know what I think? I think all that good stuff...it was in you the whole time. But sadness, missing your mom, bullying—it got in the way. Like dark glasses that made everything look gray. But it was just a filter. You were a good friend, sensitive to your dad, helped him through the loss of your mother. You helped me, too. You didn't try to stop your father and I from being together. Which means so much more than you know."

I'm biting my lip hard, tapping my foot. *Asher, DO NOT CRY.*

"You know, I think we're more alike than you realize. We're both good at reading people, figuring out what makes them tick. We observe. I've made a career out of it, helping people understand themselves. And you? Well, you've got that same gift. This year, you just...explored it in a more, hmm...roundabout way. Sure, you lied about your sexuality, but the brave person who came out? That was you. The Asher you became, the one hiding there all along...was— and is—real. And very much deserving of love."

Trying to keep my head above water, a rushing rapids of new emotions.

I'm feeling something new with Piper. Something like how my mom cared about me, and like Ethan did. Maybe it was there the whole time, and I just wouldn't let myself see it.

"I don't know who I am anymore. All the lying kind of, like, messed with my head. And Ethan? I...I don't know how I feel."

"You don't have to." Piper puts her hand on my forehead and pushes my hair back. "Everyone deserves a second chance."

"Sure."

"And don't worry about your father. I'll handle him for you. He'll get over it eventually. He just wants to see you happy."

I'm trying to take it in, but there's this parasite thing inside me, eating away. "What about Ethan? And Robbie? No fucking way they'll forgive me. Ethan told me to stay out of his life."

Piper thinks for a sec.

"Life is short, Asher. You've punished yourself enough."

It takes me out like a sniper from a mile away. Fuck. That's all I have.

She puts her hand on my knee and kisses my forehead. Holds my head with her hands and inspects the black eye.

My body totally melts. I feel so much of that hate, that hate for myself, spill away.

She gets up and starts walking away, but I jump up and rush over and give her a big hug from behind, holding her. I squeeze tight, and let my eyes do it. Wet tears, my cheeks, my face, like a big sweaty night at Pantheon.

Piper grabs my hand wrapped around her and gives it a little hard squeeze.

Is it all bullshit? Is she just tricking me into feeling better?

No fucking clue. But I start to wonder if she's right.


After stumbling back to my room in a daze, I try to watch TV, but it's not hitting.

Then I get a crazy idea. I pick up my phone, dial, don't think. It rings.

"Hello?" It's Luke. He actually answered. Can't believe I still remember his number.

"Oh, uh, hi Luke. It's...Asher." Regret it already.

"No shit. Asher Fuckin' Diamond. What's goin' on, dude?"

His voice isn't making me anxious. Kind of calming, actually. Familiar. "I've been better."

"Yeah, man. I heard what happened at that gay thing. Pretty wild. Sam got you good, didn't she? She's a beast...but, uh, you okay? Like, really?"

I can't believe he's talking to me, after everything. "Well I haven't been back to school yet. It's too...scary, I don't know. What the hell is everyone gonna think? After, you know..."

"Who the fuck knows, dude? So, uh, why'd you call, Diamond? I've got *Madden* paused and my pizza rolls are getting cold."

"Honestly, I'm not sure. I just...did it. But, um, I guess I just wanted to know if...if I'm gonna be okay? You seemed to, you know, like grow or whatever...after you left."

Luke's quiet for a sec. "You know what, man? If I learned anything this year, it's that there's always another shot. Whatever's going on, it's not the end of the world. If I could survive getting expelled for being a d-bag, then you can figure this shit out too, whatever this is."

"Are you...mad at me? For what I did? For ruining your life or whatever?"

"Dude, it doesn't matter what I think. You fucked me over, but who cares? Honestly, good on you, finally manning up. Didn't think you had it in you." I hear him take a drink of something, then talking with an ice-cube-in-mouth accent. "But I'm done with this high school shit. I moved on. Even if I did think you were being a little bitch, then, you know—own it. Be whatever the fuck you want. Be a dick. Be a good person. Apologize. Don't. Whatever. Just...just take care of yourself. You're all you've got."

Whoa. "That's...um...just, thanks, I guess. I'll let you go."

"Sure thing. Later man—"

"Oh! Uh, one last thing." I cough, from fear I think. "So...why didn't you tell anyone? You know, what I did..."

Luke's quiet for a sec, and I hear the gooey crunch of pizza roll getting chomped.

This is it. Why? Why didn't he rat me out? He could have won, given that final blow. Like *Mortal Kombat.* Finish him.

After forever, Luke talks. "I don't know what the fuck you're talking about, dude...and, uh, good luck out there."

I drop back on my bed like I took a bullet in the chest. Staring at the ceiling, under these little glow-in-the-dark star things my dad put up for me when I was eight. They don't glow much anymore.

The whole year rushes over me.

Maybe Piper's right. Maybe I've been in my room long enough. Maybe Luke's right, too. Maybe I don't have to hide forever. Maybe I'm not that bad, after all.

Fuck it. Tomorrow, I'm going back to school. Time to face the world again. See if I can salvage what's left of my friendships, my reputation, my fucking *life*. Terrifying, but I have to.

Chomp those worms, Asher. Eat them all.

## *Welcome Back*

I set my alarm extra early, so I'm *really* awake by the time I get to school. Ready for whatever shit comes my way.

All the grime and bad vibes from my week of sulking scrub off in a long, hot shower. I moisturize but skip the eye cream and other shit Ethan gave me. Gay Asher would have smudged on some concealer stuff to hide my second gnarly black eye of the year. Not anymore. I'm not perfect, can't hide my flaws. My mistakes.

I mess my hair in the mirror, hoping it'll land in the right place. But it doesn't. Just sits there like a spoiled brat. Rub some pomade through my hair—different than Ethan did. Time for something new. I put on a well-fitted plain black T-shirt and old baggy jeans. My Airwalks are dirty, and it fits. I'm scuffed up, too.

I stare at myself in the mirror. Who's looking back? Who is this guy? Some weird hybrid creature.

Old pants and sneakers, but the T-shirt Ethan picked out. Robbie's in the mirror too, with the shark-tooth necklace and Members Only jacket. My dad paid for it all, and I'm even wearing underwear Piper bought me. My mom gave me these Bart Simpson socks in sixth grade. And, of course, that shiner from Sam.

Maybe there's no one *real* Asher. Maybe I'm a little bit of everyone.

And that hole in my ear. Empty today, feels right. Not in a flashy mood.

On my drive to school, I put on "How's It Going to Be" by Third Eye Blind. Simmering in that, what's the word...melancholy, I think. Don't need to hide it. Finally.

I think about what he's singing—about a world where I'm gone. Would it be better for everyone?

I feel it, but I don't get totally sucked into the darkness, the depression. I'm fucking *here*, and I'm not going anywhere. At least not today. Gotta stay around—face my fears.

I park and walk. Feels like forever since I've been here, even though it's only been a week. Everything looks strange. I manage to remember my locker combo and grab my geometry book. Hot and damp from sitting in there so long. I know I'm not gonna look at it, but I take it anyway to decorate my desk. Mr. I deserves to see it. Literally the least I can do.

On my way to first period, I see Dean Pearson walk at me. Fuck. Gotta face him eventually. Here comes detention for the rest of my life.

"Glad to have you back, Mr. Diamond." He holds my shoulder and gives me a super-hard shake before walking away. That day in his office feels like years ago.

Thought he'd for sure make me pay for lying and making a fool outta him. Maybe he feels fine, though. Maybe he feels *bad* for me, like Piper does. Maybe today won't be that bad.

In geometry, I try my best to pay attention. No clue what's going on, but I ask a question that probs makes me sound like a total moron. Mr. I gets all excited though—I never did crap in his class before.

Some kids in class are talking shit, I think. My heart picks up, but I take deep breaths like Piper taught me, and focus on the graph Mr. I's drawing on the whiteboard.

For a real challenge, I head to the senior quad and sit on a bench right out in the open. Fucking terrifying. But that's what today's all about.

Kids whisper and stare. *Look at this random fuckup who did this psycho thing.* Then Sam and Silas walk into the quad.

My palms start dripping like waterfalls.

They sit with some of their friends who used to talk to me. Silas cradles a ball in his lacrosse stick, which, come to think of it, might be some nervous tic. Sam's ignoring me like nothing happened. Like I didn't see her with Luke, like we didn't totally make out, and like I didn't massively fuck her over.

So damn sweaty, May sun in my black T-shirt and jacket. The little people in my brain scream loud at me to run, but I don't. I stay right here.

Silas and his guy friends look at me and laugh. You know, for old times' sake.

He walks toward me, slow. Holding his lacrosse stick, cradling the ball. Rolling the stick up and down so the ball doesn't fly out. Suddenly he throws his stick up, like he's gonna chuck the ball right in my face.

I clench every muscle, ready for my third black eye. Maybe even a broken nose if I'm lucky. But, no. He stops, then goes back to cradling. He's cracking up at me flinching like a pussy.

But I know I'm not. It's totally reasonable when it looks like someone's gonna smash your face with a hard projectile. I'm over feeling like a pussy.

"Welcome back, faggot."

That word can't hurt me. Just another word. Heard it before and I'll hear it again. Doesn't mean much now after everything. Going from straight to gay to I don't know what. It's not my word to get hurt by.

Sam walks up to Silas and yanks him away. She's so close I smell her perfume, like toxic gas, making me see her blurry. Slow motion.

She walks out of the quad and flips her hair back, giving me this really quick look, and a kind of smirk thing.

We lock eyes and I feel fucking crazy. Attraction and hurt and guilt and respect. Her head snaps up, and I can't tell if she's saying *Eat shit* or giving me some weird nod that's like, *All good*. Or even *Good work, dickface*.

Guess it doesn't matter either way. I'll never understand that girl. Maybe she doesn't wanna be figured out. She's way more complex than I thought before everything happened, that's for sure.

But I survived the run-in. Time to leave the quad.

In the caf, I stand around like a loser trying to figure out where to sit. I rush past Robbie eating with some theater kids and glue my eyes to my tray, shuffling to claim an empty table in the back corner. Same one from the first day of school.

Pizza for lunch, of course. Hypnotized by the little round pie, oozing cheese and sauce like bloody pus. Bubbling sludge. I shake my head, knocking out the bleak ghosts. The pizza's totally normal.

My eyes dart around for intruders, attackers, but no one's even looking at me. Or maybe they are. *Don't think about it. Don't obsess over what other people think.* Not today.

I lift the pizza in front of my eyes, about to beat the shit out of each other in a boxing match. I take a bite, punched with pizza euphoria. Avoided pizza all year. Reminded me too much of Luke.

That call with Luke that turned everything upside down. Today, the pizza doesn't taste like revenge or victory or defeat or sadness. Just pizza. Nothing life-changing.

Can't help poking my dumb tortoise head out of its shell, looking at Robbie. My mind's going apeshit, spinning in a thousand directions. So many questions about him, who he is, what he's been through. Seems like he was just looking at me and quickly turned away. Not sure. No clue what's real—or what's just my brain fucking with me.

Been going crazy figuring how to make it up to him, what I need to do. I have an idea, I think, but does he even want to see me after my shit, hear my voice?

Fuck it. I need to do something. Can't, won't, give up on us.

I float over to his table like I'm possessed. Check my shirt like I'm walking into Pantheon. "Uh...hi." I just stand there waiting, slamming down the regret trying to bust to the surface.

Robbie fidgets with his leather cuff, gives me this nervous look, then turns to a friend. Some ESP conversation I'm not tapped into.

"I know you probably don't want to talk to me, but, um, there are some things I wanna say. You know, if you're, like, open to it. Maybe we could meet up? This weekend? Or, whenever you're free? I just, uh..." *Please say something, Robbie.*

Eventually he nods.

Fucking saved. I exhale about a gallon of air. The nod's enough. Today, anyway.

"Okay, cool...um...I'll call you." I hold my hand to my face, doing one of those dumb phone call things like a fucking dork.

Robbie squints his eyes and his lips. Suspicious? Makes sense.

Then he shifts in his seat, awkward, and zones out on the wall behind me, blinking. Is he freaked too? Do I have a chance to get him back?

Okay, he probably wants me to go.

I head back to my table, grab my bag, and toss my tray. I walk out of the cafeteria into a big outdoor hall, the kind everywhere at Palm Reef. The sun catches my eye, but the bright light doesn't feel harsh. Doesn't hurt. Makes me feel...alive. Charging my battery, the one I need to keep going.

There's someone else I gotta talk to, someone who might help me figure out, finally, who I really am.

## *Crunch*

I'M half zoned on the brown couch. Loose limbs, legs up on the back cushion, working on a sharp hangnail. The *Friends* reruns don't crack a smile.

Piper's cooking in the background, but the noise isn't pissing me off. Comforting, or something like that. Feels kinda brave, honestly. Outta my cave. Probably shouldn't stay in my room 24/7.

Clock's ticking on time at home. Graduation, then Europe if my dad and Piper aren't totally over me. Then college—still trying to figure that one out.

My mind's twisted up like my body on the couch. What do I do about Ethan?

Haven't come up with that perfect thing to say. I don't wanna show him all my failures and fuck-ups. All year I tried to come off cool and go with the flow or whatever—to mixed results. Being honest about the real me—the one I buried—makes me wanna hide. Give up all over again.

But every day I sit on my ass putting it off, the more likely I'll push Ethan away for good. That tipping point where he's just gone, like he never existed. And all that stuff I learned from him? That'll slip away too.

Prom, the kiss, Wade revealing the truth. Can't imagine what Ethan was thinking up there. What's he thinking now?

But tonight's the night. *Just do it, Asher. Man the fuck up. Listen to Luke, my new Yoda.*

I head to my room, pick up my cordless phone, and pace. Hands shaking so hard the buttons won't push right. Awkward beeps like my heartbeat. The fuck do I say? Wing it, I guess. So I call.

It rings. It's ringing. Feels like a heart attack's coming. *Throw the phone in the toilet, quick.*

But then—a voice. Ethan's mom. "Hello?"

"Oh, uh, hi Raquel. It's...it's Asher." Shit. Wasn't expecting her to pick up.

Reality sinks in. Massively disappointed her. Can't believe I fucked her over too—after everything she did to protect Ethan his whole life. The bullies, the assholes. Maybe she thinks I'm just another one.

"Hi, Asher." Her voice is flat. Doesn't call me *mijo* like normal. Doesn't chew me out either. No excitement or anger, nothing.

Punch in the fucking gut. Worse than getting ripped a new one. "Um, is Ethan around? I'm hoping to talk to him."

Raquel's quiet, then a crackle as he grabs the phone. "Yes?"

His smooth voice chills me out. Thought it would scare me shitless.

*Do it.*

"Can...can I see you? There's some stuff I wanna talk about." Ugh, so bland. Couldn't come up with anything personal. Anything real. But, you know, doing my best.

"Sure." Ethan sounds like I'm a real drag. Can't blame him.

"How about I come over tomorrow?" Shit, too pushy?

"That's fine."

"Wow, great. Awesome. Um, I'll see ya then."

Thank fucking god.

No response. Just the crunch of a hangup, then dial tone. The blank, harsh hum might as well be the soundtrack to my brain.

The rest of the night's blanking out to TV sounds, my dad, Piper. Trying to figure out what the fuck to do about Ethan. What do I even say? How the hell do I win him back?

Then it clicks. Ethan doesn't need more words. He needs proof. Something real. Raw.

I think I know what I gotta do, and for once, it feels right.

## The Truth

NEXT night, I walk around the jellybean pool, blasted with a flashback to the very first time I went to Ethan's. Nervous then, nervous now.

The rainbow sticker on the door is basically a giant *BEWARE OF DOG* sign, but I knock anyway. Fucking terrified of what's beyond the sticker.

Ethan opens the door and my heart stops. He's got his glasses on and a serious face to match. "Welcome."

No hugs like usual, and—in a snap—the hot air turns freezing cold on my skin.

Ethan turns around and I follow. On the way to his room, I see Raquel slumped on the couch. Watching the local news, flipping through a magazine. Like I don't exist. Doesn't even look up. Stab to the goddamn heart.

I shut the door behind me in Ethan's room, soft. Already caused enough chaos.

He's leaning against his desk, arms crossed, blank face.

"I, uh, brought you something." I reach into my JanSport and take out a brown paper bag from McDonald's. Chicken nuggets, fries, sweet-and-sour sauce—Ethan's favorites. I'm hoping he gets some kinda smell-memory to take him back to our first hangout, when he liked me. But then all I see is gnarly grease stains. Looks fucking disgusting. Maybe this was a bad idea. Hope I don't barf.

I'm in too deep.

I toss the bag to Ethan, and he reaches in, coming back with a nugget. Takes a bite, then tosses the other half back in the bag. "These are kinda cold." Ethan grabs my eyes with his, and raises an eyebrow. "So?"

Shit. Frozen. "Oh, right. Sorry...uh..." Focus, Asher.

I sit on his bed, real light, like a guest on thin ice. Ethan looks at me, wide eyes like he's waiting for something he doesn't think I can give.

Don't blame him. "Ethan...Uh...I...fuck." Pressure, blurry. Words aren't coming.

He sits down next to me and puts his hand on my back. Always could tell when I was starting to freak out. Skin's warm, calms me down, even though I don't deserve it. Deep, deep breath.

Ethan pulls his hand away. "You look like you're gonna pass out, Asher."

"I'm okay. I'm fine. I just, uh...I don't know what to say. Thought I had something, but my mind's, like, blank."

Ethan moves to his desk chair, puts his arms behind his head, and swivels around. "I've got time." His eyes are shiny, hungry, like watching me squirm is just another episode of *Fear Factor*.

I'd do the same, if I wasn't me.

I sit there for probably a full-ass minute. Throbbing head, shaky legs, teeth clenched so hard they might crack open. Feels like forever, but I finally spit out some words. Slow.

"So, I know what I did was...majorly fucked up. I mean...yeah.

When I first said I was *gay*, or whatever, it was so scary. I felt—"

"Not *or whatever*. You said you were gay."

"Yes, uh, sorry…yeah, so I felt, just, totally insane. The dumbest shit I'd ever done. Thought about taking it back, but…" My voice gets louder, excited almost. "Then Luke got kicked out, and everything was just so much easier."

"Easier…"

"Yeah, so I didn't know if I was gonna take it back or not, cause it was just like, way too much to handle. But then I met…you. And we became…us, you know? And…I love it. You changed me."

Ethan gives me this impatient death stare. "Wasn't there supposed to be some kind of apology in there somewhere?"

I squeeze my eyes closed and run my fingers over my head. "Yes. Yes…"

"So are you? Sorry?"

Stomach seizes, implodes. "Oh, shit, yeah—of course I am…" I squeeze my eyes tighter, harder. Fucking this up already. *No, Asher. Keep going.*

"At first, I…I didn't realize this dumb shit I was pulling was actually, like, messing things up. Messing *people* up. You told me about the soccer team, all that fucking…*pain*, and how you got through it?"

I see the harsh memory flash behind Ethan's eyes. "Well, it all just…clicked. Like, how I cheated, this new me. People being all nice and, like, respecting me or whatever. It wasn't…the *real* me, you know? Then I got totally freaked out, pulled away. Hurt you."

"No shit."

"Yeah, yes…So, then that fuckwad Wade figured it out. Started, like, threatening me? I swore I was gonna tell you at prom. The truth. Like, I was *really* going to, but then…the kiss happened, and your speech, and I...I spiraled. Then Wade, you know. Thought it was the fucking worst moment of my life. But that fight we had, outside, *that* was the worst moment of my life."

I stand up, pace. "That's what I've been obsessed about. You, Ethan, and how to get things right. It...it just needs to happen. I just...need it."

I turn away from Ethan and look above his bed, at Britney Spears. Never noticed before, but she kinda looks like she's got it all figured out. Like, she's in charge. *Learn from Britney.*

I plop down on the bed. "Okay, um, yeah...I'm sick of my own voice. What...what do you think? If..."

Ethan grabs his pink squeeze ball and sits for a sec, thinking. Then he stands up. "It helps...to hear you get it. Like, why what you did was so fucked up. Not just that you felt bad, but that you understand that what you did was, oh god, incredibly offensive."

"Shit, I know." I look up at him like a guilty toddler.

"But, I've been thinking about it a lot, and even though it was insane...I did kinda get it. You were in pain, too. You were hurting. I don't know. I guess it's complicated. Maybe I was a little too hard on you that night."

"What? No! No—"

Ethan lunges at me and covers my mouth with his hand. "Oh my god, Asher, just shut up! I'm trying to be nice here."

What the hell? Can't believe he's not killing me right now. Maybe...maybe I'm not all bad. I went through shit too.

Then it hits me. Maybe both things are true. Maybe I needed to do all that psycho shit. To save myself. Like what Luke said. Take care of myself first. Be who I wanna be. Figure out my own fucking life for myself.

But I can also be nice, generous or whatever. I can help myself and help other people. Guess things can be good and bad and fucked up and make sense all at the same time.

Ethan's pacing, squeezing that fucking pink ball. Then he stops dead. "I don't know if you *can* make things right. I don't know if I can give that to you. I think I need more time."

My stomach feels like freefall on the Tower of Terror. "I...I get that, um, it's cool...I should respect, your, um, space or whatever." I shoot up and make for the door, but Ethan grabs my hand and yanks me back.

*Zap.* The tingle, that electricity, his hand on mine. Still confusing as all fuck.

"Okay, okay, fine. You know I can't help milking the drama." He flashes a little smile, rush of sugar-free dopamine. Ethan sits on his bed and I join. Pretty sure *he's* not gonna punch me out, too. "You know, it's funny. In a way, I wasn't actually that surprised."

Frozen—almost like I was outed all over again. "What? Really?"

"I mean, what gay guy could resist?" Ethan runs his hand under his face like a cheesy model.

So fucking happy he's joking around. "Oh god, you sound like Wade." I smile and roll my eyes.

"Wade's a piece of shit. Don't push it."

I zip my lips. Not the time to be funny.

"And, yeah, Asher. I'm really fucking pissed at you. I should be. Like, what even was that?" Ethan flicks his eyes at me, with some look of, like, amusement maybe? "But it's weird. When Wade was up on stage, being classic Wade—but worse. When I figured it out...I didn't really want to rip your head off. It was kind of a...relief, I think? Like all of a sudden everything made sense. I didn't feel... crazy."

"You felt crazy?"

"Of course I did. I didn't know what was going on with us either. And I kissed you? Such a stupid—"

"You're not stupid."

Ethan gives me this irritated look. "Just let me feel stupid. I need to feel...whatever I want."

*Just listen, Asher. Chill out. It'll be okay.*

"When I first met you, way back then, you looked so...sweet and innocent. And that black eye, Jesus. My heart just melted. You looked like shit...but kind of in a hot way?" Ethan laughs to himself. "Anyway, I was really excited to meet someone like you. Nice, cute gay kid who didn't just want to party and hook up and talk behind my back. And, you know, then I tried to *change* you and everything, and...after a while, I felt guilty about it. Like, who did I think I was, trying to fix you? Like you needed fixing?"

What? No clue he could have felt that way. My assumptions are real shit. Everything in my mind was so...warped.

"Then as time went on I noticed you weren't interested in any of the guys I introduced you to. You wouldn't make out with anyone at Pantheon. That date with that kid didn't go anywhere. I was like, is this guy asexual or something? Wade was trying to get in my head about it, but I thought he was just being a bitch. I guess I thought you just...needed more time or something. And after things ended with that loser John, I think I got...confused."

"Confused..."

"I got my wires crossed, convinced myself I was in *love* with you, like you were gonna save me from all my sadness, like we were meant to be."

That word—*love*—echoes in my ears, like we're in the deepest, darkest, biggest cave on earth.

"I missed having someone special, a crush. You know me. I'm such

a tragic cliché. A hopeless romantic. So, uh, that's how I ended up...
kissing you."

Ethan's face pinks up, so I jump in. Can't leave him hanging. I'd
want him to do the same for me.

"It might not make sense, but when you kissed me, I was kind of,
like...into it? In a weird way? Not, like, sexually or whatever...I don't
think...but I felt something...good, intense. It was, like...comforting
or something. Maybe even..." I scrunch my face tight and close my
eyes. "Love? Or whatever?" A million pounds of bullshit fly off me.
"Or, like, some kind of love? I just freaked the fuck out."

Ethan's eyes get a little red.

Mine might be, too. "I knew, right then, even through all my lies
and fuckups, that what we had was, you know...*real*. I felt like a total
fake, but *we* were real. And now I'm so fucking scared that we're...
*over*." Can't stop my eyes, wet. "Are we? Over?"

Ethan runs his hand over his head, blows out some air. "Honestly,
I don't know. I'm not sure what we are." He rubs his pink eyes with
the base of his palms.

*Okay—I can handle this. Let people heal on their own time. Let*
*Ethan heal.*

"I mean, maybe you'll be this crazy story I'll tell people at NYU.
Or maybe I'll just see you around campus. Give you a little wave in
Washington Square Park and that'll be that."

NYU? No way I can go. "What do you mean, around campus?"

"Well, we're both going to NYU...right?" Ethan rolls his eyes.
"Oh, come on, Asher. You have to come."

"I just...I didn't think you'd want me there, after everything."

"Who cares? Don't give this up just because you can't forgive
yourself or something dramatic like that. Get it, girl."

I laugh, and think.

"And *don't* do it just because I'm telling you to. We've had enough mind control."

And just like that, those puppet strings, sliced. I'm free.

I stand up and reach into my backpack. One more thing. I pull out a CD and tap it against my hand.

"What's this? A bootleg of the new Britney album that'll make me forgive you for everything you've ever done?"

"I wish, but, uh...it's just a mix."

Ethan snatches the CD outta my hand. "You know I love a mix."

It's nothing special, just says *For Ethan* scribbled in Sharpie on the silver disc. Lousy handwriting. The shaky letters remind me of my name tag at the *Wizard of Oz* dance. "I thought this could say more than I could. Like, what I really want to."

Ethan rushes over to his stereo and pops it in. It starts—that familiar, bouncy guitar strum. "Teenage Dirtbag."

"Oh this is gonna be good." Ethan settles into his nice big beanbag chair, hands behind his head.

So we listen, every track, and I explain as we go. The music helps me figure out what I want to say. The words that feel impossible to come up with on my own. I spill all my brain gunk—all my thoughts. This year. Everything.

I tell him how, like, monumental it was to just sit in his car and eat McDonald's with a new friend. Cher for when we first met—strange, surreal. Jimmy Eat World, my makeover. Pantheon disco that changed my life. Good Charlotte for the Palm Reef party. Sharing about my life, even though I felt trapped. Lil' Kim from the party bus, the fucked-up stuff with Wade. Christina Aguilera for gay prom. An epic night I'll probably spend the rest of my goddamn life trying to figure out in therapy. Then—Celine Dion for our slow dance. Something I don't regret, and something I hope Ethan doesn't have to be embarrassed about.

We laugh through the fun songs. I stutter through the harder, more emotional stuff. I even let myself cry, just a bit.

But I do it. I take my time.

He tells me how he felt through everything, too, and I listen really hard. Even though some of it makes me feel like shit. His anger.

But I don't obsess, or hate myself. I need to hear it. I need to grow. Thank god he cracks jokes. We make it through.

Ethan deserves it, the truth, every word. The truth is all I have, and it's all I can give. For tonight, it seems like enough.

We walk outside, down to my car. Long, long hug. He smells like him. The feeling of his body against me, it feels so...whole. Complete. Like everything.

Safe, like my mom's hugs. Full of love and care and not in my head. That deadly hurricane of feelings, merging with Ethan's, through our bodies, and—for once—I don't fucking care what it *means*. It just *is*.

I pull out of the hug. "So, uh, what now?"

"How about we leave it like this. Go have fun in Europe, and hit me up when you're back. Or maybe I'll just see you in New York."

Disappointed, relieved, sad, hopeful. All of it, I feel it.

"Fair." I bite my lip, but it's okay. "Oh, um, another thing. I was hoping you could help me with something. It's nothing bad, I swear."

Ethan raises his eyebrow. "I'm listening..."

This is it. The final piece of the almost impossible-puzzle that might actually make all of this make sense.

## *Hi.*

I stare at my hot chocolate, trying to flip it over telepathically. Not drinking it, cause I'm too nervous for my big idea.

Right behind it is Robbie with his caramel frap. We're at that Starbucks in Barnes & Noble. Neutral turf. Didn't ask him to sit at our old spot in the self-help section. Didn't want to push it. I think he barely wants to be here as it is.

He's slurping, and I think he's getting off on making those gross, wet suction sounds. It's fine. He can do what he wants. Robbie sits quiet, like he's waiting for me to talk.

I'm picking at my cup, burning myself on purpose, and working up the courage to face this Robbie shit head-on.

"Thanks for meeting up." I shift around in my seat. "I'm really glad you're here."

Robbie takes a beat. "Yeah, well...here I am." His voice is flat, short. Clearly not wanting to act like old pals.

Suddenly I wanna speed through everything. "And, you know, again, thanks for meeting me." My leg starts shaking bad under the table, and Robbie's eyes notice. "Oh man, there's so much...so much I wanna say. That...I *need* to." Almost outta breath. Gotta pause.

"But, uh...I'm not really sure what you wanna hear..."

Robbie looks up at the ceiling, thinking. "Asher...I don't think I'm ready." He keeps staring up, looks zoned out. Finally, eyes at me. "I don't know when I'll be ready."

Gut punch.

"Oh...yeah, I mean, of course. I—fuck!" I drop my full cup too hard on the table, scalding hot chocolate almost killing me. "Agh, I really fucked up, didn't I?"

Robbie doesn't flinch. Maybe he likes seeing me get burned. "You talking about your drink or your life?"

I shake my hands off and wipe them on my pants. "Both, I guess?"

"Yeah. You fucked up."

I push my tongue into my cheek and nod over and over. "Then, uh, why did you agree? You know...to meet me here?"

Robbie takes a long sip from his green straw, squinting. Looking me over.

"Well, I think you deserve to at least hear from me, that...I don't know, you ditched me this year." His voice gets softer, and his lip starts to shake. "For Ethan and that whole...world. I felt so shitty for so long. So I know what's like to be kind of...thrown away without an explanation." Robbie's talking like he's been sitting with it for a while. "I don't want to do that to you, even if you deserve it."

"That, uh, that's really nice. Thanks."

Robbie takes another sip and looks around the store. He's rubbing his eyebrow scar, but I dunno if he's nervous or avoiding me or just wants to get this shit over with.

My body goes numb. I'm losing something. Something big. Maybe it's been gone a while. Maybe it's just sinking in now. That friendship, all those years. Something so important...just disappearing, quiet. Maybe that's just how life goes.

I realize I'm not gonna give some big apology speech, and Robbie's not just gonna forgive me so easy, like in the movies. Not gonna rush past it. We might never move on. Or maybe this talk, this meeting...maybe it *is* our way of moving on.

Without each other.

*Don't overthink. Don't assume the worst.* But I might have to be okay with it. Some shitty, sad, ugly end to us.

In a way, the anticlimax or whatever is kinda freeing. I don't have anything to earn, no convincing anyone that I'm not totally a bad guy. I can just figure out how to be myself, whoever that is, and get on with my life.

I really hope Robbie's in a good place. Seeing him at gay prom means he's made some kinda progress, at least in terms of coming out and stuff. There was that girl, so someone knows. Maybe he's got new friends, gay ones. Maybe he's gone on dates, kissed someone that's not his fucked-up ex-best friend.

I hope he gets what he's looking for, and that it doesn't hurt too bad. "But, um...there's one more thing I wanted to say, or...do."

Robbie shakes his head, annoyed. "Asher, I don't think I—"

"No! No, it's not...it's not about me. Just gimme a sec." I hold my hands out, then get up and disappear to the travel aisle nearby. I grab a gift I've been keeping for him. A peace offering. I slowly walk back to Robbie, with the present.

It's Ethan.

"Hi, Robbie." Ethan gives a nervous laugh. "It's great to meet you...again. Is it, uh, okay if I join you?"

Robbie lights the fuck up—biggest smile I've seen in years. Eyes on fire. "Oh, wow, Ethan! Hi...uh, sure, of course." His voice stutters and cracks.

"You can sit here." I pull out the empty chair. "I'm gonna...I'm gonna leave you guys to it." I stand there, awkward, looking at them back and forth. My lukewarm hot chocolate forgotten, just like me in this conversation. "I think you guys could be friends. You both deserve it."

Ethan gives me a nod, then sits down and puts his hands on the table, looking at Robbie. "Hi."

I take a few steps back and turn around, heading for the exit. Robbie doesn't say bye. I don't either. Ethan's already got him hypnotized. My goodbye doesn't matter anyway. What I gave him is more important.

Right as I reach the door, I turn one last time. There they are, these two kids who've gone through so much. I'm happy for them— I really am—and I know it's time to back away from the spotlight. But what I'm losing, with both of them, I feel it getting zapped outta my body.

I hope Robbie doesn't resent Ethan. Or, at least, I hope he can get over my dumb decisions and let Ethan in. He's got a lot to offer. They both do.

Finally took myself out. Out of my lie, out of my guilt. I don't need to be there anymore. Had my time with it, with the unpredictable, crazy, scary, fucked-up, tough, sad, frustrating, fun-as-hell gay life. I've got no clue what's next.

I walk through the big glass doors. Outside, into the hot, humid Florida air. Feels like I can finally leave it all behind. Knowing that something good—something real—is coming out of all my bullshit.

Robbie and Ethan are both in good hands.

There's still the irritating, endless question of who Asher Diamond is, without the makeover and the gay shit and the partying and the friends and Robbie and Ethan and Sam and...

How much of the good stuff can I hold onto? How much of it's already jammed into my bones, like a shiny purple geode, no matter how much guilt tries to crack it off?

After asking myself that same boring-ass question ten billion times, am I *finally* ready to *actually* find out?

Maybe

IT'S been a couple weeks since I set up Robbie and Ethan. I'm in my Nissan, driving around in the dark, no clue where I'm going.

Graduation just happened, and I'm still in my dark green gown that matches my car. Cap and gold tassel ride shotgun. Fucking hot in this polyester thing, so I'm sweating like hell.

So, graduation. Scared shitless going in. Almost bailed. But the thought of them saying my name, "Asher Diamond? Asher Diamond?" without me going up was even more humiliating than facing reality. I'd rather be an outcast than a coward.

I went, and it was fine. Turns out graduation's another anticlimax. Wasn't like in *Saved by the Bell* or *90210* or *Can't Hardly Wait*. I looked around and couldn't spot any cameras or directors or people holding big mics over our heads. Just another day.

Not many claps when they called my name. Still, I survived the walk—hundreds of people staring, knowing all the shit I pulled. Silas didn't scream out and call me a fag, at least. Guess he had better things to do.

After we got let out, I thought about running up to Robbie and giving him a hug, but I didn't. He said he doesn't want it. I faced my

305

fear by showing up, but didn't wanna hang too long and push my luck.

My dad gave me the biggest hug ever, and I thought he was gonna squish all the guts outta my body. Had to rip the digital camera outta his hand so he wouldn't make me do some embarrassing photo shoot.

I hugged Piper, too. Thought about my mom and how she didn't get to see me in my cap and gown. But in that moment, I let go of what could've been. I let Piper fill that void. It was progress.

As I dragged my dad and Piper away from the happy crowd taking pictures and celebrating the end of high school and all that, I tried to sneak a glimpse of Sam. I spotted her across the courtyard, posing with Jackie and Allie for a photo I'm sure they'll think about in eighty years on their deathbeds. Girls like that really care about this stuff.

I looked really close at Sam's face. Possessed, toothy smile, focused eyes. No fucking clue what was going through her mind. Never have. Dunno if she wanted to be there or not, or if she's excited to run away like me. I let this version of Sam replace the others in my brain. Wiping the pizza off my forehead. Falling at the party. The crazy look in her eyes after we kissed. Fist flying at my face. I'll just remember her like this. Smiling, not quite real. An enigma.

My dad and Piper took me out to dinner. Then, after thanking them, I told my dad I needed some time to myself. Piper helped distract him.

So here I am. Driving around. Hour three. I'm not bored, though.

I swung by Robbie's house, wondering what was going on inside. What I missed. I drove by Ethan's apartment and let the memories wash over. Wondering what next year in New York's gonna look like.

I've got an idea. Headed somewhere else. Somewhere important, life-changing.

It's about eleven at night, and I pull into the Pantheon parking lot. Music's leaking outta the club, and there's some people lurking around outside. Laughing, ready for a fun night out. I head to a far space and back into the spot so I'm facing Pantheon.

I turn off the radio and pop in Ethan's mix. Made myself a copy, of course. The music plays, feeling nostalgic about the year for the first time. A new era.

Now, time for the big question: *Who is Asher Diamond?*

I watch the crowd as the question pinballs around in my head. How fucking awesome and scary it felt going in there for the first time. How weird and, like, important it felt just to dance. Let the fuck loose.

So, who is this fuckface Asher Diamond I can't shut up about?

Maybe he's a boring, straight, random virgin. Maybe he's a little kid playing Beanie Babies with his best friend. Maybe he's a klutz who dropped a Yoo-hoo bottle in a cold hospital. Maybe he's a sexually ambiguous, buff-as-fuck, hotshot sex god. Maybe he doesn't exist at all.

Mind's on overdrive when I see Ethan walk up and hug Bruno. Every neutron in my body stops vibrating. Behind Ethan, trailing, is Robbie. I'm kinda far, so I can't make out his face too well—but he looks scared. Walking slow, neck hanging down. I totally get it. I've been there.

Maybe he's nervous. Maybe he's excited. Maybe he's—

Then, it hits me. But, like, for real this time. Here's the answer I've been waiting for. Here it is—the truth.

*Asher Diamond is*...someone who needs to shut the fuck up. Maybe he needs to move the fuck on. Maybe he isn't the center of the universe. And maybe, just maybe, he needs to retire the M-word

—*maybe*—altogether. *Stop asking so many fucking dumbass questions, freak. There are no answers.*

As Robbie catches up, I see Ethan grab his hand. They disappear through the doors, and strobes and lasers peek out the front. I wonder if I'll go somewhere like Pantheon again.

Are these flashing lights the last thing I'll see of a world I'm leaving behind? Or will the lights, the world, the people...will they pull me back in?

I don't have the faintest fucking clue. Ask someone else.

## *Acknowledgments*

FIRST and foremost, I'd like to thank you, Ari. Reading, editing, collaborating, giving me ideas in various swimming pools, and keeping me on a constant drip of snacks while I wrote over the past few years.

Thanks, Napalm, for this rad fucking cover art and book design. You totally nailed it.

Marcy and Francesca, you gave me such helpful analysis and ideas for my manuscript at different points in my process, and both were extremely helpful in making pretty big decisions about what this book should be.

My writing group. Jon, KK, Catie, Maggie, and Anna. You all helped convince me that this book is really a book, cheerleading me, and giving me smart notes. Thanks for letting me in.

Mom, you book addict, you read this book in one day, which really means something. Dad, thanks for questioning the title, even though I was never going to change it. And, more importantly, thanks for supporting all my artistic endeavors since I was a little kid.

My friends, my beta readers! Alex, Max, Marc, Michelle, Madeleine, Laura, Gersh, Jordana, and Louise. You actually read this.

Dinner on me, whenever.

Brian and Louis, if I hadn't met you this book literally wouldn't exist. I hope you're tickled by the memories.

Thanks to all you straight guys I could find for dealing with my insane questions about what goes on inside your minds, which apparently isn't much, and I'm still not sure what to make of that.

Last, thank you to all my friends in LA and beyond for letting me yap at you about this book for literal years. I'll shut up soon...until the next one.